Sheila—

Thank ♡ ~~~~~~~~~~ ~~~~.

your encourag~~~~~~~~

B. Fa~~~

SO

TRUST

ME

SO TRUST ME

FOUR DECADES OF LOVE AND DECEIT

BILL PIEPER

CREATIVE ARTS BOOK COMPANY

BERKELEY ❖ CALIFORNIA 2000

For information contact:
Creative Arts Book Company
833 Bancroft Way
Berkeley, California 94710
(800) 848-7789

Cover art by Joan Brown
"Wolf in Studio," 1972
Crocker Art Museum, Sacramento, California
Gift of the Crocker Art Gallery Association.

The characters, places, incidents, and situations
in this book are imaginary and have no relation
to any person, place, or actual happening.

ISBN 088739-2679
Library of Congress Catalog Number 99-61368

Printed in the United States of America

With Love and Respect to My Friend
Marc Frauenfelder, 1936–1997

ACKNOWLEDGMENTS

First, my thanks to the three vigilantes, Sidney Hollister, Dave Dawson and Harvey Schwartz, for their support, comments, criticism and willingness to read everything sent their way. My editor, Paul Samuelson, was invaluable for those same reasons. I don't know how to credit the inspiration provided over the years by John McDougall and Susan Burnet except to say that it was essential, along with John's extensive technical assistance on "The Willamette Kid."

My wife, Cathy Holden, has offered encouragement at every step as well as being a walking style manual, thesaurus and idea bank. This book would not exist without her. Annie Folk provided comments and served as consultant on the cover art, while Dave Dawson made a further contribution through his photography. Additional thanks are due Bruce McKenna, Chris Piper, Gus Koehler, Claudia Viek, Carol Gage, Susan Hayward, Jan Sterling, Marilyn Schwartz, Lynn Young, Tom Carter, Doug Hughes and Nick Pieper for their helpful feedback. If error persists despite all these efforts, the fault is entirely the author's.

CONTENTS

SO

TRUST

ME

THE WILLAMETTE KID

HAD HE MAINTAINED ACADEMIC ELIGIBILITY JOHN MCDONOUGH WOULD HAVE BEEN fencing champion of Stanford. To him, only fencing made Stanford worthwhile. John's bad luck was that fencing went from a club sport to a varsity sport his sophomore year, so the NCAA and the dean got a say in who participated.

Rollo Gans, the coach, certainly wanted John on the team. It was Rollo who called him the Willamette Kid when John, as a Portland-born freshman, began routinely demolishing his older teammates in both epee and foil. John had fenced in high school, which gave him an advantage in technique, but Rollo was more impressed with John's quickness and his instinctive feel for the spatial geometry of his opponent's body position.

Not that Stanford was a fencing powerhouse, though it always got some wins in competition against Cal, USC and UCLA as well as in non-collegiate matches against the Olympic Club of LA and Pannoina of San Francisco. And with John on board the number of wins went steadily up. John fenced until he was a first-semester junior, when he became ineligible due to low grades the previous spring. He continued to practice with the team, but within a month he ended his fencing career by storming out of the gym at the beginning of a workout. John's grades then dropped further, and his parents kept him home in Portland the second semester before sending him back the next fall.

His freshman year John had made a point of doing well in all his classes, wanting to prove he could. After that, he met his parents' constant pressure to achieve with his own determination to risk failure. They were so keen to have a third Stanford diploma in the family, John knew for once he had the upper hand. The economics major his father intended for him evolved into sociology, the least rigorous discipline John could find. In a college life increasingly devoted to shooting pool in dormitory rec rooms, playing bridge as late as possible most nights, and taking long, solitary hikes in the hills behind campus, fencing was a painful casualty along the way.

Surprisingly, beer, girls and friends weren't much part of the picture. John was usually too depressed and too alienated to want to hang around with anybody, and his irregular progress separated him from the few friends he did have. His parents always required that he live in the dorms. But, beginning with his second attempt at a junior year, John insisted on a single room. Another semester out of school, when he should have been a senior, brought John to a probable graduation date in January, 1961. Probable, but not certain, until the event occurred that would propel him into real life—he met Rebecca Minter.

⚜ ⚜ ⚜

The 1960 Big Game was in Palo Alto, on one of those crisp November Saturdays that define football weather. Sun streamed through broken cloud masses and caught the vivid red of the Virginia creeper tangled across the stadium facade. Palm trees poked up among the bare-limbed sycamores, while the remaining multi-colored leaves of the liquid-ambers flew away in a cool breeze. John, who went to football games only when his father came down for them, had actually been hoping for a warmer day so that Jack McDonough, Class of 31, would not wear the raccoon coat he brought along for these occasions.

Jack had been a lineman on the Stanford football team and still looked it. This was his thirty-year Big Game reunion, a joint affair with the Cal thirty-year team to be celebrated at a tailgate party and barbecue in the stadium parking lot two hours before kickoff. Jack had arrived from Portland that morning, and now he and John were walking at top speed out from a line of eucalyptus and across the blacktop toward a crowd standing among a circle of parked vehicles under a haze of charcoal smoke.

"Come on, Johnny, step it up," the older man called back, swinging his fur-clad arms and lengthening his stride beneath the coat. At fifty-two Jack was getting a bit jowly and florid, but he retained most of his full, dark hair and prided himself on his good eyesight.

John, six inches shorter at 5'8", had the same dark hair, but was smaller boned and much more graceful. He wore silver, wire-rimmed glasses which partially corrected for damage to his right eye in a childhood fireworks accident. The cause and extent of the injury were things John had always concealed, because he wasn't supposed to have fireworks, and in his family, you didn't admit weakness. Moreover, it had proven no handicap in fencing.

"Dad," John said, overtaking his father, "do you suppose this trip you could drop your joke about my being at Stanford on the five-year plan? You already told the cab driver who brought you in from the airport and that guy who was with us in the restroom. It's getting old."

"Why? If you're so sensitive, maybe you'll get motivated."

"Oh, great. But look, it's not even accurate. This is theoretically my eleventh semester, so that makes six years."

"The Russians never accomplish their five-year plans, either," Jack responded, enjoying his own wit.

John abandoned the topic with a familiar feeling of angry helplessness. He remembered working menial office jobs at McDonough Industries during the summers and during his two semesters out of school. Most mornings he had commuted with Jack, and in the tense silence between them, the only sound was the ticking of the dashboard clock in the big, new Lincoln Jack drove.

Jack McDonough was a man who had never desired to, and never been forced to, question his assumptions about anything. After graduating from Stanford, he returned to Portland, married Cybil Braddock and rose quickly up the ladder to succeed his own father as president of McDonough Industries by age forty. The firm was a regional power in nickel mining, timber and highway construction, and it continued to prosper under Jack's leadership. John was the one area of his life in which Jack had met a challenge he could not readily overcome.

Cybil McDonough, the daughter of one of Portland's founding families, bore her husband three children. Molly, the oldest, John, and a younger sister, Louise. All three were raised on the family's suburban estate at Lake Oswego, and the two girls, in their day, were big news on the Portland debutante circuit. Molly, now married, lived in Seattle with her husband, whom she had met at the University of Washington. Louise, "the smart one," breezed through high school a year ahead of schedule and was enrolled at Wellesley. Cybil fretted over John, but she put most of her energy into her daughters.

The Big Game reunion was well underway by the time John and Jack arrived. A growl of shouted conversation and the huddled backs of more than a hundred people confronted them as they slowed for Jack to present their tickets. Jack's was not the only raccoon coat in evidence, but that did not make him look any less foolish to John.

"Drinks to the left and food to the right," said a tweedily-dressed ticket-taker who waved them into a broad, temporary enclosure of potted shrubs. A riot of food and tobacco smells filled the air.

Jack, thinking John was behind him, headed for a low trestle-table holding a large aluminum keg, while John continued along the right periphery to face a remarkable girl who had locked her eyes onto him the moment he and Jack arrived. She was exactly his height, with the short dark hair, large eyes and delicate features that Audrey Hepburn had already made famous. She wore a European-cut, belted trench coat and a hunter green silk scarf patterned in gold. She stood alone at the edge of the crowd with a shy smile that concealed her teeth behind narrow, red lips.

Although he cut an apparently confident figure in a shearling jacket, khakis and a crew-neck sweater, John would normally clam up and hide in situations like this. Instead he found himself saying, "You don't look like a football fan, either."

"You're right, I'm not," she answered.

"Well, why are you here?"

"My father. It's his thirtieth reunion."

"Mine, too. Was your dad Cal or Stanford?"

"Cal. Is that your father in the fur coat? He's Stanford, right?"

"Right. And so am I, sort of."

"What do you mean, 'sort of?' I thought there was a blood oath."

Whether he laughed because she made him laugh, or simply because he wanted to, John didn't know. "I mean 'sort of' because I was supposed to graduate in 1959 and I'm still around. My dad calls it the five-year plan, but it's more like six."

"Older, but wiser?" she asked, still with her half smile.

"Here's how it went." John had never told anyone this and couldn't imagine why he was doing so now. "My mom and dad said from the time I was in high school that I could go to whatever college I wanted. They would pay my way through Stanford, or I could pay my way anywhere else. My dad went here, class of '31, and my mom's dad went here, class of '02, when David Starr Jordan still ran things. I didn't want to come, but I was afraid to call my parents' bluff."

"That's like me," she replied. Her hazel eyes lit up and she showed her gleaming teeth for the first time. "They can lead us to water, but they can't make us drink. Anyway, who's David Starr what's his name?"

"The first president of this place. You mean your parents forced you to go to Cal?"

"No, no. But the same idea. I wanted to do ballet, but they made me go to college. We were back east then, and I hated it."

"Where did you go?"

"Vassar. I flunked out after two years."

"Then what?"

"I came home and worked with the San Francisco ballet, as a reserve dancer in the company. I still work there."

"Wow," John nodded. "But how could this be home if your family lived back east?"

"We were always from here...Marin County. We were only back there temporarily. My father's a doctor, and he was appointed Surgeon General."

"Of what, some hospital?"

"No, of the United States. My older sister got to stay in California. She was going to Mills. My mom and I went to Washington DC with my dad. That's where I finished high school. He only resigned and came back to the Bay Area a few months ago. But my mom came back before, with me."

"Does that mean you met President Eisenhower and everything? What's your dad's name?"

"Dr. Harvey Minter. And yes, I met the President. It's no big deal. My dad has always been involved with Republican Party stuff, and he knows Justice Warren and Senator Knowland. Even Governor Brown. I've met them, too."

"OK, but it would be a big deal to most people. What's your name?"

"Rebecca...Rebecca Minter."

"I'm John McDonough." He gave a barely perceptible bow.

"And you're not from around here, I bet."

"Right. From Oregon. Portland area. My family's Republican, too."

"Good, then our dads won't have to keep us from talking to each other, and we can get them arguing about football instead of Kennedy and Nixon."

"But I want to know more about your dancing. Just from looking at you, you must be great."

Rebecca sighed and seemed to shrink. "I said I still worked at the ballet. I don't dance there anymore. Maybe I was never good enough, I don't know. Maybe I got too far out of training while I was at college. Anyway, last January I injured my knee in rehearsal, and I had to give up. It's the worst thing that ever happened to me. I cried for months, and barely left my apartment. In September, the ballet called and offered me a job helping with tickets and publicity, so I went back. That was really hard. And today is the first time I've been anywhere social since it happened."

"Oh, I'm sorry. I wish I hadn't brought it up." In a distracted way, John found himself thinking about fencing and what it had meant to him, but that was not something he was ready to share with Rebecca or anyone else.

"No. It's OK." She touched his arm. "I need to be able to talk about it."

"Well, Johnny, where did you get to?" Jack McDonough called, approaching behind Rebecca with a large, foaming paper cup in his hand. "And who is this lovely creature?"

"This is Rebecca Minter, Dad. Rebecca, this is my dad, Jack McDonough. Rebecca's father is an Old Blue. He played for Cal in 1930."

"Hangin' out with the enemy, are ya? Hope she understands we beat 'em 41-0 back then." Jack winked at Rebecca. "What's your dad's name? Maybe I knew him."

"Harvey Minter. But you probably didn't. He wasn't a player. He was the student manager. He kept track of equipment and taped ankles and things like that. He says it helped him get into med school. He also says Stanford hasn't won any games so far this season." She pointed to a tall, trim, slightly balding, gray-haired man in a beautiful camel overcoat who stood with his back to them about fifteen feet away. "That's him, right there."

"I think I'll go over and say hello," Jack responded. "Maybe he knows some of the Cal folks I was looking for and can't seem to find. And don't get too cocky. Big Red will be putting up a win today." He began to walk in the direction Rebecca had pointed.

"Say," Jack shot back over his shoulder, "did Johnny tell you he was at Stanford on the five-year plan?"

"Yes he did, Mr. McDonough," she answered sweetly.

John's face went blank. He should have known that asking Jack to drop the five-year plan joke would produce the opposite result. And John had heard about the 41-0 victory over Cal for most of his life. In games since then, wins by lesser margins, not to say defeats, Jack took as proof that 1930 had been Stanford's golden age.

"I see why you explained the five-year plan right away," Rebecca continued, once Jack was gone. "I got a lot of that kind of thing when I was flunking out. But I want to ask, are you going home to Portland for Thanksgiving?"

"No. I have no plans. I'm supposed to stay around Palo Alto and study."

"Why not come to my family's place in Belvedere? I'll check with my dad to see if it's OK, but I'm sure it will be."

"I could. But I don't know where Belvedere is, and I don't have any way to get there."

"It's in Marin, just north of the Golden Gate. Take the train to San Francisco, and I'll meet you at the station in my little Plymouth."

"That might work," John said. "But for now, can I get you a drink?"

"Yes, thanks. A glass of wine, if you can find one. White or red, I don't care."

✹ ✹ ✹

After a launch so effortless what could go wrong? Jack was greatly impressed with Harvey Minter and with Rebecca, and Rebecca's family immediately took to John when he joined them for Thanksgiving dinner. The Minters had a gorgeous 3,000 square-foot split-level home high on the southeast slope of Belvedere Island with dramatic views of the bay and the San Francisco skyline. Everything was on the scale of the house John had grown up in, but more contemporary in style. And Dr. Minter couldn't have been in a better mood. Not only had Cal avenged the 1930 pasting by winning the 1960 Big Game 21-10, Democratic Governor Pat Brown had just appointed him to a seat on the University's Board of Regents. Past personal ties between the two men, it seems, counted for more than party affiliation.

The one off-note was that the Minters' older daughter, Priscilla, who was very protective of her sister, virtually interrogated John about his background and future prospects. But Priscilla's husband, Lloyd Combs, a broker at the Pacific Stock Exchange, was a nice enough guy, and he did what he could to keep things mellow. When Rebecca was out of the room, the family all agreed that she looked happier than she had in years.

Once John saw Rebecca's San Francisco apartment the following weekend, he gained an entirely new sense of purpose. She lived in the upper right flat of a new four-unit building at the corner of Vallejo and Baker in Cow Hollow. The white stucco walls and tile roofs of the Marina District fell away to the north, and when the fog was out, there was a clear view to the bay, the Golden Gate, the Marin headlands, and to Rebecca's parents' place in Belvedere. She had antiques, Asian art, a fireplace and a fully equipped kitchen. There was now no doubt that John would be graduating when the semester ended, and that he wanted to find a job in San Francisco. With Rebecca in the picture and graduation taken care of, maybe his parents would accept his defection from McDonough Industries, at least for a while.

By the week after Christmas, John and Rebecca were spending passionate nights in her apartment at every opportunity. He was in love with her, in love with the city and in love with the idea that his life might actually become his. She was tender and daring in bed, and her slim, muscular, small-breasted body excited him like no woman ever had. John's previous experience was almost entirely of hired sex or of nervously dating the secretaries at McDonough Industries to flout his father's prohibition against doing so. But rather than making him concerned about his own adequacy, Rebecca seemed delighted with whatever John did, and his doubts melted away.

Rebecca occasionally drank more wine than John thought she should, but it was not unknown for him to join right in. They also had to do a good bit of sneaking around, because her father owned the building and knew the other tenants. The honor system applied in all spheres of life, Harvey Minter liked to say, and he was proud of having raised his daughters to know their moral duty. The fact that Priscilla was apt to come by unannounced on her frequent trips into town from San Mateo was another reason for watchfulness. Still, John's term papers and final exams notwithstanding, it was an idyllic time.

Jack and Cybil, too, conveyed positive feelings. If this girl gave John reason to graduate, that was a plus, and she was certainly a prize catch. Even if he stayed in California for a while, he could always come home to Portland later. And when it turned out that he did graduate, and that he wanted to stay in California to be near Rebecca, John found his family amazingly supportive.

Jack got on the phone to his old Stanford cronies and quickly lined up a job for John at the San Francisco headquarters of Grenville Sugar, as Assistant to the Vice President for Sales. The Grenville family no longer ran the business, and were only minority shareholders, but clout was clout. And though there was no graduation ceremony on campus at mid-year, the McDonoughs and the Minters celebrated the event in Palo Alto with a dinner at Ricky's Hyatt House which ended with John's being left in possession of a new, silver-blue Austin Healy that Jack had arranged to be delivered to the restaurant by the dealer. John was agog. This was more parental approval than he had received in a lifetime, and the glow of the moment pushed aside any thoughts about the strings attached to such a gift.

✸ ✸ ✸

Everything in John's new life went perfectly for more than a month. After some hurried shopping at the Union Square Brooks Brothers for suits, ties, and the like, he began his job on February 1. A few days later he found a one-room, Murphy-bed apartment in the Columbus, an unfashionable building at 1492 Pacific on the back side of Nob Hill. There was a parking space for his car in the alley behind, and he could take the California Street cable car to the Grenville Building in the financial district. He also had easy access to Rebecca's, about a dozen blocks west.

Of course, John spent almost every night at Rebecca's, so most of these considerations were moot. He didn't bother to get a phone, and he unpacked little beyond his immediate wardrobe and toiletry needs. Nonetheless, the place gave John an address of his own and somewhere to sleep on those few nights when Rebecca was occupied with her mother or sister.

Even the weather cooperated. February often marks the beginning of spring in San Francisco, with the sun gaining strength and fog rarely a factor. Yellow branches of acacia blossoms drape over fences, the Japanese plums make cascades of pink, and the surrounding hills, customarily a golden brown, are green enough to be taken for Ireland. Occasional cloudbursts produce rainbows above the bay, seeming to refresh and cleanse rather than batter like the storms of December or January.

Most evenings, John and Rebecca went out to dinner at Scoma's, La Pantera, the Brighton Express and other restaurants in North Beach or enjoyed the view and Rebecca's excellent cooking at her place. They were also movie-goers, to foreign films generally, and they liked the dixieland jazz at Earthquake McGoon's. Weekend trips to Carmel and the Napa Valley in the Austin Healy were other reminders to John of how much his life had changed.

Although he rarely showed interest in Rebecca's work at the ballet, John usually volunteered a flow of information about Grenville. If they were home, meaning her place, they would build a fire after dinner, dim the lights, and drink wine while watching ships come in and out of the Golden Gate. This could lead to talking, making love or both.

"Tell me again what you fixed us tonight," John said. "I've never had anything like that before."

"Veal piccatta. I'm really glad you liked it. I use lemon, garlic, black pepper, and capers, but you have to know where to get good veal." She sat long-wise on the couch with her feet and lower legs across John's lap.

"As far as my family's concerned, veal is for veal cutlets. And you always have such great bread. Where do you get that?"

She blushed with pleasure. "Boudin's...Becky's little secret. But go on about what you were saying at dinner. How you never spend any time in your office anymore, and you think you're getting a new assignment."

"Well, at first they had me read up on the beet sugar industry and learn who our main competitors and customers are, so I was in my office all the time. Then I did that tour of the refinery in Manteca. Now all I do is go to meetings with my boss, the sales VP, Bob Harcourt. He's making sure I get to know everybody and understand how to interpret the sales reports. I'm supposed to learn as much as possible about the way he thinks and reacts so I can go to some of those meetings on my own and represent him. It's weird, though. I don't actually do anything."

"You will, just wait. So, what's next?"

"I think I'm getting assigned to this special project—developing a new line of restaurant and supermarket products to be sold in small quantities. Up to now Grenville's been strictly an industrial supplier...you know, to canneries, bakeries, wineries, soft drink companies. We sell by the ton or by the freight-car load. But Harcourt says that stuff's all gotten ultra-competitive now and profits are low."

"Sounds exciting. Too bad the health news on refined sugar isn't so great."

"I know. I've heard your dad talking about that. But look, sugar's a staple. Everybody all over the world uses it. And Harcourt says why sell industrial at $2.80 a hundred-pound bag when you can get ten or twenty times that price for little packages? Those restaurant packets are free advertising for the company, too."

"Who's going to be running the project? Will Harcourt let you?"

"No. That's where things get tricky. Ted Fulton, the president, has picked this guy Charlie Houndsley to run it. Charlie has been a product manager under Harcourt, but they don't get along. Charlie's known as a bullshit artist who's married to a half-sister of Fulton's wife, and Fulton's wife is a Grenville."

"Sounds like you'll be moving in the top circle, anyway." Rebecca pulled herself closer and started stroking his arm.

"Yeah, maybe. But I think my main job will be keeping an eye on Houndsley and reporting back to Harcourt."

"I was going to make that Joe's Special you like so much tomorrow night," Rebecca segued. "But Priscilla and Lloyd have invited us down to their place. Would that be OK?"

"Sure, I suppose. Why not?"

"There's a little of this dry semillon left," she said, handing him the bottle. "Let's finish it. We can both drink from your glass."

Most mornings, John was out of bed and quietly down the stairs before the other tenants began to stir. He would retrieve his car from around the corner and head to his place to shower and shave. This was the mode Rebecca preferred. But he also began leaving a few personal items hidden away in her closet, and sometimes would bring his suit and clean shirt for the next day so they would have time for breakfast together before he left. Although John had clearly not been Rebecca's first lover, he knew it was important to her to maintain a fiction of noncohabitation for the sake of her sister and parents. He never understood why, nor did he ask. Concealing things from one's family was second nature to John.

✻ ✻ ✻

Fault lines began to appear at work and at home about the same time. John couldn't escape a pervasive sense of uselessness regarding his duties at Grenville Sugar, and he couldn't avoid the realization that he and Rebecca didn't have that much in common. She stayed away from the ballet, because it remained too painful for her to attend a performance, but her taste ran very much to high culture. She was always promoting trips to the opera, the symphony, and various museums. Her favorite was the Palace of the Legion of Honor, in the Seacliff area, which had the ironic twist of having been a lavish gift to the city from none other than Anna Grenville in 1924.

John couldn't have been less interested in any of this. Moreover, beyond a casual enjoyment of movies and restaurants, he couldn't say what interested him. If he thought about the question at all, it was to define himself in opposition to his father. As a result, John had no idea who he was. He just knew he wasn't Jack. Even fencing had the good fortune to be the one sport Jack disliked. "A bunch of loony tunes in white suits," Jack called it. In San Francisco, John's only real idea of fun was to go for walks around the city or on Mount Tamalpais. But with or without her knee injury, aimless walking had little appeal for Rebecca.

One Tuesday night, they were sharing a white-bean and sausage cassoulet and a bottle of zinfandel in the exposed brick interior of the Brighton Express when Rebecca pointed to a large, magazine-piled table at the rear reserved for patrons dining alone.

"If you didn't have me," she said tentatively, "that's where you'd be. Reading a magazine by the light of a Tiffany lamp, or trying to pick up one of those women."

"If I didn't have you, I'd be under lock and key at home in Portland after a day of some kind of work at McDonough Industries. Grenville seems pretty stupid, but it's not as bad as that."

"What's the latest on your project?"

"Nothing. Just waiting for the production line to go in at the Salinas plant so we can manufacture the little restaurant sugar packets with the custom-printed labels. Houndsley has the sales force contacting every restaurant in Northern California, and I'm logging all the maybe's and no's into a follow-up list to get key-punched into the computer. For this you have to go to Stanford?"

"Come on. Don't be so negative. It's going to be important."

"Maybe. I know the company hasn't been doing well and needs the profit from this stuff. And that's what has Harcourt all on edge. If it doesn't work out, he gets the blame, 'cause it was his idea. If it does work, Houndsley is set up to take the credit."

"There'll be credit for you, too, I bet."

"For what it's worth. But no matter how hard I try, I just can't take it seriously.

You should see this guy, Houndsley. Always in tweeds with his hair waved back just so. He's from Sacramento, but he tries to put on sort of an English accent. What a phony."

"I'd still like to meet those people some time."

"And the whole project team goes to the upstairs cafeteria every morning for coffee break. Houndsley makes this big production about having his English muffin toasted exactly right. He'll send it back two or three times. The cook hates his guts and the rest of us think he's an ass. Those muffins aren't even really English."

"I know, but that must be funny, in a way."

"And all they talk about is college sports, and how they did this or that in college, or their kids are going to this or that school. Shows how bored they are if college was the high point of their lives. Though I gotta' say, Stanford doesn't seem so bad looking back from here."

"Why don't you try introducing some other topic? Maybe something more serious."

"Like what? How health reports show that people already eat way too much sugar, but all of our jobs are to sell them more of it."

"Oh, let's drop the whole thing. I hate to see you upset. What about I try to get us symphony tickets this weekend?"

"OK, if that's what you want." John was struck again with how beguilingly beautiful she was. No doubt about it, when he walked into a place like this with Rebecca, most of the guys at the other tables dropped their forks.

❈ ❈ ❈

In early May, something happened at Grenville that John really did find interesting. The workers at the four refineries went on strike, and management decided to keep two of the plants open, one shift a day. Every available office staffer and non-union plant supervisor was mobilized to go to either Salinas or Marysville. In John's case, it was Marysville, and he was assigned to be a centrifuge operator.

This meant being away from Rebecca for what could be a week or more, a prospect that made her churlish and tearful. But it also meant being away from Charlie Houndsley and his coffee break antics. The company chartered busses to take John and the others across the Central Valley on a hot Monday evening and deliver them to the ramshackle, brick Hotel California on Marysville's run-down main street. Each morning, they were bussed out to the refinery to be escorted across the picket line by a cadre of Yuba County sheriff's deputies. The reverse occurred each evening.

The six days he was there, John never failed to get a rush of adrenaline crossing the line, though he felt some compunction about doing it. The hundred or so pickets, an amazing ethnic melange of men and women, wore blue work shirts, neck bandannas and wide-brimmed hats. As the busses approached, they whistled, hooted, and waved placards. Then an eerie silence fell, and hard, menacing, seemingly personal glares were directed at each passenger and the deputies. Once the busses were clear, the whistling and hooting resumed. All of this took place against the backdrop of a grimy, two-story, two-block-square, cement structure sprouting dense clusters of exhaust and vent pipes and ringed with rusty, creaking conveyor lines to haul materials in and waste or byproducts out. A half-dozen silos holding various grades of finished sugar towered above the roofline at the right, beyond which a swarm of crows wheeled over a huge, bone-white pile of quick lime.

The centrifuge area was on the second floor, where every inch of every surface was sticky, brownish-black and reeked of molasses. Five centrifuges about the size of upside-down Volkswagens were suspended side-by-side along a set of parallel I-beams. Up a flight of narrow metal stairs from each one was an operator's booth giving a vantage into the whirling cylinder so the sugar could be released when it reached the proper color. Carl, a young engineer not five years older than John, taught him to run machine number 4. The steps were: engage the clutch to move the cylinder in under the operator; turn on the flow of barely-liquid, sugar-laden raw molasses until the cylinder filled; move the cylinder away to the middle of the beam; activate the centrifuge so it spun at 1,000 plus rpm and drained the molasses water, a valuable byproduct, out the bottom into a catch system; and finally, move the cylinder further away to dump the load of sugar crystals onto a conveyor leading down to the dryer. When things went right you could move a load through every five minutes.

John caught on quickly, and within an hour he was running his centrifuge solo while Carl, with a few glances back in his direction, went on to number 5 to train someone else. What a lifetime, or even a year, of doing this work would be like John had no way of knowing, but a week of it was exhilarating. He made every motion as precisely and economically as possible, and worked to avoid abrupt stops or starts. During his time there, before the strike was settled the following weekend, his machine was never down, and he was getting loads through at between 4 and 4.5 minutes, on average. The non-stop, roaring noise and the hot swirl of steamy-sweet air not only didn't bother him, they added to the challenge of taming the mechanical beast.

"From what you told me before you left, I thought it was going to be hell," Rebecca said when he phoned her from the hotel lobby the second night. "How can you say it's the best job you ever had?"

"Because it is," John laughed. "It's real. It takes skill and concentration. It's what work should be. If you screw up, gooey stuff gets dumped all over the floor, and there's no question who's to blame."

"You're strange, John McDonough. But I miss you so much already. I had to drink my cabernet all by myself tonight, and I hate it. I need my lover-man to come home."

"I miss you, too, Becca. But I'm doing OK. This is a colorful town. The best Mexican food ever. And it's a railroad junction, so there's hobo campfires all around the river bottoms at night. We're not supposed to go out alone. They tell us the strikers might try to beat us up, but I've been sneaking out anyway."

"Oh, no. Now I'll be worried sick."

"Don't be. Carl, one of the plant engineers, says the picket line is pretty much all for show. It's high harvest for the beets that were in the ground over winter, and everybody knows the workers have the upper hand. Management can only produce a token amount of sugar in one shift. Besides, I've mastered the art of being nondescript."

"I'm still worried. Please call me every night, OK?"

"I will, but bye now, love. I've got to go. Other Grenville people need to use the phone."

"Bye, love," she answered, her voice not quite under control.

John had a romantic reunion with Rebecca when he got back the following Sunday night. And she called in sick on Monday so they could lay in bed to celebrate a special day off Grenville had granted the returned strikebreakers. John's familiar rhythm of vapid days at the office and pleasant evenings with Rebecca then reestablished itself, though it proved impossible to entice her into prowling around the Mission District to hunt up Mexican food like he had had at the Cafe Centro along the Yuba River levee during the strike.

Another brief separation followed when John visited his family in Portland over Memorial Day weekend. He told them the story of his work at the Marysville plant during dinner one night, and got a lecturing reply from Jack.

"Good going, Johnny. Sounds like you and Grenville showed that bunch of commies what for. Ever since Kennedy let Castro kick our butts at the Bay of Pigs, I've been expecting the unions to start something."

"No, Dad. It wasn't like that at all."

"Sure it was. You just choose not to see it. You'll have to wise up when you come back here and start getting serious about your career. And by the way," Jack added, "when are you going to get a phone in that apartment of yours?"

"There's been some kind of backlog on hookups in that area lately," John lied. "But I've gotten so used to the pay phone down in the lobby, it's no problem. And you can always leave messages for me at Rebecca's. Just don't call Grenville. They don't like us doing personal stuff there."

"I don't blame them," Jack said. "I tell my people the same thing."

"You've been very good about calling us this year, Johnny," his mother put in. "Much better than when you were at Stanford."

"How's that car doing?" Jack asked, pushing himself back from the table.

"Great," John answered. "I love it."

⚡ ⚡ ⚡

Tuesday, June 20, seemed a morning like any other at Grenville Sugar when John completed his fog-bound walk from the cable car and slid behind his desk about 8:10. But it was not usual at all to be summoned into his boss's heavily-carpeted, wood-paneled office at 8:25, when John was busy preparing for his daily meeting with the restaurant products team. John saw that Harcourt's long-time secretary, Bev Tinley, an always pleasant and immaculate graying blonde whose Navy husband had been killed in the Pacific, was already in one of the two chairs facing the desk.

Harcourt himself, sitting stiffly in a dark blue, banker's-stripe suit, was behind the desk and motioned John to close the door and take the other chair. Harcourt's salt-and-pepper hair looked freshly combed and his thoughtful eyes were alert, but his face was pale and John could see a tremor in his hand when he extended it for John to shake.

"I suppose you've already heard," Harcourt began.

"Heard what?" Bev answered, abruptly sitting forward in her chair.

"Nobody's said anything to me...except good morning," John added.

"Well, American Sugar's taking control of Grenville in a stock buyout. It's been hush-hush so far, but they'll be in charge in a matter of weeks. Accounting, finance and production control will be shut down here. All that stays is a regional sales office, and they'll rent out whatever space in the building they don't need for that."

"What about our jobs?" Bev broke in.

"You'll be OK right here, Bev. Don't worry. John, they'll probably transfer you to New York or New Orleans for training. Who knows after that, but they'll keep you. I'm out, myself. American is sending one of its own regional sales VP's to take over. Ted told me this morning."

"Oh, Mr. Harcourt, how awful!" Tears ran down Bev's face, the only uncontrolled act John had ever seen from her.

John himself was stunned, though he did manage to mumble a few comforting words to each of them. New Orleans? he thought. New York? There was everything wrong with those places. Not only did John not want to go there, his parents would insist on Portland instead. And either way, it would raise unavoidable marriage issues with Rebecca.

"Well," Harcourt said, standing up. "Better that both of you got the news from me first. And don't worry about my situation. I'll be fine. I was heading for retirement in a year or so anyway, and the same with Ted Fulton."

"What about restaurant products?" John asked, standing also. "What happens to the project?"

"Canceled. American already has the whole restaurant line covered, and they certainly aren't going to spend money competing with themselves."

"What about Houndsley?"

"Who knows? But that son of a bitch has always been able to float on nothing."

John sat vacantly at his desk for about five minutes, then he walked to the elevator through a storm of anxious office chatter, rode down to the lobby, and headed out the shiny brass doors. The fog was beginning to burn off. Feeling like he was encased in a transparent bubble, John turned left for no reason, crossed Market Street in the rumbling eddy of a green and yellow trolley, and kept going toward the massive abutments of the Bay Bridge until he reached the Embarcadero at Pier 23. He had never been in this part of town.

An undulating swell of dirty greenish water filled the empty slip to John's left as an out-bound tug cleared the end of the wharf and blatted its horn before turning north toward Alcatraz. Those lucky guys had real jobs, John thought, and he'd bet there were no management trainees on board. In the slip to his right stood the imposing, sixty-foot-high prow of a faded black and rust-red ocean freighter. Between the two slips, almost concealed behind piles of randomly stacked wooden pallets, was the white plywood front of a box-like building whose large, hand-lettered sign identified it as Red's Java House. Everything was pocked with sea gull droppings and exuded a funky, kelpy smell. Still in zombie mode, John walked into Red's and found himself blinded by a blast of sunlight.

All white inside and out, Red's stood on pilings over the water and had walls of windows at the back. Once his eyes adjusted, John could see Berkeley and Oakland across the bay and Treasure Island framed by the Bay Bridge in the foreground. With the fog receding to the west, the sun shone full in from the southeast and was amplified by glare off the water.

"Have a seat, young fella'," came a voice. "What can I bring ya?"

John turned to take a chrome stool at the varnished mahogany counter. "Coffee, please."

"Can do," said a short, blocky man with a ruddy-brown complexion, a black crewcut and intense dark eyes. He wore an oversized, white apron on which he was wiping his hands.

"Sure is quiet," John said, realizing that he was the only customer among the dozen or so tables and at the counter. He couldn't remember how he had gotten here, but for the moment, he felt safe.

"Always is this time of day. We start breakfast at 5 A.M. for the stevedores and warehousemen going on shift at six, then we serve a bunch of guys getting off shift, then coffee break business up to about nine, and lunch from ten until we close at three." The man put in front of John a large dun-colored ceramic mug that would weigh almost as much empty as it did full.

"Are you Red?"

"That's what everybody calls me, but the name's actually Josh. Darlene and me bought this place off Red Halleran back in '55 when I quit the service after Korea. Two wars was enough. But we kept the name, 'cause I like the joke."

"Joke?"

"Well, red's a tricky word down here on the docks, if you know your history. Besides, I'm a Hoopa Indian from up in Humboldt." He laughed. "All these years, I still think it's funny."

"OK, Red, good to meet you. I'm John."

Red nodded. "Well, Johnny Boy, we don't get much white-collar trade down here, and Darlene ain't around, so you'll have to tell your troubles to me."

"Easy. I lost my job today." Taking a sip, John noted that the coffee was not the usual watery, greasy-spoon brew.

"That's always tough," Red agreed. "But you're young, and that suit you're wearing tells me you ain't poor. The docks are picking up, so downtown will, too. Unless your boss caught you stealing, I bet you're workin' again by next month."

"No, no stealing. Nothing like that."

The door banged shut, and a swarthy man with a prominent nose and a deeply-lined face took a seat at a corner table away from the windows. He wore a black watch cap and an Army surplus jacket. "Hey, Red," he called. "What's for lunch?"

"Hey, Lou," Red answered. "I can whip you up something, but Darlene's not back from the market yet. If you wait, she's gonna be doing artichoke omelets."

"I'm no dummy. I'll wait. But gimme a coffee."

"That's Lou Caggiano," Red told John. "Retired longshoreman and big-time union guy from when Harry Bridges started running the show down here. Look, I gotta get busy. We'll be full in another fifteen minutes. But good talkin' to ya, and keep your head up."

"Thanks."

"Hey, Frank," Red called to another old-timer who came in to join Lou. "Retired cop," he said to John on his way across the room with two mugs of coffee.

Darlene, a petite peroxide blonde with a big voice, came banging in the kitchen door before John had finished his coffee, by which time half the dining area had filled with a boisterous assembly of hefty men in caps, jeans and woolen work shirts. John stayed at the counter, largely unnoticed, for a second cup of coffee and a toasted cheese sandwich with some kind of tasty green chilies in it. Then he waved at Red and left. He decided to walk home by an indirect route up the Embarcadero through North Beach and Chinatown.

Two and a half hours later, after progressing from stevedores and winos to departing cruise passengers to muttering Italian grandmothers to beatniks and to jostling throngs of Chinese shoppers and street vendors, John arrived at his apartment. He had not bought any live chickens, but he hadn't been able to avoid buying a small bag of almond cookies to snack from as he climbed the last hill. Leaving the shades down and not even removing his trousers or shirt, he pulled out the Murphy bed, crawled in and took a nap, something he hadn't done since his darkest days at Stanford.

The next sound he heard was his landlady, Mrs. Lipiski, out in the alley bullying her toy poodle in a harsh whisper. "Go pooh-pooh, Fifi! Fifi, go pooh-pooh! Go pooh-pooh!"

Since this performance normally took place at 11 P.M., John jumped from bed and lunged to the window to check his watch. Only 6:10. Thank god! He'd be half an hour late to Rebecca's, but nothing serious. He combed his hair, threw on some casual clothes, ran down to the Austin Healy and gunned it out of the alley toward Broadway. A little luck with the left turn off Larkin and the light at Van Ness, and he'd be fine.

Parking out of sight around the corner from Rebecca's building, John walked rapidly to the entryway and up the stairs. Part of her subterfuge with her family was that she would not give him a key. He avoided the brass knocker and tapped lightly with his knuckles. Their secret knock. The door opened immediately.

"Hi!" Her eyes shone. "You're late. I was worried." She pushed herself into his arms.

"Hi," he answered, kissing her forehead and neck. "Sorry. I got sidetracked with Mrs. Lipiski when I stopped at my place to change."

"That's OK. Come in and open the wine. It's a pinot noir, and were having eggplant moussaka."

"Sounds great, whatever it is."

"Well, what happened at work today? Anything special?"

"No, nothing much. Just the usual meetings. I'd rather talk about your day at the ballet."

⋇ ⋇ ⋇

John could not remember making a conscious decision to deceive Rebecca about his situation at Grenville. He never thought of himself as having a choice. He had barely been able to work there before American took over, and he certainly wasn't going back now. But she just couldn't know. Grenville was the key to his San Francisco legitimacy. And his parents couldn't know either, of course. Something else would turn up, and he would announce a job change later with full fanfare. But to cover himself, he did tell Rebecca the next night about the takeover, assuring her that his job was safe and that he had been assigned to a new, and highly secret, project he wasn't allowed to discuss with anyone. He then used her phone to give his family the same news.

"And be sure not to call me there," John reminded his father. "Everybody's walking on eggs, and I don't want to get in trouble. I've told Rebecca that, too."

Meanwhile life went on as before, except he wasn't bringing in any money, and he started each day at Red's and spent the rest of it wandering around the city. John kept his suit pants and dress shirt on, but threw a jeans jacket or sweater over them to be less conspicuous. He got back into his coat and tie at the end of the afternoon before meeting Rebecca. Then he'd change for the evening at her place. On the last day of June, he called Grenville from a pay phone and asked for Bev.

"John, hi," she answered, recognizing his voice. "What happened to you? Where've you been?"

"I'm OK, but tell Harcourt I quit. I'm working someplace else, selling insurance."

"I don't really blame you. It's a mess here. And Harcourt's gone. The new guy from New York, Steve Weller, has already arrived."

"Too bad. How're you doing?"

"I don't know. It's pretty much chaos, and Weller has terrible dandruff. He drives me nuts. But you should see Houndsley suck up to him. I don't know whether to laugh or cry."

"Look, could you take care of my final check? I have a few days pay coming since the fifteenth. Just make sure it gets mailed to my home address."

"Sure. No problem. I have the address, but Personnel doesn't have a phone for you. I've been supposed to call, and then they told me to draft a letter, but I can't get anybody to take time to approve it."

"That's all right, I don't have a phone and I don't need the letter. But thanks a lot for looking out for me. I really appreciate it."

"Glad to," Bev replied. "And John, give a call once in a while to keep in touch. There aren't many people around here now I feel comfortable with."

"I will," John said, realizing that inside information on Grenville would come in handy if he was going to be pretending he still worked there.

John bought a book of detailed city maps and carefully planned the neighborhoods he would visit during his unexpected days of freedom. He avoided the financial district, where he might run into Grenville people or Rebecca's brother-in-law, Lloyd, and he also avoided the Civic Center and Cow Hollow, where he might run into Rebecca herself. Often he would devote two or three consecutive days to the same area, driving and walking to cover it thoroughly. The Mission District seemed wondrous to him. Ethnic restaurants galore, not just Mexican, but Salvadoran, Peruvian and Argentinean. In addition, there was the Silver Follies Burlesque Palace and the Mission Dolores, with its namesake esplanade of billowing palms.

From there he branched out to Potrero Hill, China Basin, Twin Peaks, Clement Street, Irving Street, the Tenderloin and the remnants of Japan Town. All he did was lurk about, but it was lurking surrounded by people whose lives were much more real than his own. And he couldn't get enough of Golden Gate Park, Ocean Beach and the greenbelt of cliffs stretching northward from the ruins of the Sutro

Baths around to Fort Point under the Golden Gate Bridge. Something about the quality of the light hypnotized him and drew him on. Only later, when he saw a revival of the film *Vertigo*, did John realize that Hitchcock's camera had already captured the city in the way he was seeing it.

More and more, John contrived to shower at Rebecca's, and he began to store additional clothes there as well. When he was late with his July rent, John persuaded Mrs. Lipiski to apply his last month's deposit and allow him to move out as of August 1, even though he hadn't given the required notice. She had always liked him, and readily obliged. This was a risky maneuver, but despite the extra cost of a post office box and the bother of having his mail forwarded, it saved him a major expense. He put his few household things and his unpacked boxes from Stanford in storage at Busvan's and began to keep his working wardrobe in the trunk of his car. Each week John told himself he would read the want ads and look for a job, but each week it didn't happen.

Nonetheless, with Red's as an alternate base of operations when he couldn't finesse things at Rebecca's, he managed to keep his hold on the status quo. As far as he could tell, she had no inkling that he was no longer working at Grenville and that the apartment at 1492 Pacific was no longer his. Rebecca sensed something, though. Relations between them grew strained, and she was getting noticeably drunk most nights. Any hint of withdrawal on his part reduced her to weeping fits of need. The most despicable thing John did during this period of lies and deceit was to use Rebecca's emotional fragility to his advantage. Yet he was initially oblivious to such concerns, because he was caught up in the excitement of floating so many lies and getting away with them. Think of it: John McDonough from Portland, Oregon leading a double life.

Red's, where he was seen as a frustrated job seeker, began as John's only personal haven. He found a second in August, when Rudy, another of Red's regulars, put him onto the California Historical Society library on Jackson at Octavia. Now John could pursue the written history of any part of the city in an opulent, mansion-like setting with a spacious and generally vacant men's room where he could also shave and change clothes when necessary. He presented himself as an impecunious, would-be graduate student and made the most of what was offered. With two such havens, plus Rebecca's, lots of restaurant meals, and regular trips to the dry cleaners and laundromat, he found he could live rather agreeably. It did take money, though, and his checking account was dwindling fast.

Of course, he had a major asset in his car, and what forced the issue was bottoming out hard on one of the impossibly steep ridges in Bernal Heights during a day of wandering. The ensuing noise from his transmission was like an icy hand around John's neck. He tried to ignore it, but it got so bad that Rebecca insisted he do something. Finally, a visit to the Austin Healy dealership in late August confirmed the worst: $400, and a long wait for parts from England.

Selling the car to the dealer for $3,600 under these circumstances seemed a master stroke, but John also knew that the whole game had fundamentally changed. No semblance of the life Rebecca and his parents thought he was living now remained. But for the moment, he had a bunch of money, and the excuse of parts coming from England explained away their having to use Rebecca's Plymouth for a Labor Day trip to join her parents at Tahoe and for subsequent outings around town. Without his car trunk as a private space, John secretly kept more of his wardrobe at Rebecca's, and the rest in a couple of boxes stashed at Red's. Then a third haven unexpectedly appeared.

John's time at the Historical Society had been growing, because it was an easy walk to Cow Hollow in the evenings. The Monday following Labor Day, a little past five o'clock, he left the Society and detoured to nearby Lafayette Park to enjoy the view. The weather was balmy by San Francisco standards and the park was crowded. Both tennis courts were busy, one side with three young boys hitting balls every which way, and the other with a group of old men who could barely run playing round-robin doubles. After about fifteen minutes, John headed west on Sacramento Street, thinking to cut back to Vallejo along upper Fillmore.

At 3125 Fillmore, he came to a shabby, double-wide store front he had never noticed while driving by. The place was dark, though a faint light showed over a partition at the rear. In black-outlined gold lettering, each of the two front windows said:

Salle d'Arms

Hans F. Bierstadt, Master

Fencing Instruction, Inquire Within

Fencing—the word produced a surge of emotion, yet John hadn't given it a serious thought in years. He pressed his nose to the glass. In the gloom he saw a hardwood floor bisected diagonally with a wide linoleum strip. Two narrower strips paralleled the side walls, along which were waist-high racks holding almost invisible masks, foils, epees and sabers. He considered pounding on the door, but looked for a phone number instead. None visible. Damn! And no business hours posted, either. But he'd be back.

"Baby, baby, what's happening to us?" Rebecca wailed from the kitchen door after John arrived for dinner and all but ignored her. "I can see something is tearing you up. Can't you tell me? Is it this project at work or what?" She had had who knows how much wine before he got there.

"That's part of it," he said wearily. "A lot of change, and a lot of New York assholes running around contradicting each other. And you know the new boss, Weller, drives me nuts. He's unapproachable, but somehow Houndsley has become his right hand man. Also, I'm in the dumps about my car." He hoped this sounded convincing. It did to him, anyway. The part about his car was true, and thanks to Bev, there was a germ of truth to the rest as well.

"Time will take care of all of that. And we have my car. When you get down like this, it scares me."

"I'm not that down. I just don't want to talk right now. Don't let it get you."

At her instigation, they went to a movie that night at the Clay Theater, one block down and across the street from the Bierstadt Salle d'Arms. John stared at it while they were waiting to buy tickets, and he couldn't think about anything else once they were inside. The movie was some boring Ingemar Bergman thing that passed him right by. Later, in bed, Rebecca did whatever she could to rouse him. He responded, but when she drifted off to sleep, he swung back and forth between the unwanted recognition that he was a shit for lying to her all the time and long-buried memories of Stanford fencing.

The next day, just after 12:30, John arrived at 3125 Fillmore in his business suit. Again, no one was visible, but the door was unlocked and he let himself in.

"Hello," John called across the unlit room.

"Ja...who iss dat?" came an answer in heavily accented English. The lights switched on and an erect figure in a black beret and turtleneck, charcoal trousers, and discolored tennis shoes walked toward him.

"Are you Maestro Bierstadt?"

"Ja...but call me Hans. I make only the teenagers call me Maestro Bierstadt." Hans was perhaps sixty years old and hadn't shaved that day. He was about John's height, wore thick tortoise-rimmed glasses and had strands of silver-gray hair combed back over his ears. No doubt he was bald under the beret.

"I'm John McDonough. I think I want to become a student."

"Good. I can help you. Saturday times are now all taken, and we are closed Sunday and Monday. But any weekday before two, when the kinder get out of school, we can set up a time. Come into the office and sit down."

John ran his eyes around and took a deep breath. Talk about atmosphere! Vintage fencing photographs adorned the walls above the weapons racks, and the smell was intoxicating. Floor wax, metal polish, sweat, and a hint of cigar smoke. John followed Hans into an office that was so unkempt it bordered on being a landfill.

"Here," Hans said, lifting a stack of sports equipment catalogues off a plain wooden chair. "The fee is $25 for each four lessons, payable in advance." He sat at a deeply piled desk on which a heavy scheduling ledger comprised the top layer. "Have you fenced before?"

"Yes, some. But not in a long time."

"What weapons?"

"Epee and foil."

"Then it will be foil. I no longer teach epee. Foil and saber are my specialties."

"OK. I have the $25 now. How about 1 o'clock on Tuesdays and Thursdays? I only work part time, so I'm free those afternoons."

"Ja...that would be good. We will begin at 1:15. The lessons are thirty minutes, but you must arrive beforehand to warm-up. And two lessons per week?"

"Yes, I really want to push myself."

"Dis is Tuesday. Shall we start?"

John was taken aback. "I wasn't really planning to. I have no equipment with me."

"We can loan you equipment. And the sooner we assess your skills, the better. Later, if you need them, I can help you order your own foils and other gear by mail from Castelli in New York. This is the best source I know. There is nowhere to buy such things here."

Foil is the classic weapon. Unlike epee, where points are gained when the tip touches any part of the opponent's body, or saber, where both the tip and the edge of the weapon may be used, points in foil require that the tip touch the opponent's torso. Offensive moves must be more subtle, and defensive stratagems are more difficult to penetrate.

Within a few minutes John was wearing an old pair of Hans's elk-soled fencing shoes that had not been white in a long time, a padded white vest, and a wire-mesh mask tipped up on the back of his head. In his hand was a good, but well-used foil selected from one of the racks. John stood near the rightmost linoleum strip, lightly hefting his weapon to check its balance and blade angle. These operations felt both strangely familiar and utterly foreign. Above John's head was a three-by-four-foot poster of fencing immortal Lazlo Krasge at the 1928 Amsterdam Olympics. John remembered that Krasge, a Hungarian, had there become the only man in Olympic history to win gold medals in all three weapons in the same competition.

While John was crouching and bending a few times to stretch his muscles, Hans arrived, wearing a black fencing jacket and having changed into soft black leather shoes. He held a foil in one hand and his mask tucked under the other arm. "Now?" Hans asked.

"Yes," John answered. He stepped onto the strip facing Hans. They bowed slightly to one another and pulled their masks into place.

"En garde. Ready? Fence," said Hans.

Each wanted the other to attack immediately, but each was too experienced to do so. John already knew that Hans, like himself, was right-handed, and he noted that Hans favored the pronated grip. This information helped John, who preferred a more supinated grip, decide what he should and should not attempt. Hans was filing away the same information about John as they stalked one another up and down the strip with feints, lunges, and retreats.

Hans made what John felt sure was a feint to the left as though he would come under John's foil for a touch on the opposite side. Rather than react and leave himself open to counterattack, John faked the parry for an instant, then snapped his wrist to bring the tip of his foil around in a blur of metal. Hans was hundredths of a second late with his parry, allowing John a solid touch on Hans's right abdomen before Hans's blade briefly slid against John's.

"Ja...touch. Very good. You are fast." Hans stepped back and squared himself. "En garde."

This time John did attack immediately and got away with it. He drew Hans to him by jumping backward a step, then suddenly unleashed a crouching forward lunge that closed on the older man before he could retreat. With his foil trapped above John's arm, Hans took a light upward touch to the side of his chest.

"Touch again," Hans acknowledged. "I must take my new student more seriously."

The next touch was scored by Hans after a prolonged stalemate of feints and parries. Hans maneuvered John's feet badly out of position and thrust so unexpectedly that John stumbled instead of making a successful retreat. Hans quickly scored again on an elegant time-thrust that deflected John's attack and touched him above the right hip an eye-wink before John could parry and launch a riposte. They had been fencing no more than fifteen minutes, but John was exhausted. Hans himself was breathing heavily.

"One more," Hans said. "En Garde."

Hans began a sustained attack outside, from John's right. John worked to force back Hans's blade and create his own offensive opportunity, but Hans expertly maintained controlling leverage. When John finally did gain an opening and lunged to exploit it, he remained alert for Hans to repeat the previously successful time-thrust. Hans tried, but John stopped him. Hans then parried away John's attempted riposte. Hans, too, had been ready. But after a few more feints to the outside, Hans shifted his feet for what John assumed would be an inside attack. Instead, Hans came at John head-on, attacking toward the base of his foil and pushing it away. The tenth-of-a-second it took John to recover was all Hans needed to land a solid touch at the upper right.

"Touch," Hans said, having clearly surprised John with a strength move that would be daring even for a man who was much larger than his opponent. John removed his mask and bowed. "I have much to learn."

"You have less than you think," wheezed Hans, mask in hand and returning the bow. "That was an old man's last trick. Let us sit."

He led John to a small, windowless living area off one end of the office. In addition to a plain linoleum table, matching chrome chairs, a double-burner hot plate, an ancient refrigerator and a neatly-made army cot, there was a wall of books and an obviously expensive hi-fi phonograph system. Like the office, this room was separated from the main space by partitions that did not extend all the way to the ceiling. A small bathroom with a stall shower and fully finished walls was inset behind the office. In the far back, John learned later, were a few lockers, a makeshift closet, and additional storage space.

Hans took a carafe of chilled water from the refrigerator and poured them each a glass. "We will not do that again," he said, "but it was valuable. You have problems with the footwork and your riposte is slow, but you defend well. And you have fenced much. Where?" He sat heavily at the table.

"In prep school, then two seasons at Stanford about four years ago."

Hans's eyes wrinkled in a smile. "You fenced for Rollo? A wonderful man. I have had many saber matches against him."

"Yes, that was his weapon," John answered. "How did you know him?"

"Ten and fifteen years ago, I fenced with the Pannoina team. He came to San Francisco all the time to find competition. There was none in Palo Alto then." Hans looked closely at John. "Tell me again your name."

"John McDonough. I live here now."

"I know you! Ja...from Stanford. The one Rollo called...what was it?...the Whamit Kid. I saw you win a match against Cal in Berkeley."

"He called me the Willamette Kid. It was embarrassing. The Willamette is a big river in Oregon near where I grew up."

"Ja...I know it. But you broke his heart when you quit. Why did you do that?"

"It's a long story. One I don't like to tell."

"Is the extra thickness of the lens on the right side of your glasses perhaps a clue? A little more probing, and I might find a weakness there."

"No," John said with a smile. "That was a childhood injury. My left eye more than makes up for it." But, John thought, the old fox was observant and, like any good fencer, eager to take advantage. Those heavy attacks to the outside had been intentional.

Hans nodded. The outer door banged and footsteps came across the fencing floor. "I must go," said Hans, pushing himself up. "My next students have arrived."

Two handsome Japanese-American brothers, fourteen and sixteen, were donning their gear in one corner of the large room as Hans and John emerged from the back. They jumped to their feet and bowed. "Good afternoon, Maestro Bierstadt," they said together.

Hans bowed in return. "John, I want you to meet Matt and Tom Yasuda. They are fine young men. Boys, this is John McDonough, a new student who fenced at Stanford."

Upon this news, Matt and Tom ran to shake John's hand, followed by a round of bows.

"Stay and watch, if you like," Hans told John.

"Thanks, I will for a while. Then I'll just slip out. But tell me, did you know Krasge?" John pointed to the Olympic poster under which they had been fencing. He had suddenly remembered that Rollo once mentioned something to him about a famous old German fencer in San Francisco.

"Ja, I knew him very well...in Berlin. Those were great days. Painful to think about now."

"Maybe we can trade stories. I've never told anyone why I stopped fencing, but I'll tell you. One thing, though...please don't let Rollo know you have seen me."

"As you wish, but I see him almost never these years." Hans stood quietly for a moment. "Until Thursday, then," he said, moving off to begin work with his young students.

From the doorway, John watched Hans drill the two brothers in foil and have them practice new moves at reduced speed. When they switched to saber, which the boys, of course, preferred, John left and walked aimlessly south toward Geary and the Negro neighborhoods clustered near there. That had been quite a successful two hours. If he didn't think about Rebecca, he felt good, and there was always plenty to see on the streets.

∗ ∗ ∗

Before his second fencing lesson, John picked up a deli sandwich and went to the Salle early. Hans was eating scrambled eggs in the back and, as John had hoped, he asked John to join him. But rather than talk, Hans wanted to listen to a stately, booming orchestral work that was playing on his hi-fi. John's only option was to relax and try to let the music carry him along.

"Haydn," Hans said after the finale. "Symphony 104 in D, also known as the *London*. Now that I am old, I listen only to Haydn. The symphonies and the string quartets. Oh, and to Django Reinhardt."

"Who?"

"You don't know Django? Jazz guitar. I will introduce you when we have time. I brought his original recordings with me from Europe."

Nervously honoring his offer of two days before, John raised the subject of Rollo Gans and why John had left the Stanford fencing team.

"I want to tell you what happened at Stanford to see if it makes sense to anyone besides me," he began. "I didn't have the grades. There's no argument about that. But it's absolutely standard for ineligible athletes to continue to practice with the team. Happens all the time in football, track, tennis, you name it. Rollo had even done it before."

"Ja."

"But my parents complained to the dean. They wanted me punished. My father is an alumnus, and so was my grandfather. They've donated money to the Stanford building fund over the years. So the dean talked to Rollo and told him I shouldn't be allowed to even practice with the team until my grades were good enough.

"If fencing had still been a club, like it was when I started, grades wouldn't have mattered. But Rollo didn't stick up for me. He could have told the dean I should be treated like everyone else. But he didn't. He explained that he was sorry, he wanted me back the next semester, but I had to stop coming to practice. I told him to go to hell."

"Not Rollo's finest hour," Hans agreed. "But why were your grades so low? I cannot believe you are a dumkopf."

"I didn't always know the answer to that question. My parents made me go to Stanford. They made me major in economics, which I hated. To flunk was the only way I could fight back. And it worked. It drove my father crazy. But I didn't want to flunk out, I wanted to fence. My parents turned fencing into one more way to control me."

"There is a saying in German, and in English also, about the foolishness of giving someone a stick to beat you with. You must see now that is exactly what you did."

"Yes, I do. Now I do. I should have either called their bluff and refused to go to Stanford at all, or I should have done the work while I was there."

"Did Stanford teach you Kierkegaard?"

"Yes, some. The first so-called modern philosopher. Danish, right?"

"Ja...I will quote him. Kierkegaard said 'Life can only be understood backwards, but it must be lived forwards.' And you, of course, must go forward from here."

"Sure, you're right. That's all anyone can do."

"Now we shall get on with the fencing," Hans said. "You need conditioning drills, especially lunges and backstepping. Then I will work you in slow motion—a very useful technique I have adapted from Tai Chi. Another day I will tell you about Krasge."

The following week John lunched with Hans before his lessons on Tuesday and Thursday, and he stayed through the afternoon both days to talk and to help Hans with the other students. This was clearly to be the new pattern. John had already reclaimed his own foil and other equipment from Busvan's, and he moved them into a battered locker at the far back of the Salle. He could also shower and change at the Salle when necessary.

Red's began to fall by the wayside, so John went down one morning at the end of September to say goodbye. He told people there he had gotten a job selling sports equipment for a company in Daly City, way across town. The few regulars in the room shook his hand and made a fuss. Darlene gave him a kiss, and Red staked him to a free piece of homemade banana cream pie. Feeling a little sheepish about his duplicity, John was sitting at the counter enjoying the pie and the last of the morning lull when Lou Caggiano, the retired longshoreman, came in and sat next to him.

"Crazy weather," Lou announced. "Blowing fifteen, twenty miles an hour out there." He unbuttoned his army jacket but left his cap on. "Long time no see," Lou went on, giving John a craggy smile. "But, tell me, what the hell do you make of this? Wind wrapped it around my ankle a couple blocks back."

Lou reached into his pocket and handed John a sheet of beat-up white paper. On one side was a line of faded, purple mimeographed words in oversized, block letters: "DO LIKE YOU ARE TOLD." Then, at the bottom, in smaller, even more faded letters, it said, "Waterfront Gospel Mission, 441 Brannan Street." By this time Red had brought Lou some coffee and was craning over the counter to see, too.

John didn't know what to say, but Red jumped right in. "For you, Lou, that could be an important message. I mean, when was the last time you did what you were told?"

"Can't remember," Lou laughed. "But who's doing the telling? Does it mean God or the wife?"

"There's a difference?" cracked Darlene, leaning crosswise in the kitchen door. "Don't let Red find out." They all laughed.

"But I'm half-serious here," Lou said. "It came whipping down the street and stuck to me like glue. What's it supposed to mean? Far as I know, God's never been real clear about sending advice my way."

"Maybe it's not God," Darlene answered. "Maybe it means you should listen to what Red calls the inner voice."

"What's the inner voice?" John asked, painfully aware that in his own life his parents did the telling, because he always let them define the alternatives.

"Kind of an Indian thing," Red answered. "When you need to figure out something in your life, you seek the inner voice by fasting and by going through physical hardship. You know...cold, wet, isolation, walking long distances and like that. It's helped me."

"Think I'll wait for God," Lou said. "I got enough of that other crap working longshore."

"Speakin' of working," Red changed the subject, "Johnny, here, finally got a job. And we ain't gonna' be seeing him down this way, 'cause he's gonna' be in Daly City."

"No shit?" Lou responded, sticking out his hand. "Congrats. Doin' what?"

They shook and John told Lou his made-up news while getting himself ready to leave.

"Well, kid, good luck," Lou said. "But don't let them screw you over. From what I've seen, bosses are all the same, and they'll all try."

These were good people, but John had deceived them anyway. What was worse, they probably would have been just as accepting if he'd told the truth to begin with. But once you create the web of lies, how do you get out? John crammed the contents of his two stored clothing boxes into a suitcase he had borrowed from Hans, lugged it over to Third Street, and took the bus back to Fillmore.

By now, though, spending time with Hans came as naturally as breathing. And Hans knew more of the truth than anyone, which was a relief. Since John always arrived and departed in a suit and tie, it was easy to let Hans believe he was working irregular part-time hours at some kind of sales job. But otherwise John explained that he lived with his girl friend not far away, that her parents were unaware of this arrangement, that he had left Grenville Sugar, that he had sold his car and given up his apartment to keep expenses down, and that he was extremely concerned his parents would somehow force him to come home to Portland to work in the family business if they knew any of this. John did not add that his girl friend was as much in the dark as his parents.

"Ja..." Hans said after John provided this information. "You and I have much in common. We are both from wealthy families, we both disappointed our parents at the university, we both refused the family business, and we are both fencers. This is something, is it not?"

As best John could piece the story together, Hans had been born in 1902 or 1903. He was a much-loved only child from Bremen, where his father ran a successful import-export and shipping business. Hans had been young enough to avoid WWI, and his family survived the disastrous Weimar inflation because they had access to reserves of foreign currency. He had fenced from an early age and had always been good. By the mid 1920's, Hans was enjoying the life of a university dilettante in Berlin when he fell in with Lazlo Krasge, a fencing prodigy from Budapest who was a few years older. To his parents distress, this effectively ended Hans's academic studies, and he spent the next decade in Berlin as a sometime fencing instructor, a sometime commercial representative for his father's business, and a sometime denizen of the infamous cabarets of that era. The rise of the Nazis ultimately propelled Hans to London along with his parents, and after the war, Hans propelled himself to San Francisco.

"You see in the Krasge poster?" Hans asked, pointing above John's head. "I was there. That is me standing in the background with the German team, behind Krasge and to the left. I am the only one holding a weapon."

"Amazing," John said. "The event of a lifetime. But didn't Krasge fence for Hungary?"

"Ja, always. And that brought trouble."

"How so?"

"Krasge was from a German-speaking family with blood ties to the old nobility in both countries. He lived in Berlin most of his adult life. He could easily have fenced for Germany, but he would not because of anger at the German role in drawing Hungary into the 1914 war. This was not an issue in 1928, the year of his great triumph. But as Nazi influence grew, in 1932 and especially for the Berlin Olympics in 1936, much pressure was put on him. Finally, he was denounced as a Jew and forced to flee to Budapest before the games. He was threatened with arrest at the border if he tried to return."

"Krasge was Jewish?" John looked at the architypical Aryan figure in the poster.

"Ja, apparently in some way on his father's side, though his parents were both dead by then and he had only his sister left. I myself was a Jew in the eyes of the Nazis. And in the eyes of the Israelis, I am still." Hans walked into the living area and lowered himself into one of the chairs. John followed.

"And that's why your family went to England?"

"Ja...my mother's mother was Jewish. That means my mother was a Jew and so am I, because in Judaism, the blood descends through the mother. I am automatically a citizen of Israel, if I choose to go there."

"But you came here?"

"Ja, and now I am an American. Better, I think. Nothing in my family was ever Jewish.

We went to Dutch Reformed Church, even my grandmother. To be a Jew is as foreign to me as to be an Eskimo."

"Where is Krasge now?"

"Dead. He and his sister both. They were killed by the Nazis in the camps. Or they died there. It is the same thing. But he was a remarkable man. The best I have ever known. He taught me not just fencing. He taught me life."

"And your parents are dead, too?"

"Ja, but I give my father great credit. He was ready when the trouble came, and he got us out safely on one of his company's ships. He had many business ties in England. We were not poor when we lived there."

"Then they died after the war?"

"Ja...the air raids were terrifying, and they were very hard on my mother. She was never well after that time. She died in 1948, the year I came here. My father died a year later. They are buried in England. None of us ever returned to Germany."

"And you had to learn English."

"I always knew some English, and so did my father. My mother never learned. She would not try. And I can read and write English better than I speak." Hans reached to the bookcase and pulled a couple of yellowed paperbacks from the middle shelf. "And here is how I learned American."

John took the books from Hans. Murder mysteries, and very lurid-looking ones at that— Red Harvest and The Big Sleep. John smiled. Kierkegaard, then this; what next?

"Dashiell Hammett and Raymond Chandler," Hans bragged. "I have all their books. The hard-boiled private dicks. I love these people."

"Hans, you're full of life. Why do you keep calling yourself old?"

"Because I am sick. And because I feel old. I have seen much—two wars and three countries."

"Sick how? You beat me three touches out of five when we fenced."

Hans sighed. "I have the stomach ulcers, a very bad case."

"Then what are these doing here." John pointed to a line of empty wine bottles along the wall leading to the office door. From the labels, Hans obviously had a taste for Medoc, the best he could afford. "I remember my uncle saying he had to give up wine because of his ulcers."

"Ja, my doctor says the same. And stop my cigars, too, he says. But I have only this one life. I am responsible for it, and I live it as I choose."

As John got to know him better, he saw that Hans had good days and bad days. At times Hans would vigorously demonstrate fencing techniques and fence for a few moments with each student. Other times he taught almost entirely from a chair. And one Thursday, when John arrived for a pre-lesson lunch, he found Hans still lying in his cot wrapped in blankets from the night before. John made him some soup, did solo fencing drills, and stayed to teach the two remaining afternoon lessons on his own. Fortunately, the students involved were accepting of this. The next afternoon, John went to the Salle unexpectedly, and was relieved to see Hans up and about, working with a blonde, female student from San Francisco State named Janice, who was quite a good fencer.

Not surprisingly, John's fencing also showed steady improvement. And while there were no further personal revelations on either side, Hans added to the fencing instruction the project of advancing John's cultural education. Hans's collection of Haydn string quartets came out, and he would play them loudly, periodically stopping to explain musical points. Number 77 in C, the *Kaiserquartett*, was Hans's particular favorite, despite its Deutschland Uber Alles theme, and John got so he could recognize almost every bar. He did not respond to Haydn as Hans did, but he was certainly listening with new ears.

Django Reinhardt was another story. Hans's scratchy, old 78's greatly interfered with the sound, but what Hans called the Hot Club Quintet had the innocent joy of dixieland coupled with an intense, driving beat. The violin, played by Stephan Grapelli, exchanged ingenious riffs and solos with Django on every line of popular standards from the 20's and 30's like *Charleston* and *After You've Gone*. Of course Hans loved it. This was the music of Hans's Berlin party days as a young man. John wondered if Rebecca knew of the Hot Club Quintet. There was no doubt she would like it as much as he did. And when he learned that Django, a Gypsy who could not read music, was missing a finger on one hand, John was completely entranced.

✹ ✹ ✹

"What's that, sweetie?" Rebecca asked as John arrived one October Tuesday evening holding Hans's copy of *The Big Sleep*.

"A trashy murder mystery. A guy at work was reading it. I thought it looked like fun, so he offered to pass it along. The author uses such incredible language you can't help but keep going."

"Let's see," she patted John's forearm lightly and took the book. "What a funny old edition. It's practically falling apart. You know, I think they made a movie of this one with Bogart and Bacall."

"No kidding. That would be a kick to see if it ever comes around at one of the art theaters."

Rebecca smiled glowingly. "You've been in so much better a mood this last week or so. I'm really, really glad." They exchanged a long kiss. "I didn't see how it could be my fault, but I didn't know what was wrong. You haven't said you loved me in a long time."

"I know, and I'm sorry. I do love you, Becca. I need to say it more."

She stood with her head on his shoulder. "I want to celebrate tonight. Let's go someplace special."

"OK. How about Le Trianon? I'll keep my suit on and you can dress up."

"I'd love that. Give me about twenty minutes." She pulled away and took a few steps toward the bedroom. "Oh, honey," she said, turning back, "Daddy called at work and asked me to have you call him in the next day or two."

"Yeah, OK. What's that about?"

"He wants to take you to lunch at the Pacific Union Club in a few weeks, when he gets home from his trip back east."

"Really? That's new. I'll call him tomorrow, I guess."

This development might not be ominous, but John couldn't help being concerned. Then again, maybe the threat of a formal audience with Harvey Minter would prod him into extracting himself from the all-encompassing mess he had turned his life into since June. If John lined up a new job, he could tell Rebecca he was taking a few weeks off in anticipation of the change and stop the whole Grenville charade. And the Salle gave him such perfect cover in terms of living arrangements that she probably wouldn't mind if he told her he was getting rid of his apartment. Finally, with the assurance of money coming in, he could buy a cheap car of some kind and say that more problems had been discovered with the Healy and he had given up on it. John was actually beginning to see a way out. All he had to do was take things one step at a time.

The softly-lit dining room at Le Trianon was no more than half-full, and there had been no wait. They ordered champagne. Rebecca looked perfect in a black sheath dress and pearl choker. John could see her facing him against the background of a gray-green brocaded wall, and also in profile in a gilt-edged mirror to her right. She was fragile, he knew that, especially when she was drunk. But she had backed off on the drinking lately, and there was no doubt that she loved him. They made a silent, intimate toast when the champagne arrived. And god, she was a babe! That was one thing about her you couldn't miss.

"Do you have any idea why your dad wants to talk to me?" he asked while they were sharing a salade Nicoise. "I mean, the Pacific Union Club. Yoiks!"

"No, not really," she answered in a tone that told him she almost certainly did. "But I know he likes to go there, and you are a McDonough, after all."

"Maybe I could change my name," he joked. It seemed time to push a little. "Anyway, Becca, I've been thinking. You don't suppose he's so old-fashioned he's going to ask me what my intentions are toward his daughter. Could that be it?"

She smiled enigmatically. "Well, he is that old-fashioned. It's embarrassing, but I guess he might be up to something along those lines."

"My intentions are honorable. You know that, don't you?" He looked steadily into her eyes. Then he broke a sly grin. "But I wonder what I'll tell your dad when he asks?"

She simultaneously blushed and giggled. "Mr. McDonough," she asked in mock anger, "has a lady ever thrown a glass of champagne in your face?"

That Rebecca was happy was evident to their waiter and to all the adjoining tables. She leaned across to feed John tastes of her salmon mousse and begged him for bites of his coque au vin. Over a dessert of apple tart, he began to carry out his new plan.

"Did you know that I was on the fencing team at Stanford?"

"No, you never told me. How exciting! I love the dueling scenes in operas."

"I only fenced about two years. I was actually fairly good, but I got kicked off for bad grades."

"What a shame. How come you're telling me now?"

"Well, I hadn't thought about fencing in years, but the other night after work, I took the Pine Street bus and got off at Fillmore so I could be outside and walk over to your place. Anyway, just across and down from the Clay Theater, there's a fencing academy. I'd never seen it before, and it was closed when I was there. But now I'm thinking I might like to start taking lessons."

"Oh, you should. That would be wonderful. And right close by. Did you get the phone number?"

"No, I looked, but it wasn't on the door or the windows. The sign said the fencing master is named Bierstadt. I looked him up in the phone book at the office the next day, but for some reason he isn't listed. There's nothing at that address in the yellow pages under fencing, either. I'm going to go over on Saturday and see how things look."

"I want to come, too."

"Could you do me a favor and wait a while? The guy might turn out to be a jerk, and I know I'll be rusty. It would make me self-conscious if you came now."

"OK. But I really want to see my man sword fighting some day."

"Some day you will, I promise."

The whole thing about Hans and the phone was odd. Despite being in business, Hans wanted his privacy, and refused to list or display his phone number. John had learned the number, Fillmore-6-6643, because Hans gave every student a business card showing all the relevant information. That way students could mail in checks if they wanted to, and could give the phone number to their families or use it to cancel or reschedule lessons.

When John asked Hans about this and told him he should at least have an ad in the yellow pages, Hans was curtly dismissive. John still remembered his response word-for-word. "Ach, no," Hans had replied. "I do not wish to deal with strangers on the telephone. There must be chemistry between the students and the master. They must first meet me face-to-face. And they must be sincere enough to come to the Salle and find me, as you did." What a purist Hans was, John mused, watching Rebecca finish the last of her coffee.

"Thank you, sweetheart," Rebecca whispered in John's ear while he was driving them back to Cow Hollow in her car. "The dinner was heavenly. Too bad we have to work tomorrow. I'd like to go dancing at the Starlight Room right now." She cuddled against him in the front seat, and he kissed the top of her head.

As John eased the car into the parking area under Rebecca's building, she gently pushed herself away from him. "I have an idea," she said. "You know your good glen-plaid suit, the brown one, that's in the far corner of my closet?"

"Yes."

"It looks so sharp on you, I'm going to have it specially cleaned and pressed so you can wear it when you go to lunch with my father."

"You don't have to do that, Becca. I can take care of it."

"No," she said, leaning against his shoulder again. "I want to do it."

❄ ❄ ❄

The following day, John dropped in and used Hans's phone to call Dr. Minter at home, and they set a lunch date for the first week in November. Everything was cordial, and John had to admit that Harvey Minter was a pretty good guy. You could do a lot worse for a father-in-law, that's for sure. Look what Rebecca would be getting if John ended up marrying her. And while he was there, John confirmed to Hans that he would be coming to the Salle on Saturday to visit for a while. Hans had been urging him to do so. That's when the better fencers were around, he said. Hans wanted John to meet them and perhaps to fence a few matches. You are ready, Hans reassured him. Hans himself looked pale and was moving more slowly than usual, but he was in good spirits and full of charm.

The next few days John paid close attention to the *Chronicle* and *Examiner* want ads when he was at the Historical Society. There were possibilities, and Ada, one of the librarians, generously let him use her phone to make some calls. At least that got the ball rolling. And with the end seemingly in sight, John appreciated more fully what a critical bastion of calm the Society had been before he met Hans and things were at their worst.

Saturday morning John left Rebecca's about 9:45 to walk the ten or so blocks to the Salle. Earlier, Rebecca had made him a wonderful breakfast and had been all aflutter when he left. It was a beautiful mid-October day, the time of year when San Francisco weather is at its peak, just before the winter rains begin. The bay, a striking midnight blue marked with whitecaps and a myriad of sailboats, came into and out of view as he headed east on Broadway. And once he reached the Salle, everything went splendidly.

The atmosphere was more like a festival than a course of instruction. No wonder Hans was closed on Sundays and Mondays. Anybody would need two days to recover from this. Ten to fifteen people were there at all times, though the faces changed as students and onlookers drifted in and out. The three strips were busy non-stop with lessons or the clashing metal of bouts arranged by Hans, who moved irrepressibly to and fro, teaching, observing and interrupting to whatever degree he thought necessary. The Yasuda boys came for a while to learn by watching the older fencers, and so did some of the other weekday students.

Hans introduced John around, and made sure that he fenced the 35 year-old stockbroker son of a famous writer as well as two former Cal fencers whom John vaguely remembered as upperclassmen when he was a Stanford freshman. He lost a close match to one of them, beat the other handily, and tied the stockbroker four touches apiece after Hans insisted they stop at a not-so-friendly draw. Having no winner this time, Hans claimed, would heighten the future rivalry. For breaks, everyone had brought coffee, sweet rolls, sandwiches, sodas or something of the sort, which they were anxious to share.

John radiated well-being when he returned to Rebecca's at 3 that afternoon. It was the best time he could remember having in years. All the nagging contradictions and dangers associated with his personal swamp of deceit fell away when he had his foil in his hand, and John knew he had fenced well.

"You were there a long time," Rebecca said, meeting him with a kiss at the door. "That must mean things went OK."

"Better than OK," John exulted. "The master, Hans, is an old guy who is really cool, and the students were friendly. I'm way out of shape, but I can still fence. They loaned me some equipment to work out with, passed sandwiches around, and the next thing I knew it was five hours later."

"How lucky you happened to see that place."

"Sure was. Anyway, now I'm set up with lessons Tuesdays and Thursdays at 5:30, which means I won't be here until about 6:30 on those days."

"That will be so good for you. And remember, pretty soon you have to let me come and watch. By the way, I picked up your brown suit at the cleaners today. It looks great."

"Oh...thanks. How about I take you for a picnic on the bluffs at the Palace of the Legion of Honor tomorrow? Then we can go inside to see those Monet water lilies you like so much."

"Sounds wonderful. And the weather is going to be perfect. But I heard on the radio the first big storm of the season is supposed to come in by Tuesday."

Monday and Tuesday went by slowly. When you're ripe for change, John remembered from his dismal last year in Palo Alto, the familiar becomes claus-trophobic. He checked his post office box several times and lingered restlessly at the Historical Society. Along with his usual reading, John caught up on the want ads, something he couldn't do when he was with Rebecca, made a few calls, and actually got a 3:30 interview set up for Thursday afternoon at the Patterson Employment Agency downtown on Sutter Street.

They seemed to specialize in sales and marketing jobs, where John could maybe draw on his Grenville experience, and they had management trainee slots listed, too. Another office job didn't sound that appealing, but god, it was change, and it was a way out of this mess. The new season signaled by the Tuesday arrival of the cold, blowy storm Rebecca had warned of gave John further impetus. You couldn't be prowling the streets all day in this kind of weather.

Hans was perky for John's Tuesday lesson, though he taught mainly from his chair. But to make up for it, Hans had John fence long sessions with Matt and Tom Yasuda, something all four of them greatly enjoyed. John then stayed to visit and listen to Haydn and Django before walking to Rebecca's in a downpour that had forced him to borrow Hans's umbrella.

Wednesday John made a fascinating discovery. Ada, at the Historical Society, acquainted him with the work of Amado Muro in the form of stories and articles from the *Bakersfield Californian* that she pulled from the archives. Muro, whose real name was Chester Seltzer, had been born in 1915 in Cleveland, Ohio, the son of a wealthy Republican newspaper baron. After college, Seltzer drifted off to the Southwest, was jailed as a draft resister during WWII, married a Mexican woman, changed his name and published dozens of semi-autobiographical pieces on hobo life, fruit bums, desert loners and the gritty tag ends of the wild fron-tier. Hans had to hear this. Muro's was a transformation more complete than Hans's own, and beyond anything John would dream. Not something, however, that Rebecca could be expected to appreciate.

Hans was having another off day that Thursday. He was up, but pale and shaky. His eyes were pouchy under his glasses frames and his trademark beret was miss-ing. The beret would turn up by tomorrow, Hans insisted, and everything would be fine. John offered to cook something, but Hans didn't want to eat, and that meant John would miss lunch, too. Having nearly been late for his lesson, John had not had time to bring his usual sandwich. He'd have to get a snack later, after the interview. From a chair, Hans put John through a rigorous workout of calis-thenics and lunges up and down the strip, stopping a little early because he knew John had to leave. John showered and dressed carefully before taking the bus downtown. The weather was still glowering, but it hadn't rained since morning, so John ignored Hans's offer and left the umbrella behind.

And things went OK. Nothing like a Stanford degree to wave in people's faces, and John's story of being forced out by the takeover at Grenville along with his boss and other likely references aroused no suspicion. Patterson had seen a number of ex-Grenvillites in past months. By the end of the interview, they were ready to refer him the following week as a candidate for management trainee at Equitable Life Insurance or for sales trainee at Folger's Coffee, and both jobs paid salaries comparable to what he had been making before. He should call Monday to get the addresses and times. If things got serious, John knew he could track down Houndsley at Grenville for a reference, but he hoped he could get by without it.

The bigger question, John realized in the rush-hour body jam of the westbound Pine Street bus, was could he really return to that life? He wanted the money, he wanted the status, he wanted to keep his family at bay, and he wanted the latitude to be open with Rebecca. But if he was going to give up all of his free time five days a week, why couldn't he do something real like run one of those big centrifuges or work on a tugboat and have those other things he wanted anyway? Was life always about irreconcilable choices? And if it was, why couldn't he make them? For some reason, John had forgotten to discuss Amado Muro with Hans when he was at the Salle before, but that was just what he wanted to do when he got back.

It took John almost a block of walking to realize that the lights and commotion he saw on the sidewalk up ahead were centered around an ambulance backed in toward the door of the Salle. And even then, as he quickened his pace, his first thought was an injured student. You could break a hand or an arm fencing if you fell wrong, and John had seen some nasty welts in saber. But when the gurney came out with what was unmistakably a blanket-wrapped Hans strapped to it, John began to run.

By the time he had covered the last fifty yards, Hans was already in the ambulance and only the bald, vulnerable top of his head could be seen. Among a small cluster of bystanders, one uniformed attendant was closing the ambulance's wide rear door, while another slammed the front door of the now-dark Salle and checked the lock. The ambulance looked like a hearse, except that it was white.

"What happened, what happened?" John yelled, out of breath and weak from a crunching knot in his stomach. He recognized a couple of people from the neighboring shops who had arrived on the scene ahead of him.

"It looks like Mr. Bierstadt collapsed," said a woman in a bulky gray sweater who had pulled her hands up into the sleeves. "This could be worse than last year."

"Such a wonderful man," said an unidentified voice.

John pushed against the back of the ambulance and tried to look in. All he saw in the glass was a distorted mug-shot image of himself.

"Are you family?" the taller attendant asked him. He had the most pronounced cleft chin John had ever seen.

"No...a friend," John answered. "I was just coming to meet him. What happened, for god's sake?"

"We don't know for sure. He called in himself, said it wasn't an emergency. But when we got here he was out. We're taking him to General. They radioed to say some guy—his lawyer, I guess—would meet us there to take him somewhere else."

"Well...is he alive?"

"Yeah, he's alive, but the pulse is real weak. Back off, will ya'. We gotta go."

They cranked up the siren and the bubble light, took the first right turn off Fillmore and went shrieking away to the east. John caught a couple of the people who were dispersing up and down the block, but he already knew almost as much as they did. The ambulance had been there maybe ten minutes total, and no one had seen or heard anything prior to that time. He scanned the sidewalk for the woman who had said something about last year, but she was gone.

John considered going into the Rooster Club, the bar across the street. They had pickled eggs or sausages he could eat to take the edge off his hunger, and he wasn't due at Rebecca's for over an hour. But he needed Rebecca. He could talk to her about Hans, and from there he could call San Francisco General and try to find out more. And what was the deal about Hans's lawyer arranging for him to go someplace else after General? If it took Dr. Harvey Minter's clout to crack that nut, so be it. At 5:30, when John still had several blocks to go, the rain blew in again. Not as heavy as that morning, but a steady, soaking drizzle.

In addition to being hungry, John was damp and cold by the time he reached Rebecca's door, but he was in such a powerful swirl of emotions that his lack of physical comfort barely registered. He rolled his knuckles lightly against the wooden surface in their secret knock. She was home already, he had seen a light in the window. No answer. He knocked again a little louder. She wasn't expecting him until 6:30. Maybe she was in the bathroom. "Becca," he called, knocking louder still. Finally he rapped hard with the knocker, three quick beats, then three more.

"Go away," came a faint voice inside. He wasn't even sure it was her.

"Becca, is that you? What's wrong? Let me in."

"Go away." Louder now, and clearly her.

"Please, Becca. I need to talk to you about something important."

"Go away, liar!"

"No, Becca, please no. What do you mean?"

"You know what I mean, liar!"

And, yes, sickness upon sickness, suddenly he did know what she meant. But how could she mean that? "Please, Becca, I'm begging."

"Liar! Liar! Liar!" She shouted, then broke into a wail that ended in a frightening crescendo of sobs.

He waited for her to quiet. "Becca, Becca, I'm sorry. Let me in. We have to talk."

"I'm not talking to you," she said hoarsely. "Go away!"

"What happened?" he said, lowering his voice and aiming it directly into the crack between the door and the doorjamb.

"Priscilla saw your car at Stonestown."

"So?" The car, he thought. The goddamn car.

"The driver said it was his. He bought it used from the dealer. Priscilla called around. You sold that car, you haven't worked at Grenville in months, and you don't have any apartment on Pacific Street. The fencing school is probably a lie, too!" More sobs and a heavy, deep breath.

"What can I do?" he asked plaintively.

"I told you. Go away. And never come back!"

"Becca, no. I really need to talk to you."

"Too late. And Priscilla will be here any minute. I told her to come at six, but you already forgot your lie about fencing until 6:30."

Priscilla, John thought. Oh, great—the grand inquisitor. Once she arrived, that would be that. "It wasn't a lie, Becca. Hans is sick."

"I don't care. I hate you!"

"OK," John said, "I'll go. But I'm coming back tomorrow to get my stuff, and we can talk then."

"Don't bother. You can get your stuff right now. It's in the garbage. I threw it out."

"The garbage?" He waited, but she remained silent. "OK, Becca, I'm going. But we still have to talk."

The damp and cold now registered on John full force. Starting to shiver, he turned and went down the wrought-iron supported concrete staircase toward the street. That must have been quite a show for the neighbors, he thought. In the naked city, who needs TV drama? John cut back under the stairs into a longitudinal alley along the carport wall. Having taken out the garbage many times after Rebecca's elaborate dinners for two, he knew right where to look. And there, in a line of battered, crud-smeared cans, was an uncovered one with the left shoulder and arm of John's good brown suit hanging over the rim like a corpse waiting to be discovered by Philip Marlowe in a Raymond Chandler novel.

Moving closer, John saw that a soggy bag of vegetable parings, fish scraps, coffee grounds and egg shells had been thrown in on top. He extracted his suit-coat and shook it off. In layers below, stained with rain and garbage drippings, were trousers, his blue blazer, underwear, several pairs of socks, and two dress shirts still folded from the Chinese laundry on Union Street. Groping around inside the can for his toilet kit, John thought about climbing in himself. Why not? He felt like garbage. Finally, he found the kit, pulled the brown coat up over his head like a parka, and heard the sound of a car door followed by what must have been Priscilla's sensible pumps plonging angrily up the stairs.

Where would he go? With Hans around, the choice would have been easy. Even without Hans, there was no practical alternative. John knew a spare key to the Salle was wedged behind the gas meter at the back of the south wall. Hans had shown him so John could use it if he ever needed to. Retracing his steps in the rain, John stumbled along with his head down. And when he did look up, the orangey-yellow lights of the Golden Gate Bridge mocked him in the distance. He understood why people went there and jumped off.

John had to try three times to get the key positioned properly in the Salle's worn old lock so the bolt would release. His shaking hands didn't help. Pushing the creaking door ahead of him, John entered a familiar space that was now unfamiliarly dark and eerily quiet. But the smell was still right.

"Hans," John called out. "Hello, Hans." He knew there would be no answer, but the old man's presence was so palpable, John couldn't help himself.

He locked the door behind him and tiptoed—why did he need to tiptoe?—down the diagonal fencing strip toward the office and the living area beyond. Rain intermittently pattered against the windows and dripped loudly from the gutters outside. John's eyes adjusted, and he could now navigate easily enough by the refracted light from passing traffic and nearby streetlamps.

John felt his way through the deeper dark of the office and switched on the bare-bulb fixture above Hans's dining table. After plugging in and turning on a small electric heater he had seen Hans use occasionally, John aimed it at his legs, sat, and grabbed for the phone. His fingers were stiff as crochet hooks, and dialing Rebecca's number was hard. It rang and rang and rang.

"Hello." Finally a voice. Priscilla's voice.

John hung up, but no more than thirty seconds later, he dialed again.

"John, that must be you," Priscilla answered coldly on the first ring. He said nothing, and she continued a few seconds later. "Rebecca is not going to talk to you, so you might as well give up and stop bothering her. If you don't, we'll have the police hunt you down and arrest you. And I want you to know, I've called my father and he is already trying to reach your father in Portland."

"Priscilla...please," he choked. John remembered having fallen down an embankment at Lake Oswego when he was a kid and lying breathless on the muddy beach with the wind knocked out of him.

"Don't give me any of that please crap! You'll have to find yourself another meal ticket. We're done!" She slammed the phone down.

John sat dumfounded, yet it was no more than he had expected. That's how the Minters would feel. And John didn't doubt that Harvey Minter could and would have him arrested if John pushed things. The man was not only politically influential around here, his straight-ahead, old-fashioned morality would be in overdrive by now. It would be as impossible as fighting the McDonoughs or the Braddocks in Portland.

Shivering harder despite the electric heat, John knew he had to get warm. His toilet kit lay on the floor near the heater unit, and he picked it up and headed for the shower. He blasted himself with the spray, as hot as he could stand, and his shivering gradually subsided. There were clean underwear and socks in John's locker, over which he put a pair of Hans's dark wool slacks and a black turtleneck and heavy black sweater from the shelf of Hans's makeshift closet.

John then poured himself a tumbler full of Medoc from an open bottle on the cluttered, kitchen counter and drank half of it in one gulp. His next step was to rummage behind the curtain of Hans's tiny pantry to find a can of soup—chicken noodle, that would do great. He turned one side of the hotplate on so it would preheat while he opened the soup and mixed it in a pan. He placed the pan on the heat and returned to the table with his glass, the wine bottle and a skinny red, white and blue sack containing the last of a sourdough baguette. The little heater was now doing its job, and the whole room had begun to warm up.

Reflexively, John reached for the phone again, noticing for the first time that it was on a long cord that would reach both here and to the desk in the office. But after dialing the two letters of Rebecca's exchange prefix, he made himself stop. He imagined her tear-streaked face on the other side of her door, and his own eyes welled up. He drained his wine glass and poured more. Putting the bottle down, John's hand brushed against something soft. Hans's beret. It had been placed near a boxed set of LP records, on top of which were several pages of folded-over white paper. John pulled the beret onto his head. The effect of his shower had diminished, and the extra warmth felt good. He got up and went to the hotplate to check his soup. It was ready, or close enough. He slurped some right out of the pan.

On his way back to the table with the saucepan and a spoon, John saw that the outer side of the folded-over white pages had his full name written on it. His scalp tingled as though he had been shocked, and the spoon clanged from his hand onto the table. Putting the soup aside, John stretched to grab the pages. They had been sitting on Hans's beloved Haydn string quartets. He folded open the pages and saw that they were in typescript, undated, and with xxxed out corrections and smudged o's and p's from the worn, re-inked ribbon of the vintage Underwood in Hans's office.

My Dear New Friend,

I do not know when you will receive this, but I am preparing it in advance, and in stages as time permits, so I can say here all that needs to be said. By the time you do receive it, I may already have told you some of its contents, or you may have learned them from others. No matter, as long as we do not have the sins of omission.

As I begin, I know that we have both kept secrets from each other. Important ones, in my case, perhaps less important ones in yours. It is unlikely that I will ever learn the truth, but there is something about this job of yours, with the floating hours and the duties of which you never speak, that has seemed suspicious. And the same with your lady friend, who never appears, and about whom you never really speak, and who, therefore, may not exist. I can only believe that you have had good reasons for keeping these secrets, or I may be wrong, and you do not have the secrets after all.

You may have speculated about my secrets, also, but I hope I have been so devious that you have not yet had the motive. First, my friend, I do not have the stomach ulcers, I have the stomach cancer. Last year, before you knew me, I was in the hospital for many months and the Salle was closed. But I was lucky, and the cancer went into remission for a time. Of course, no one knew for how long it would stay away. Yet this gave me the chance to settle my affairs and live each remaining day exactly as I wanted to live it. And how I wanted to live was in my Salle, teaching fencing. These have been very good days, and in you, I was even sent a wonderful new student. But just as my wonderful new student appeared. my body began to tell me that this period would soon be over. So I have treasured you.

Now I must ask something. I have arranged with my lawyer for my life to end with as much dignity as the doctors can manage. Only a few of my oldest and most trusted students have any knowledge of my real illness or of my plan. I wish to remember all of you, and for you to remember me, as we knew one another in life—as fencers. Therefore, when I become too ill to continue my life in the Salle, my lawyer, Otto Casperson, will place me in a special home some miles away that is devoted to helping the cancer patients through their final days. Please do not try to find me or to see me after I leave. Otto will not tell you where I am, and it is my express wish that neither you nor anyone else have contact with me again. I know this will be hard for many of my students, but I believe that they will all come to see it as for the best.

My next secret is much more difficult to reveal, because I fear it will make you hate me or misunderstand my feelings for you. I tell you to prove to myself that I have the courage and in the hope that you will find the courage to confront your own secrets. In truth, I am homosexual, something my parents could never accept, and something that I have had great problems myself in accepting. You see, I was for many years Krasge's lover. He had no Jewish blood, as I do. The Nazis tried to use the sex to blackmail Krasge into fencing for Germany, and when he would not, they cracked down on him and his whole circle. That is why he had to flee and was later put in the camps. But my family hated Krasge. They held him responsible for corrupting me, which was completely false. They made me choose, and when the Nazis went after them, too, I chose them. It saved my life to go with my parents to London; it broke my heart not to go to Budapest with Krasge. After the war, to spare my parents the pain brought to them by these sexual desires, I came to San Francisco. I know this separation caused my mother to lose years from her life, and probably my father as well. But I myself have found peace here that I do not think would have existed for me anywhere else.

The sex has been dangerous also for the fencing. Parents would not send their children to me for lessons, even the girl children, if they thought I was a man who loved other men. Thus I have had to pretend to be a much more odd thing, a man who loves no one. Some of my associates, for example Rollo, may have had suspicions, but I have lived very carefully. I do not think any from my current group of students, even those who know about the cancer, know of my sexual life. Nor have I ever betrayed the trust of my students, the young ones or the older, by being sexual toward them. I have of course done things in the matter of sex that now shame me, but I think few among men of any kind can truthfully say otherwise.

I emphasize these points because I do not want you to have doubts that you are my friend. In earlier years, I might have the other kind of attraction to you, but those fires have declined and are now destroyed by the cancer. Do not think that my friendship has been for your body, except as a fencer, or that I would ever be the peeking Tom while you were here in the shower. And because you are my friend, and I sense that your secrets may bring you to need a new life, I offer you the chance to have the Salle and to become a fencing master. You do not have the experience, but you have the talent and the students already like and respect you. I have no family left and no children. I have also only a little money from what I inherited from my parents many years ago. This I need for my last medical care. But if you wish to accept my offer, I have done two things to make this possible. The lease on the Salle is paid in full through the end of May next year, 1962. Also paid for some time in advance are the telephone, gas and electricity. Please talk to Otto about other details. I have instructed him to help you. Unlike me, he is listed in the telephone book.

Here the typescript ended and the letter continued in pen in the same strug-gling hand that had written the words John McDonough on the outside page.

26 October, 1961

You fenced beautifully with Matt on Tuesday. Today I did not myself have the ability to test you, and there will not be another chance. Now you must choose, as I had to in 1936. Will it be Hans or your family? There is no absolute right or wrong in this. You must know your heart, and then you must act. You cannot have both things in the way you tried to at Stanford, and you must not let your family's money be the sole consideration one way or the other. I have left out for you the Haydn, because sometimes the *Kaiserquartett* helps with the thinking.

With deep affection,

Hans

John did not begin to cry until the mention of "peeking Tom." Tears then poured down his face, with a few hitting the bottom of the page below Hans's signature. When he had finished the letter, John put it down, lay forward on his arms and wept in great heaving bursts. He wept for Hans, he wept for Rebecca, he wept for himself, for his mother, his father, Harvey Minter and Priscilla. He wept for Red and Darlene, for Lou, and for Ada. He wept for Harcourt, he wept for Bev, he wept for Mrs. Lipiski, he wept for Rollo, he wept for Hans's parents and he wept for Krasge. He wept for nearly fifteen minutes, more than he had wept in his whole life combined until that day. On the table, his filled wine glass sat and his pan of soup grew cold.

A police siren screaming south on Fillmore left silence in its wake, and John realized the silence included him. Could he even move? He could, and though he was beyond hunger, John had to make himself eat. The saucepan felt as heavy as a manhole cover when he lugged it back to the hotplate to warm again. While it was heating, he tore at the bread and drank another swallow of wine. Luke-warm soup was delicious, too. He again drank it from the pan and only used the spoon to get the last of the noodles. He carried the pan to the sink, put it in to soak, washed his hands, leaned his hip against the counter, and took several long deep breaths.

Hans was right. John had to make a decision. And no matter what the Minters told his parents, John knew the way would not be closed to him at home. He'd dodged plenty of bullets in the past, and he'd always managed to get back in good graces. But Red was right, too. There was an inner voice. John removed the *Kaiserquartett* disk from the box and pressed the power switch on Hans's hi-fi, turning the volume two notches above the previous setting.

It was the Amadeus Quartet performing on a Deutsche-something German label, and it was so thrilling that it seemed from another world. Every note led to the next and echoed the last. When the second, or poco adagio part began, John boosted the volume further and went into Hans's office. Under the glow of a dented, olive-drab goose-neck lamp, John found blank bond paper and a heavy European fountain pen in the desk drawers. He cleared a space on the desktop, measured out his planned text and began to write. Haydn's exquisite melodic variations swelled behind him as he worked.

John wrote slowly in large letters. Waiting briefly for the ink to dry, he took the paper and walked out across the dark fencing floor to the front left. Against the fading background of the Kaiserquartett, the boards creaked softly underfoot and rain continued to splash down. He placed the paper carefully against the glass in the lower corner, standing it up in the cracks of the side and bottom molding. John then went to the door and let himself out, taking a few steps onto the rainy sidewalk before turning back to look. If what he had done was OK, he would do one like it for the other window. The sign in front of him now read:

Salle d'Arms
Hans F. Bierstadt, Master
Fencing Instruction, Inquire Within

Or Call John McDonough
FI-6-6643
To Arrange Lessons or
for Further Information

Rain ran from a crease in Hans's beret and dripped down John's nose. But he didn't care. He thought the new sign looked great. Was October too late, John wondered, to get an ad in next year's Yellow Pages? And shouldn't the Salle start selling weapons, masks and other equipment? There had to be money in it. Before long he'd have rent to pay.

WINNEMUCCA ROSE

[1970]

THE GRAY-GREEN RIBBON OF REEDS, SAGE, AND IRRIGATED ALFALFA THAT IS THE Humboldt Valley began to unroll against the brown hills and distant mountains of northern Nevada. Brian McAlpin was at the wheel of a blue camper van, trying to maintain a smooth 75 mph among the erratic flow of cars and trucks eastbound on Interstate 80. His wife Susan, her sunglasses flipped up into her burnished red bangs, was studying a map laid out between them on the front seat.

"God it's hot," she said to no one in particular. "Even in this halter top and cutoffs I can't get comfortable."

Nor could her three companions on this cloudless, early September afternoon in 1970. The van, still relatively new, had jumping trout decals on the side doors, and like many vehicles at that time, was without air-conditioning. The few windows that would open let in a stifling rush of heat and highway noise, and five hours remained before the sun would find the western horizon.

Two forms sprawled across the L-shaped benches behind the McAlpins. Marc Ficetti, his dark curly hair and bushy mustache in shadowed silhouette, gazed blankly out the window. A flushed and damp Phil Beaumont hunched himself forward, awakening from a nap. They had all talked seemingly non-stop from Berkeley to their lunch outside Reno, but had fallen silent since then. To Phil's relief, though, it was a benign silence and he had dozed off.

"How much further is Winnemucca?" Phil asked, stretching and sitting up.

"That's what I'm checking," said Susan. "We left Fernley twenty-five minutes ago, so that means at least two more hours. Go back to sleep if you can."

"Any time you want, Brian," Marc put in, using his T-shirt sleeve to wipe sweat from his forehead, "I can spell you with the driving."

"Thanks, man. It's hot as hell, but I'm fine. I'll finish out today, and you can take it in the morning." Brian, who looked not unlike John Lennon, complete with wire-rimmed glasses and pony tail, swung his head toward Marc for a moment and added, "Tell us more about this Basque hotel where you think we should stay."

"It's great." Marc waved his hands animatedly as he talked. "Maybe three stories high, down by the railroad yard, clean, cheap. I forget the name, but we can find it easy. Has a great bar and restaurant, too. Shepherds, cowboys, truck drivers and railroad guys are the regulars. And communal bathrooms. When I was there last spring, I heard this guy gasping and coughing in the shower while I

44

was taking my morning piss, and god-damned if he didn't step out with a lit cigarette in his mouth and start drying himself off." Phil had heard this story before, but pulled along by Marc's enthusiasm, he joined in the McAlpins' laughter.

"Susie and I love funky hotels," Brian responded, "and we really dig the Basque restaurants we've been to in North Beach. How'd you get on to this place?"

"A friend in Denver who used to hunt sage hen around Winnemucca with his dad. Told me to be sure and stay there a night when I left Colorado to move back to Berkeley. And Winnemucca's a real kick. Except on the main drag, the casinos aren't neon plastic like Reno or Vegas, and the red light district makes you feel like you've walked onto a movie set."

"Oh, Brian's heard lots about the red light district," Susan said sweetly, flashing her husband a look. "And, of course, we're all going tonight. It's Saturday and things should be jumping."

A surprised smile crossed Phil's face. A few months ago, when Brian and Phil began planning this week of camping and fly fishing in Idaho, neither had known about the Basque hotel, but the Winnemucca red light district had become a private joke between them. Their night in Babylon and all that. But now Susan was in on it, and it was no longer sounding like just a joke. Exactly what the McAlpins had in mind was hard to tell, but Phil did know they could be very crazy together.

How Marc would react was another matter. He had met the McAlpins only that morning, so his first thought would probably be that Susan was engaging in verbal titillation for sport. Marc also knew that Phil had the hots for her, and could no doubt see why. Susan was a very attractive woman, with her clear green eyes, her scattering of freckles, her girlish body and her anything-is-possible manner. But Marc wouldn't play along if he thought Susan was trying to captivate him, too. Marc never liked to be bested in anything. He looked directly at her and threw down a challenge.

"I don't think you've got the concept," Marc said. "All the help, so to speak, in those places is female, and those are the only women they let in. Everyplace has a bouncer. Otherwise they'd have an endless run of ugly scenes with angry wives and girlfriends. I think there's even a city ordinance against women on the street in that part of town."

"Sounds like you're a veteran," she shot back.

"I've cruised around a bit and stopped into one of the joints for beer and conversation," he said. "But it's not my thing to pay for sex."

"Oh, come on, man," hooted Brian. "You always pay for sex. Everybody knows that. What was that stuff a couple of hours ago about how your ex in Colorado got the house and you had to move out?"

Phil, trying to take the edge off, jumped in, "Well, how much does Susan charge you?" They all laughed.

"You're the accountant, Beaumont, not me," Brian answered calmly. "All I'm saying is every human transaction has a cost. Maybe not money, but a cost."

Susan let this go and picked up where she had left off. "Anyway, tonight I'm not paying. You guys are going to get laid, and I'm going to watch. Or if I can't watch because of what Marc says, then you're going to tell me all about it. In detail."

"Whatever's right, baby," said Brian, archly blowing her a kiss.

Marc started to respond, but swallowed it, rolled his eyes and turned back to the window. Brian and Susan continued their occasional front-seat chatter while Phil again settled as best he could onto the sticky bench and tried to sleep.

⁂

Phil had known the McAlpins a little more than two years. At twenty-eight, he was the same age as Susan and six years younger than Brian. He met Susan first, through her work as an editorial assistant at the Sierra Club in San Francisco, where Phil had also worked. She was the most appealing woman he'd ever seen, and for some reason, she sought him out. Phil had begun living with Karen Scharf in a rented Berkeley cottage about that time, yet Phil had nearly rejected Susan as a friend when he learned she was married. She wore no ring, which had initially thrown him off.

After repeated urging, Phil finally agreed to join Susan and Brian one day at a nearby downtown lunch spot, and everything quickly moved to another level. Together, the McAlpins made Phil feel alive in a way he never had before. They were smart, funny, and carelessly free. Both had gone to Stanford, though not at the same time. But for both it had been the Stanford of a cozy, pre-Vietnam bohemianism, not the rah-rah Stanford of the Big Game. Now they lived in a large, top-floor Victorian flat in Presidio Heights crammed with books, California landscape paintings, oriental furniture and hand-thrown pottery, while Brian ran a successful family printing business he had taken over when his father died.

A skilled black-and-white nature photographer, Brian had met Susan through Sid Hartley, a photographer friend of his whose book she was editing. Brian was also an excellent fly fisherman and a grower of powerful marijuana under lights in the back bathroom of their flat. Had Susan been married to anyone else, the friendship wouldn't have worked for Phil. As it was, he was on for the ride. Phil wasn't always sure what it took to be hip in Brian's eyes, but he certainly hoped to measure up.

The only flaw was that, while the McAlpins seemed to like Karen well enough, she never really liked them. Still, the two couples spent a fair amount of time together, because Karen understood there would be no gain for her in provoking a confrontation.

"Everything's too easy for those people" she complained privately to Phil. "They're not real. Did you know you start to talk and laugh like Brian when you're around him?"

"No. And I'm not sure I believe it."

"Well, you should. It also drives me crazy that Susan's so un-feminist."

"Wow," Phil replied, "I sure see her as a feminist. But she's a personal feminist, not a political feminist. She thinks politics are irrelevant, because all change takes place on the personal level."

Karen, who resembled Joan Baez, sighed and pulled at her hair. "What do you suppose gets the word out and makes people realize that they need to change on the personal level? Politics, that's what."

Marc and Phil were friends from their undergraduate days at Berkeley. They had met the winter of Phil's freshman year playing squash in Harmon Gym. Phil was from Ohio, while Marc, a junior, was from Oregon. They were both about average height, and evenly matched in squash, but as the oldest of three sons, Marc assumed a big brother role in all other spheres. Phil didn't mind. He was an only child, and had never had much mentoring from his distant and preoccupied father.

It was the call of the mountain west that brought Phil to Berkeley in the first place, so he eagerly absorbed Marc's extensive knowledge of fly fishing and backpacking. Some of Marc's other tastes and mannerisms transplanted themselves to Phil as well. The exception was learning to attract women, something Phil, slender and pleasant-looking, with a mid-length shock of light brown hair, found daunting. Karen was actually his first serious girlfriend. Marc, Italian-Swiss and a vivid physical presence, never suffered a lack of female attention.

The end of Marc's MA in European history coincided with the end of Phil's BA in economics, giving them nearly four years together in the Berkeley of the Free Speech Movement and the salad days of student activism. Their interests hadn't run much to LSD or radical politics, so they emerged basically unscathed. Yet, as with many college friendships, they had seen one another only rarely since.

Marc had gone to Boulder to pursue a doctorate, but he got married, had two sons and launched a teaching career at a Denver-area community college without completing his dissertation. His now ex-wife taught there as well, and the word was she would be marrying Marc's former department chair by the end of the year. Marc had returned to Berkeley a few months back, when his divorce became final.

Phil had stayed in the Bay Area, working first in the membership office of the Sierra Club, and currently, much better paid, as an accountant for the City of Berkeley. Marc phoned Phil after he decided to pull up stakes in Colorado, and they quickly renewed their past connection when Marc arrived. It was a bonus for Phil that Karen seemed as pleased with Marc as she was wary of Brian and Susan. At some level, though, Phil recognized that Brian had now assumed the role in his life Marc once held. Would Marc care, Phil wondered, or even notice?

In any case, Marc readily found work as a crew boss for an Oakland painting contractor, a job he'd had off-and-on during his previous Berkeley years. Hopefully, something better would turn up, but aside from missing his two boys terribly, life was good. He was once again a personage in the bookstores and coffee shops of Telegraph Avenue, and he was waking up more and more in the bed of a charming anthropology student down the hall in the rambling old apartment block where he lived.

For Phil, adding Marc to his planned Idaho trip with the McAlpins was a natural. They were receptive, and Marc openly wanted in. Karen, a counselor at Berkeley High, was an avid Sierra Clubber and hiker in the East Bay hills, but had no interest in fishing and, as she put it, "sleeping in the dirt." That meant four of them were going and she was gladly staying home.

As the date approached, Phil realized that his having assembled this group gave him an extra interest in making things go smoothly. He began by briefing the McAlpins about Marc, and vice versa. They seemed intrigued when Phil told them that Marc, the son of an intellectually-inclined Portland dock worker, was brash and emotive, had strong opinions and loved to bullshit.

"He was always my Zorba," Phil explained. "The one who sent me messages saying 'Have found wonderful green stone, come at once'." At this, Susan gave a smiling nod.

"Sounds cool," Brian said. "Just have him bring an air mattress so he doesn't have to sleep on any green stones. Oh, and a couple of jugs of decent red wine. There probably won't be much to buy up in mountain country."

Marc's expectations, on the other hand, related largely to fishing, and he mentioned several times that this would be his first chance in more than a year. When Phil told him that his companions-to-be were given to prankish games, that Brian's wardrobe was a blue button-down shirt and plain blue jeans over black cowboy boots, 365 days a year, and that Susan could show up in anything from a Chanel sheath to coveralls, Marc had only one question.

"Does she fish, too?"

"No," Phil answered. "But she cooks like you wouldn't believe."

⚹ ⚹ ⚹

As Marc had promised, the Basque hotel was easy to find. By shortly after 6 P.M. they were already checked in and signed up for the 7:30 serving in the family-style dining room downstairs. Phil and Marc were on the second floor in a tiny, wood-paneled room with two squeaky metal-frame beds. The McAlpins had a larger room on the next floor up. The plan was to get out of their road clothes and meet in the bar before dinner.

"A shower is going to feel great," said Phil, peeling off his sweaty shirt. Then, turning to Marc, "Well, what do you think, so far?"

"It's been fun. And my first real chance to unwind in a long time. As you know, this hasn't been the greatest year of my life."

"Right, but I mean them. What's your take?"

"Pretty much what you said to expect. I can see you really dig him. He's a colorful guy, and obviously knows his fishing. Hangs back a bit on the personal stuff, but hell, he's barely met me. No problems, if that's what you're asking."

"And her?"

"Can't say yet. She operates on a lot of levels. But you told me she was a fox, and she is."

"In those cutoffs she was wearing today, that would be hard to miss."

"One thing, though. How far are they going to push this whorehouse scene? Seems weird to me. Or are you in on it?"

"No, I'm not. And I don't know how far they'll push it. I doubt they even know themselves."

The hotel bar was dark, smoky and packed. Brian and Susan, sharing a glass of something called Picon punch, were pressed into a corner near the dining room door when Phil and Marc arrived through a noisy crowd that seemed to include at least one of every kind of white person in Nevada. Before Marc could order a Picon of his own, a chuckwagon bell sounded and they were expelled into a low-ceilinged room filled with long, narrow tables swathed in red. Swords, crests, Pyrenees travel posters and jai-lai photographs covered the walls.

Acting as though they had rehearsed it, Brian and Marc eased through the confusion and each staked out a pair of spots opposite the other. Brian was already pouring Marc some red wine from a nearby bottle when Susan, still nursing the Picon, directed Phil to a seat next to Brian while she went around to join Marc. They soon found themselves flanked by dozens of other patrons eyeing one another across mounds of sliced sourdough bread and steaming tureens of soup. Brian was in his standard uniform, although he had donned a fresh shirt since their long drive through the desert. Marc wore a black turtleneck, Phil a rust-orange western shirt with pearl buttons, and Susan a high-cut, sleeveless denim jumper with a Navajo necklace.

Brian raised his glass in a toast to Marc. "To great fishing. We've heard a lot about you, and we're glad you're back in California. This hotel is dynamite, by the way."

"Thanks, man. I've heard great things about you guys, and I can see Phil wasn't making it up."

Wine flowed freely and the courses kept coming: dry salami, olives, salad, ravioli, green beans with roasted red pepper, chicken, french fries, roast beef, fruit, cheese, and flan. A team of stocky, dark-eyed waitresses in red blouses and black skirts plunged among the tables bringing whatever was needed. With impatient hand gestures, they informed the uninitiated that the heavy glass tumbler at each place was an all-purpose wine glass, water glass and, finally, coffee cup.

"Those have to be the best french fries ever," Phil said.

"They didn't come from a freezer bag, that's for sure," Susan added. "But I've got a question. Why are there Basques?"

"Because God made them," Brian deadpanned.

"No, I mean why are Basques here? And around through the Sierra and southern San Joaquin? I thought Basques were something out of Hemingway or San Francisco ethnic restaurants."

"It's a holdover from the open range days of the sheep industry seventy-five years back," Marc volunteered. "And thanks to a loophole in U.S. immigration law, they're still coming."

"They all came as shepherds?" Phil asked.

"The men, yes," Marc went on. "Since they were escaping extreme poverty at home, they were willing to tolerate the months of isolation that went with the job. But like any immigrant group, they sent for relatives once they got established and also expanded by intermarrying."

"What's this loophole?" Susan wanted to know.

"Basque shepherds get preference and automatic visas if they sign up to work for two years, I think it is. But they get no wages and hardly have a chance to learn English. For all practical purposes, they're slaves. We'll probably see some as we head north the next few days. And you can imagine the ranchers would fight to the death to keep them coming. Those bastards pay next to nothing for grazing rights on public land, why should they pay for labor?" By now, Marc had become quite impassioned, and stares from elsewhere in the room were being directed their way.

"The Sierra Club ought to be interested in this," Susan said to Phil. But while he was getting ready to respond, he lip-read the words Sierra Club coming from the mouth of a florid, beefy man across the table a few seats to his left.

Brian saw it, too, and jumped in quickly. "Speaking of Hemingway," he said, leaning forward to catch everyone's eye and then dropping his voice, "just because he killed himself up in this country nine years ago doesn't mean we have to do it now. This is Nixon America, remember." Then louder, "Oh, and I brought Hem's *Collected Short Stories* with me for the trip."

Marc, of course, got Brian's drift in a flash and so did Susan. "What a great idea, Brian," she said in an ironic sing-song. "Something we can takes turns reading around the campfire."

"Phil and I would definitely be up for that," Marc smiled, having clearly enjoyed the friction he'd caused. There was a general scraping of chairs as dinner broke up, and the four of them, groaning that they were too full to move, left the hotel through a side door.

It had already cooled noticeably, and the sun was shooting its last beams from behind a barren range of mountains in the distance. Venus was plainly visible. Promising another treat, Marc led them along a rutted dirt road several hundred yards west to a stunted grove of box elders and willows on the berm of a drainage canal overlooking the railroad yard. Twenty-five sidings a quarter-mile long fanned out below them, spaced along which were engines and rail cars of every description.

"Wow, it's huge," said Phil. "Hobo heaven. Looks like a godzilla model train set from here."

Behind him, Brian had lit a perfectly rolled joint, and was now taking a hit. He passed it to Susan, who did the same, and she then tried to pass it to Marc.

He waved it off. "With that great food, all the wine, a classic rail yard, and a sunset, I don't need to gild the lily."

She passed it to Phil, and he took a hit, too. Then he offered it to Marc again. "Go on, man, at least have a taste," Brian urged. "It's home grown. Hand pollinated and no seeds. We call it McAlpin Gold. Only the privileged few get to smoke it."

Marc relented, and took a shallow drag. "Yeah, Phil told me you have grow lights." He took a second shallow drag and passed the joint to Brian. "I don't smoke much anymore, so a bit might get me royally stoned."

Brian drew deeply. "It's strong," he said on the exhale, "but not that strong. After you waved the red flag at all those ranchers in the restaurant, I wouldn't figure a little dope would bother you."

Marc continued to abstain while the other three smoked the joint down to a generous stub which Brian secreted in a snuff can in the pocket of his jeans. After arranging to meet Phil and Marc on the hotel porch in twenty minutes, the McAlpins left to get dressed for what Susan called the "evening's entertainment." Marc and Phil stayed where they were, watching a train pull out as the stars brightened and grew more numerous in the night sky.

"We're calling their bluff, right?" asked Phil after a period of silence.

"To a point. But what if it's not a bluff?"

"I haven't thought that through," Phil admitted. "For all we know, they could be back on that porch right now in clown suits playing the kazoo."

"Ah, yes," Marc sighed, "the merry pranksters. But I did have fun tweaking them with a little hot politics at the dinner table. Did you see them cut and run?"

"You were tweaking everyone within earshot, more or less. Perhaps you've forgotten how *Easy Rider* ends." Phil paused, then went on, "Anyway, that doesn't solve our main problem. I mean there's part of me that's always wanted the bordello experience. It's a big theme in male folklore, and here it's even legal."

"Of course there's still disease, exploitation, and Karen to worry about," Marc pointed out. "It's legal in Mexico, too, but it ain't pretty. I made a no-sleep run to Tijuana all the way from Portland with some of my buddies the week after we graduated from high school. I felt dirty for months after that, and it's not something I plan to do again just to make Little Susie happy."

"The difference is, you've had the experience, so you can reject it. I never have. And remember, Montgomery Clift met Donna Reed in a whorehouse in Hawaii."

"*From Here to Eternity* was a movie, too, for Christ's sake! Now I know you're stoned."

They started back to the hotel and, true enough, Phil could feel the dope working in his brain. The night air and the wildly chirping crickets rushed at him in waves of pleasure.

"Besides," Marc continued, "if I'm in Nevada, and I have to worry about bluffing, I'd rather play poker."

Two denim-clad men in western hats slouched in the shadows against the front corner of the hotel, but there was no sign of the McAlpins on the dimly-lit porch.

But as Marc and Phil drew even with them, the two men looked up and Brian's voice materialized from the figure on the left.

"This here's my new friend Sam," Brian said with a nod toward his companion, "and we propose to go out and get us a piece of ass. What do you boys say to that?" He paused for dramatic effect, and added, "Say howdy to Marc and Phil, Sam."

"Howdy, boys," Susan croaked, just before she and Brian disintegrated in prolonged howls of laughter. Phil, and even Marc, found it impossible not to join them.

The McAlpins were close enough in size that Brian had been able to dress Susan fairly convincingly in an extra set of his all-purpose clothes. She wore the jeans bloused into her boots to take up some length, and had added a jeans jacket with a dark blue bandanna at the neck to make her look more muscular. Together they had used her make-up kit to give her a five o'clock shadow, darken her teeth, and put sagging age lines under her eyes. The hat, an old one Brian used for fishing, shaded her face and allowed her to tuck her hair up out of sight. In bright light, she would look absurd. In dim light, she would automatically pass for a man. Brian rounded out the effect by also wearing a jacket and hat.

Suddenly, Phil knew without the slightest doubt that he would be heading to the Winnemucca red light district for some Saturday night fun. He managed to quiet his laughter and said, "Hope all the pretty ladies don't just chase after Sam and leave the rest of us in the cold."

This provoked a few more laughs before Brian turned to Marc. "Lead on, man. You're the one who knows where the fleshpots can be found."

"About four blocks from here," Marc said, pointing. "Go down to the left fifty feet or so where this street ends. Head east there and follow the street that parallels the drainage canal until you see a gated compound on your right. You can't miss it."

"Ya' mean to say yer not comin'," Susan croaked again, as stoned as Phil had ever seen her. "Mr. Sam would be proud to buy you a sarsaparilla or a shot of whatever else yer drinkin'."

"Nope. I've got a lucky casino in this town that's up the other way. Poker is the vice for me tonight, and anybody who wants to come along and watch is more than welcome." Marc started to walk off. Despite everything that had been said, Marc's refusal still caught Phil by surprise and for an instant, he was torn.

"Hey, man! What are you doing, man?" exclaimed Brian, also very stoned. "Come on! It'll be fun. What can it hurt?" The McAlpins had obviously smoked the rest of that joint upstairs while they were getting dressed.

Marc turned and spoke angrily. "This is bullshit, man! Do what you want, and you have to live with it! I don't!" This time he walked determinedly away, gaining speed as he went.

"Whoa!" said Brian quietly. "Things are getting weird."

"Sorry, guys," said Phil, experiencing an unwelcome clearheadedness. "I didn't know for sure what you were up to, and I never thought he'd react that way."

"But we were up to exactly what we said all along we were up to," answered Brian in a baffled tone.

"That's probably what confused me," Phil countered.

"It's OK, Phil," Susan said in her real voice, "as long as you're coming. Mr. Sam would hate to pull his six-gun on you."

"You're hopeless," Phil laughed, and the three of them started walking the route Marc had outlined. The moon was up, a thin gothic slice amid the brilliant desert stars. Along the drainage canal, frogs now joined the crickets in a dense panoply of sound. And with the temperature having dropped a few more degrees, Phil began to wish he, too, had a jacket.

They apparently weren't too stoned to follow directions, because the compound Marc had described began to show on their right just where he said it would. A couple of slow-moving cars passed from behind as they walked, and a slow-moving pickup passed going the other way a few seconds later. No one paid them the slightest attention.

A hundred feet or so before they reached the gate, which was secured in an open position, a Winnemucca police cruiser rolled by, entered the compound, slowed further to make a crunching U-turn across the full extent of the wide, graveled parking lot, and came back to face them. After a cursory look, the officer waved and disappeared as silently as he had arrived.

"Congratulations, Sam," said Phil, "I think you've just been accepted as a member of the male sex."

"It's a start," she replied. "Is there a secret handshake I get to learn?"

"What I'm having a hard time with," Brian said wonderingly, "is imagining that the cops could possibly be on my side when I'm out getting laid."

They now found themselves entering the northwest corner of an enclosure more than an acre in size and bounded all around by whitewashed, wooden fencing and well-tended shrubs. An open, circular, graveled space occupied the center, bordered by a number of huge cottonwood trees.

Four lighted structures and a fifth that was dark were scattered among the cottonwoods, facing inward toward the gravel. It looked like an exceptionally neat, old-fashioned motel court. A few cars and pickups were parked around the edges of the lot, and a door thumped shut as someone went into one of the structures to their left. There was a low murmur of voices from another direction and several competing strains of faint music mingled in the air.

"Great," Brian said. "We got here early enough. A guy I was talking to in the men's room at the hotel told me that there's a sort of a dinner hour rush on Saturdays and then a real crush later on. Between 8 and 10, though, he says it's usually quiet. Except during hunting season, when he says it's totally crazy right straight through."

"I wonder what the guys tell their wives they're hunting," Susan whispered to Phil.

They began to wander in a leisurely, clockwise arc, and Phil noted that Susan had even adopted a more masculine stride to go with her disguise. Two of the lighted structures turned out to be extra-wide mobile homes with frontier-style false fronts. One was called Fannie Anne's and one was called The Casbah. The other two lighted structures were wood-frame buildings with porches and white clapboard siding. The smaller of them, a single story affair, was called LuLu's, while the other, two stories with a sharply pitched roof, was The Ritz. No neon anywhere. Each sign was custom-done and tastefully floodlit. To the right of the Ritz was the final structure, dark, showing no name and seemingly closed down.

"Marc was right," said Phil, feeling pleasantly stoned again. "What a jewel of a spot this is." Actually, Phil thought, Marc always knew his way around. You could count on that.

Outside LuLu's was a funky, beige pickup from the back of which issued loud, drunken snoring. A pair of elaborately tooled cowboy boots were angled up from the bed onto the top of the closed tailgate. It seemed likely that the guy's friends were inside and he'd been too wrecked to accompany them.

"Just think," Susan said quietly in her Sam voice, "if Marc hadn't gotten all freaked out, he could have come down here with us and had a little nap."

Her remark gave Phil a pang, but it quickly passed as he realized that he already had half a hard-on. Through LuLu's front window, partially obscured with loosely-tied gingham curtains, they could see a bar with some beer signs behind it and an entwined couple dancing. The guy was dressed not unlike Phil, and the woman was wearing far less, most of it sheer nylon.

By unanimous vote, they picked The Ritz. It not only had architectural merit, it sat directly adjacent to an impressive patch of dark. They walked toward the entryway. Mr. Sam tapped Brian on the shoulder and spoke to him eye-to-eye in a voice that Phil couldn't pick up. Brian shrugged and walked toward Phil.

"Looks like Sam has to take an urgent piss," he said in a measured way. "Let's go on and he'll catch up with us."

Susan and her Sam persona drifted off to the right, beyond the massive trunk of the nearest cottonwood, and carefully proceeded down the side of the building along a dark, overgrown lane. A moment later, Brian and Phil were on the porch.

"Here we go, man," Brian said. "Good luck."

Far too orderly to be either Sodom or Gomorra, the interior looked more like a suburbanite's rec room decorated for the annual Valentine's party. A knotty-pine bar faced the door, set ten or twelve feet back. Almost everything else was pink and adorned with sequined cupids—the walls, the frilly gauze curtains, the lampshades and the bartender's voluminous mu mu. A linebacker if Phil had ever seen one, she had impossible red hair, wide chrome glasses, a two-inch layer of mascara and a turquoise cigarette holder. Presumably, she was the madam or the manager.

"Howdy fella's," she said pleasantly as the outside door closed. "Come on in." Then, aiming her voice through a half-door in the wall to their left, still pleasant but a bit louder, she called, "Girrlls, you've got coommpany!" Phil and Brian veered rightwards into a lounge area furnished with tables and chairs, a vintage juke box, and a pair of Victorian love seats.

Brian took a chair on the far side of a large table in the back corner, with a window behind him and the stairway to the upper floor straight ahead. Phil followed without thinking, sitting on the near side. Now he really did have a hard on, and he was certainly stoned.

Five women and a cloud of perfume surrounded them before Phil could completely sort out where he was. The basic uniform was heels, panty hose and a low cut bra, with variations in the color and cut of the slinky, see-through teddy or dressing gown that comprised the outer layer. Having run his eyes furtively over the whole group, Phil could see that they were all between twenty and thirty, passably good-looking, and with varying facial features, coloring, height, and hairstyles.

Looking back toward Brian, Phil saw him touch the wrist of a short-haired brunette and wave her to a chair facing the window. Phil followed the two legs closest to him up to a shapely midsection, nice breasts and a pair of alert green eyes. This was when he learned that to make definite eye contact in this situation is to make a selection, because the other three women immediately walked with waggling butts back toward the bar. They were not to remain idle, however, because the door opened and three more men entered.

Without sitting down, Ms. Green Eyes bent forward, held out her hand and said, "Hi, I'm Rose. What's your name?" It was only then that Phil really saw her, and realized he had picked a woman who looked a great deal like Susan. Her hair was darker, the freckles were lighter, her breasts were bigger, and she was not quite as tall, but shit! Could Brian fail to see this? And out the window, could Susan herself?

Rose pulled a chair from the next table and sat with her knee and calf pressed to Phil's nearest leg. "You do have a name, don't you?"

Brian, meanwhile, was paying no attention and was flashing his eyes at his pretty brunette, stroking her hair and making sotto voce comments. But to Phil, the window seemed like a giant lens zooming in for a close-up.

"Hey, over there," Rose called to Brian. "Does this guy have a name?"

Brian laughed. "He did when we came in. It was Phil."

"OK, Phil," she said, dropping a hand lightly into his lap. "We've got that covered. Where ya' from? I mean everybody's from someplace."

"Sorry," he said sheepishly, "I was having a little out-of-body experience there. I'm from Berkeley, how about you? Where you from?"

"Phoenix," she answered with a twinkle. "A hot babe from a hot town." Then a shadow hovered briefly over the table, and Phil found that Brian had somehow ordered four small glasses of barely-bubbling, viscous-looking champagne.

"Thanks, Betty," Rose said to the madam's mu mu-clad derriere as it returned to the front of the room.

"It's been a while since the camel's nose was under that tent," Brian cracked.

"Oh, you'd be surprised who comes in here and why," his brunette replied, giving him a pouting kiss on the cheek.

"This stuff doesn't taste all that great, but it's cold," Rose whispered in Phil's ear, lightly touching her glass to his forehead. Then she nodded toward Brian and said, "So, cheers. My name's Rose."

"Cheers," Brian answered, as he and his date sipped their champagne, and Phil reached to do likewise. "Nice to meet you, Rose. I'm Brian, and you already know Josette. Phil, meet Josette. Josette, that's Phil."

Phil and Josette exchanged nods, and she said, "How about we all dance?"

"No, not me," Brian replied. "I'm not a dancer. But come sit on my lap." Josette did, and they resumed their private talk.

Rose stood and took both Phil's hands. "How about you. I bet you dance."

"You're right." Phil stood also. "I'll dance." He put his arm around her, and they walked to the juke box.

"Kind of quiet tonight," he said.

"Won't be for long," Rose assured him.

The apricot teddy she was wearing clung to every inch of her body, showing off her tits and her smooth, round ass as she leaned on the front edge of the neon-lit machine. "Free," she said. "All you have to do is pick something. How about a waltz? Can you waltz?"

"Sure," Phil said. "Play your favorite."

"OK." Rose pushed a button seemingly without looking and turned to step into his arms. An old, amazingly sweet orchestral version of *The Tennessee Waltz* came on, and they began a slow glide across the floor. She wrapped around him in a way that shouldn't have worked for dancing, but did. The here-again, gone-again hard-on Phil had felt earlier began to reassert itself.

"You're good at this," she said breathily in his ear. "And I think I feel something down there, Mr. Berkeley Boy. What could it be?"

"Oh, I can't imagine. But maybe when the music's over I'll have you check it for me."

"My, my," she cooed, "we're making progress. Are you a student, then, Mr. Berkeley Boy?"

"No, but I was. Now I'm just a twenty-eight year old working guy."

"Twenty-eight, huh? That's exactly how old I am. Were you a bomb-throwing student or an LSD-taking student?"

"Neither," Phil said, though he remembered Susan's having asked him that same playful question when they first met, and remembered giving that same answer.

"What's the matter," Rose asked, as the music wound down. He made no reply, and she led him back to their table. Phil sat, drank the rest of his champagne and reached the inescapable conclusion that his bordello experience had come to an end.

Brian and Josette arose and walked languorously, arm-in-arm toward the stairway. Josette started up first, so that her tight little fanny showed above Brian's shoulder as Phil and Rose followed their progress. At that point, Brian turned fully around and made an exaggerated, orchestra-conductor's bow, looking not quite at Phil, but past him and out the window. Then he turned back, put both hands on Josette's rear and pushed her up the stairs.

"Oo la la," Josette laughed, as they disappeared from sight. "You bad boy!"

"So what's happening," Rose asked. "I can't really hang around like this if nothing's happening. You understand that, don't you?"

"Yeah, I understand. And I'm really sorry, but nothing's happening. It's not you, it's me."

"That's OK, I guess. I'm sorry, too." She stood up and moved to the bar, but her pronounced sexual affect was gone. It was just regular walking.

Phil sat another minute trying to figure out what actually was going on. Then he got up and headed glumly across the room to the door. Rose gave him a little, half-hand wave from her bar stool as he went by. Betty glowered and said nothing. The other girls were busy making deals with their dates. Two inbound customers passed Phil on the porch, and one gave him a knowing wink.

But once he was outside, he immediately felt better. He went down the steps and headed to the big cottonwood. In it's shadow, he called softly, "Mr. Sam. Hey, Sam. You still around?" There was movement only a few feet away, and Susan came toward him with her head down, not meeting his eyes. Blood pounded in Phil's ears like a berserk metronome.

"Let's get out of here," Susan said, walking past him. He turned and did a double-skip to catch up. They crunched across the gravel and out the gate at a rapid pace.

Finally, she spoke. "God, these boots are killing me! We've got to slow down."

Instead, Phil stopped and grabbed her by the shoulder. "Are you all right?"

"Yeah, I guess. Except my feet. But it was a lot harder than I thought."

"What was? Were you able to see, or did you have to just wait around?"

"Oh, no. I saw everything. Until they went upstairs, that is."

Phil started walking again and she followed. "Well, what did you expect?" he asked.

"It was pretty much what I expected. I mean I knew what Brian was going to do, and everything. Our plan worked great. I just didn't realize how much it would hurt to see him like that. You know, with her. What was her name?"

"Josette, but probably not her real name. Chicano trying to pass for French would be my guess."

"Was she nice?"

"Let's say she was good at her job. But I think we're all going to end up wishing we hadn't done this."

"Oh, I don't know. Maybe by tomorrow it'll seem funny."

"If you say so," he replied. She reached to take his arm, and he let her. "But if you start hanging on me like that, Mr. Sam, the cops are going to think we're a couple of homos. And those probably are illegal in Winnemucca."

"The hell with Mr. Sam. I want to be a girl." She pulled off her hat, shook down her hair, studied the hat for a second or two, and then pushed it onto Phil's head. "Looks better on you, anyway." She again took his arm and pulled herself closer.

Now, for the first time, he could really see her. From the corners of her eyes, faint streaks ran down through her age lines and five o'clock shadow. Craning in her direction, he sang in a soft falsetto, "Take a good look at my face. You know my smile may seem out of place..."

"OK," she cut him off by giving him a shove. "I cried. And I didn't even feel the tears at first. I told you it was harder than I thought." She paused. " But what about you? Why didn't you go upstairs, too?"

"Chickened out."

"Maybe that's 'cause Karen wasn't watching outside with me."

"Are you nuts? If Karen was along on this trip, she and I would've been up with Marc at the casino. The only way she'd ever go into that compound would be to hand out feminist literature at quitting time."

Susan gave a squeal of laughter. "You know...you're right." She removed her bandanna and used it to wipe at her eyes and at the remaining makeup. "But I bet Karen was still the reason."

"Yeah, maybe." Making himself form the words, Phil asked, "Did you notice anything about Rose, the girl I was with?"

"No, nothing in particular. But I was mostly watching Brian. Why?"

"Just wondered," Phil answered, incredulous that Susan had seen no likeness to herself.

"She seemed pretty," Susan said. "I saw the two of you start dancing, but right then a security guard came around and swung his flashlight my way, so I had to get back for a while. What happened with you and Rose after that."

"Not much."

"Brian doesn't dance," Susan went on. "It would have killed me if he'd danced with that Josette. But I saw them go upstairs. Did you catch his bow?"

"Oh, yes. And, of course, that was for you."

"I think that's when I cried. How much does it cost to go upstairs?"

"I didn't get far enough to have that discussion. You'll find out all about it from Brian."

"I certainly will," she said.

By now they had rounded the last corner and were less than half a block from the hotel. What an amazing woman she was, thought Phil. If he were into voyeurism, he'd have a hidden microphone in their room tonight to hear the first conversation between her and Brian. But a flash of guilt quashed the smile that idea had produced. Approaching the hotel porch they slowed and heard loud footsteps coming from the other direction.

Head down, shoulders hunched, hands in pockets and heels slamming the pavement, a figure that was unmistakably Marc approached rapidly. "Shit!" he exclaimed. "Shit! Shit! Shit!"

Phil could feel Susan tense up. "What happened?" he asked, speaking for both of them.

"I lost all my fucking money is what happened. And in not even two goddamn hours."

Phil grimaced. "Not such a lucky casino after all. What were you playing?"

"Five card stud. It started good, then everything got fucked. I never lose like that."

"I'd be angry, too," Phil said reasonably, "but tomorrow you can cash a traveler's check and pretend it didn't happen."

"I did cash my traveler's checks, asshole! Want to see what I have left?" He reached into his pocket and dumped some change into Phil's hand. "A dollar and thirty-five fucking cents! That's what!"

Susan walked directly to Marc and gave him a quick hug. "I'm sorry," she said. "And I'm sorry for what happened before. We all came on this trip to have fun. Brian and I shouldn't have leaned on you like we did."

Marc was touched, and softened immediately. "You're right...both of you. Tomorrow we'll figure something out." He reached for the coins Phil was trying to return and asked, "Want to go into the bar and have one of those Picon punches? I think I can just afford it."

"Thanks, but no," Susan said. "I need to sleep."

Noting Phil's newly-acquired hat, Marc finally thought to ask, "Where's Brian?"

"He's with Josette," Susan answered firmly, turned to give Phil a hug, and went into the hotel.

Marc looked at Phil. "Things must have gotten heavy."

"You could say that...yes."

"Let me guess. He got laid and you didn't."

"That's the short version. I mean Brian and I did go inside, and she did watch through the window. But somehow Winnemucca Rose and I didn't get it on."

"Winnemucca Rose?"

"That's my name for her. But look, if we're going to talk, lets do it in the bar. I'm cold, and I can't stand the thought of you not spending your last dime."

They went in and settled at a small table. The bar was nowhere near as crowded as before, but was far from empty. A Picon punch, they learned, cost $1.50, so Marc brazenly lifted the fifteen cents he was short from a departed customer's tip and made a show of paying his own way. The murky, bitter-sweet drinks were a mirror of how the day had gone.

"You already know all you need to know about my night," Marc stated. "Tell me what went down with you guys."

"Not yet," Phil responded. "I've got a question. Did you lose so big because you were stoned?"

"I asked myself that, but no. I hardly had one real hit, and I didn't feel any buzz. Maybe knowing what you guys were up to made me more reckless. Whatever, man, it's on me, not you. So, come on. Tell what happened."

Phil did, and in considerable detail, although there was no mention of Susan's tears or of any possible resemblance between Susan and Rose.

"Great story," Marc acknowledged. "And The Ritz," he laughed. "What a name. Right out of Hemingway."

"Not at all the place where Jake Barnes might go to have the perfect martini."

"Guess not. But there's one thing I don't get."

"What's that?"

Marc, gesturing emphatically with his hands, continued, "How could Brian go through with it? I mean Susan was right there, and you know there's going to be dues to pay. If you had gone upstairs with Rose, so what? Karen's not around, and you'd've had your—what did you call it?—bordello experience. But Brian, geez! None of us would put him down if he'd left instead of you."

✳ ✳ ✳

That night Marc slept well and Phil didn't. But when Marc got up, Phil feigned sleep and saw him only later, in the dining room, sitting with the McAlpins over the remains of their Sunday breakfast.

"Well, here he comes," called Susan. "Good morning." Her sad, puffy eyes of the night before were gone behind an unexpected sparkle.

Brian, also seeming well-rested, looked up and gave Phil an odd smile. "Early to bed, late to rise," he said with a hint of sarcasm. "Sounds backward. Anyway, it's almost 8:30, and we've got a lot of miles to cover. Think you can be on the road by 9?"

"Yeah," Phil answered. "Sorry, but at least I'm packed. What's for breakfast?"

"Behind you," pointed Marc, indicating a large, wood-inlaid sideboard on the opposite wall.

"Like my college semester in France," Susan added. "Bread, jam, fruit, cheese, and cafe-au-lait in bowls."

Marc, too, looked relaxed and alert. Was everyone but him impervious to wine, dope, and anxiety, Phil wondered. He'd already spent the pre-dawn hours marveling at Marc's gift for sleep, and he was certainly not going to ask the McAlpins what time Brian had gotten in or how the two of them could possibly have had a peaceful night.

"We've got my money thing worked out," Marc said when Phil returned from the buffet with a brimming bowl of black coffee and a plate piled with food. "Brian is going to call McAlpin Printing first thing tomorrow and get $200 wired to a bank in Ketchum. And since I see you all the time in Berkeley, you're going to write him a check for it, and I pay you back when we get home. You may need to front me a few bucks between here and Ketchum, but I'll take care of that when I have cash."

Phil knew this was a good plan. Unless you brought a letter of credit, getting cash away from home could be a real pain. Moreover, Phil kept a few loose checks tucked into his wallet, and he understood that Marc would be more comfortable owing him money than owing it to the McAlpins.

After keeping Phil company for a few minutes in the now depopulated dining room, his three friends got up to finish their packing.

"See you in the lobby," Brian waved. He and Susan left, but Marc lingered.

"Those people are cool," Marc said. "I don't understand them, but they're cool. The minute he saw me, Brian apologized for getting on my case last night, and then started brainstorming a way to get cash. And neither of them let on that I'm basically a jack-off for being in this situation in the first place."

"Glad to hear it," Phil said nonchalantly, though he was feeling relieved. Some of what had been keeping him awake turned out to be no big deal after all.

"But you should know," Marc went on, "I may not be able to repay you anytime soon. With child support and rent every month, what I lost at the casino is all the spare cash I had. I'll have to work some overtime to replace it."

"No problem," Phil answered, having already guessed this might be coming. "By the way, did I miss any revelations?"

"Nothing said and nothing asked," Marc assured him. "If we're lucky, it's already blown over. The last thing I want is to get caught in a bloodletting between those two."

By only a minute or so after 9 they actually were on the road. And having gassed up at the end of the previous day, they headed directly out of Winnemucca on Highway 95 toward eastern Oregon and southwestern Idaho. Marc was at the wheel, with Phil next to him and the McAlpins in back.

They soon left the Humboldt Valley and entered a land of overt desolation. From a base elevation of 4,000 feet, ridge after ridge of rocky, bare, block-faulted mountains spread to the north at 20 to 30 mile intervals through a high-desert moonscape of basin and range. Winnemucca was now well out of sight, though not out of mind.

"Good," Susan said, "we can finally talk. There were too many straight people back at the hotel for us to say anything."

Phil knew what she meant, but he pretended otherwise. "Like what?"

"Like Brian's exploits last night. Or don't you care that Josette was pretty hot and it cost $60?" By parading this knowledge, she was clearly trying to make it her own. "That was for a straight fuck. For half-and-half, which is partly a blow job, it costs $75. And, of course, he used a rubber."

Showing no reaction, Marc kept his eyes on the road. Phil's neck hairs were tingling, and he wished he, too, had a way to block the subject out. Here was the rest of what had been keeping him awake last night. But he was trapped into listening, and had to override his unease.

"Does Brian himself have anything to add?" Phil asked as lightly as he could.

"I don't know what spooked you, but I thought it was a far-out experience," Brian answered. "The only whorehouses I've been to before were in Mexico a long time ago, and they were pretty gross. Because this is legal and aboveboard, it's a whole different scene. The place was so clean and low key, it was like going to visit your girlfriend when you were in high school, but her mom brings you drinks, her sisters all come by in their underwear to say hello, and then she takes you up to her room and fucks you. It was unreal."

"At least now I know how to dress when I really want to turn him on," Susan added, gently pulling at her husband's hair. "But tell them what else you did."

"Once we got upstairs and got the price worked out, Josette starts washing me off and giving me this pecker inspection. Good idea, I guess, disease-wise. But to have something to say while this was going on, I told her what we had done. You know, that my wife was outside the downstairs window dressed like a man and everything."

"What did she do?" Marc put in, laughing in spite of his attempt at disinterest. This twist had been too outrageous to ignore.

"She freaked. Absolutely wouldn't believe it. Went on and on denying it no matter what I said and called me crazy and her 'little madman.' But I think it turned her on. You know, as a fantasy."

"What would she say if she knew it was true?" asked Phil, who could not help sounding amazed.

"Hell if I know," Brian replied. "If you hadn't finked out, you could've asked her yourself."

Josette was real. Phil had seen her. But did any of the rest of this actually happen, or were he and Marc just being had? Did Susan herself even know? And why was Marc seeming to take it all at face value? He'd been warned about their pranks. Phil was tired of the whole thing. All he wanted was to get on with the fishing and whatever else they had come on this trip for. Now that the inevitable topic had been aired, maybe they could get beyond it. And for most of the day, they did.

Marc started the new tack by singing a few bars of *Me and Bobby McGee*, a song he claimed was the best open-road tamer ever written. This inspired Susan to dig out her autoharp, and though she didn't know the chords to *Bobby McGee*, she knew the words and got a good rhythm going by drumming on the sounding board. Delighted to have a diversion, everyone pitched in to sing it three times back-to-back. Susan then played and sang a lovely version of *Shenandoah* and was rewarded with spirited applause.

"Actually, Phil can do a pretty fine Smoky Robinson falsetto," Susan volunteered, catching Phil's eyes for a moment. "Maybe I should've brought him in on the 'Away, oh, look away' part."

Phil knew she was referring to their walk back from the red light district last night, and he felt good about what had happened between them then. Meanwhile, the desert sailed by and they passed a sign saying they were in Oregon.

"Oregon, isn't that Marc's home state?" Brian asked.

"Sure is," Marc replied, "but not this godforsaken part. No self-respecting Swiss would be caught dead here."

"Thought you were Italian," Brian said.

"Trying to pick a fight?" Marc waved a fist in the air.

"But you look Italian," Susan put in, passing around sandwiches and drinks from the camper's propane refrigerator.

"So do a lot of people from our part of Switzerland. But I've got blonde, Heidi cousins there, too. And in terms of attitude, my family was old-country all the way."

At a two-building outpost on the Oregon-Idaho border known as Jordan Valley, they branched onto an unpaved road for about forty miles to connect them to Idaho Route 78. Then they paralleled the Snake River gorge until they wound down to cross the Snake at Mountain Home. This was stark and dramatic country, with the first hints of pine trees on the high ridges and periodic sweeping vistas down the gorge itself. Stacks of clouds raced above them, somehow making the sky seem bigger. Occasionally, one of the shepherds Marc had predicted they'd see appeared in the gray-brown distance trailing plumes of dust and surrounded by masses of slowly-moving white specks. The faster-moving specks around the edges were their dogs.

Back to singing, the group discovered they knew the words and melodies to a number of songs from *Sergeant Pepper*, and the Beatles' whimsicality expressed the improved mood of the day. They extended their rendition of *A Little Help From My Friends* by adding made-up verses, but Susan fell off key and dropped out when Brian substituted "a little help from Josette" for the real chorus. From where Phil was sitting, he couldn't tell if she had any other reaction.

More and more pines and less and less sage shone in the dying Sunday light as they took Route 20 northeast to a KOA campground just beyond Bellevue, picking up a pizza and a six-pack in town when they passed through. Munching away, they threw together an impromptu, fireless camp with Susan and Brian in the van and Marc and Phil outside under the stars.

The Monday plan was to head for Ketchum shortly after sunup. Brian would call San Francisco, and then they would eat and do some shopping while waiting for the banks to open and Marc's cash to arrive. Their twenty mile morning route followed the Big Wood River and completed the transition into mountain country—luminous blue sky, warm sun, pines and cool air. Susan drove, while the men pointed at the river exclaiming over promising-looking trout water.

Ketchum was quite a departure from the other Idaho towns they had seen. Not lavish or Disneyfied, but clearly prosperous, it had sidewalks and municipal landscaping. On a wide, tree-lined main street and a couple of thriving cross streets there were banks, gas stations, food markets, restaurants, and a variety of other businesses. The newer buildings had been designed to blend with the brick or false-front construction of the older ones. Ketchum is where Trail Creek joins the Big Wood from the east. And up Trail Creek a few miles is the plush Sun Valley ski and summer resort, for which Ketchum serves as a supply depot, shopping center, and source of quasi-urban delights.

"Rich people are good for something after all," Brian declared. "This'll be a great spot to take care of business."

"One of those rich people was Hem," said Phil, reminding his companions of what they already knew. A home on the north outskirts of Ketchum had been Hemingway's last permanent residence and the site of his 1961 suicide.

Within two hours they had made the necessary phone call, eaten an acceptably good breakfast, mailed off postcards to Karen and to Marc's kids, bought the additional food items Susan needed, and received $200 for Marc. Phil then gave Brian a check, and Marc reimbursed Brian and Phil for travel expenses that only he'd been keeping track of. Their last stop was a large store called All Season Sports, where they intended to pick up fishing info, detailed maps and some locally-tied dry flies.

The best flies on Idaho rivers at this time of year were said to be a tiny mayfly emerger called a Yellow Sally and the Royal Wulff, a high-floating, deer-hair cousin of the Royal Coachman. The men each got an assortment of those patterns, plus a few old favorites. They learned that no change was expected in the weather, that the fishing had been decent of late, and that by waiting until after Labor Day, they would have the country largely to themselves. With Brain back at the wheel, pointedly grumbling that he'd forgotten to buy a postcard for Josette, north they went, about ten more miles up the Big Wood to where it leveled out in a series of pine-clad hanging valleys 2,000 or so feet below its source on Galena Summit.

Brian took a dirt road cutoff at random and they found a beautiful meadow campsite twenty yards from the river. Blue-green mountain vistas spread in all directions, there were no other camps nearby, and firewood was plentiful. Finally, a chance to unpack the van and use the things they'd been hauling for the last 600 miles. Around the blackened rocks of an existing fire pit they soon set up two folding tables, four chairs, a large wooden chest of cookware and staples, a

Coleman lantern, a two-burner Coleman stove, a sides-rolled-up sleeping tent for Marc and Phil, and strung a line from which to hang fishing vests, waders and spare clothing.

After adding flannel shirts to their jeans, they polished off the last of Susan's pre-prepared sandwiches and got ready for an afternoon of play. This would be fishing for the men, although Brian intended to check out the photographic possibilities as well. For Susan, it would be sunbathing, reading, foraging for wild edibles and preparing a pot of black-bean chili. The evening's menu was trout and chili, assuming the fishing lived up to its reputation, with baked apples for dessert.

"If things could be improved, I don't know how," said Phil, sitting on a fallen pine trunk and rigging his fly rod. On the ground to his left, Brian and Marc were in differing stages of doing the same thing, flanked by the slumped shapes of their waders.

"We could have brought Josette along," Brian joked. "I'd share."

Neither Phil nor Marc laughed. Susan was near the van some distance away, apparently out of earshot. She'd ignored Brian's mention of Josette earlier in the day, but she hadn't seemed pleased.

"Give it a rest, man," Marc replied. "This is supposed to be a fishing trip." Unfazed, Brian smiled back impishly.

Phil interceded by arranging that Marc would hike downstream and fish back to camp, Brian would fish the first 500 yards up from camp to have easy access to his camera equipment, and Phil would circle beyond Brian's beat to fish upstream from there. The exhilaration of fishing then took over. They would meet back here by 6:30, share information and study the evening rise. Other days they would trade spots.

Phil's stretch of the Big Wood had a narrow, rocky bed with few good lies and a press of surrounding brush. Conditions he could handle, though, having experienced them many times in the Sierra. Slap-casting a number 12 Royal Wulff into the white water chutes so it floated semi-submerged got him several hits right away, and he landed two nine-or-ten-inch fish within the first half hour. But wading was tough. Lots of rocks and obstacles, and he was in and out of the water constantly.

After Phil picked up a third fish about the same size, he snagged his back-cast badly and lost the fly and most of his leader. Time for a break. Stretching out on a smooth streamside rock, he folded his fishing vest into a pillow and stared at the sky from beneath the brim of his fishhook-studded brown hat. Then he pulled a copy of The New Yorker out of his vest, rolled his shoulders to get more comfortable, and began to flip through the pages.

Re-rigging his line about an hour later, Phil could picture exactly where his two friends were and what they must be doing. He already knew the lower Big Wood was Marc's kind of river. Limpid green in the shade and almost transparent in the sun, its broad flats, isolated pools and occasional rocky riffles would show-case Marc's ability to cast a long line and still drop his fly softly on target. Mid-afternoon conditions were less than ideal, of course, but Marc was an aggressive wader, and he would work the patches of fast water tirelessly with a number 14 Royal Wulff. Marc never, or nearly never, came back without fish.

Brian would have little alternative but to explore his piece of stream, take a few tentative casts, and decide to wait. There in the meadow, he had almost all crystal-clear gravel shallows overhung with willows and elder. To wade in the afternoon light would spook the fish, and to cast without wading would mean a tangle every time. But there was real potential for later, especially if Brian used the smallest Yellow Sally he had, a near-invisible size 22, and dropped it right over the swirls of cruising fish.

What he'd do first was park his fly rod, vest, and waders near one of the best-looking spots and walk back to camp for his camera. Maybe Brian would take some photographs, maybe he wouldn't. Phil never really understood what moti-vated him. But once back on the stream, Brian would wade with painstaking care and wait as long as five minutes after every step or two. Occasionally, when he sensed the slightest movement in the water, Brian would release a short, smooth cast, and almost every cast would produce a fish. A nice one, too, more often than not.

Phil, Brian and Susan were already in camp when Marc returned about 6:45. They had started a small fire, and an open jug of wine sat on the dining table, along with a few plastic cups. A tantalizing aroma of garlic and chili spread in all directions. The light was fading rapidly, but everyone knew there would be a long period of alpenglow on the surrounding peaks.

"Hey, Marc," Susan called, as he shrugged out of his fishing vest and began to strip off his waders. "How'd it go?"

"Yeah, man, you were gone a long time," Phil added. Brian poured Marc some wine and walked it over to him.

"Did OK," Marc answered. "Beautiful water. I got five and kept three." Marc took a hurried gulp of wine that left a red trickle on his chin. "Thanks, man," he said to Brian. "Here, take a look."

Marc reached into the cloth shoulder bag in which he also carried his landing net and held up three gorgeous rainbows, the smallest just under fourteen inches and the largest over fifteen. They were deep-bodied and silver-green with glowing roseate markings down their sides.

"How'd you guys do?"

Phil had a half-dozen pan-size rainbows to show, and Brian contributed an-other three, somewhere in size between Phil's and Marc's.

"Yeee-haaw!" Susan cried. "Trout and chili tonight, and trout with cottage fries and wild onions for breakfast."

And when she served it up, trout and chili was quite a treat. The fish, moist and tender in a crispy corn-meal breading, subtly complimented generous bowls of deeply flavorful chili garnished with whole roasted garlic cloves and astringent green leaves. Susan had also fashioned an oddly attractive centerpiece of wild flowers and raw broccoli spears that shone in the Coleman lantern's white light. The wine jug was one Marc had brought and he made sure everyone's glass was topped up.

"Balducci House Red," Brian announced, reading the label. "New one on me, but damn good."

"Sure beats Carlo Rossi or Gallo, doesn't it?" Marc replied. "And same price."

"I'm too hungry to do anything about the evening rise, but I bet they're really churning in the flat water all over this meadow," said Phil, looking toward the river.

"They are for sure," Brian agreed. "That's where I got mine, but I spent about half my time with the camera and only fished the earliest part of the rise. Those tiny Yellow Sallies are deadly."

"We've got four more nights to perfect our technique," Marc added. "Let me tell you what I found downstream, and I want to hear about upstream conditions, too."

"Hey," Susan joked, "what do you suppose wine snobs recommend with trout and chili? If wine snobs eat trout and chili, that is."

"This stuff, if they're smart," Phil answered, taking a long swallow.

The meal was a perfect progression of flavors Susan could never repeat, with or without a recipe. She was very pleased. She dished out seconds to all, and they ate contentedly, finishing Marc's wine with the baked apples. Then Brian started a joint of McAlpin Gold around. Marc again abstained, this time without comment from anyone.

"So, Susan, what were those herbs on top of the chili?" Phil asked.

"Not herbs, watercress," she replied. "I found it weaving in the current of a little side stream that also has wild onions growing along the banks. And I found some not-quite-ripe blackberries and blueberries, but those are for another day."

"Ms. Natural strikes again," Brian joked. "Unless Josette learns to cook, I'm keeping you." Susan flushed and glared at Brian, but he pretended not to notice. Getting past the corrosive effect of Winnemucca, Phil thought, was starting to feel hopeless.

"How did you get into all this eating off the land?" Marc asked, turning to give Brian a piercing look of his own. Brian ignored that, too.

"My parents," Susan answered, relieved to take the conversation in a new direction. "I grew up in Marin...Fairfax, if you know where that is. Our yard backed onto Mt. Tam, and all of us were hikers. We only ever cooked with wild thyme, wild sage, wild bay leaves and rosemary that had run wild out of a neighbor's garden. It was a game for my sister and me, and my brother, too. What could you find? What was it? How could it be used? And we'd trick one another into eating the grossest things we could get away with."

"Ever pick wild mushrooms?" Marc followed.

"My father used to. He was the expert. It was really fun. My mom and brother and sister thought mushrooms were yukky, but I think they're delicious. My dad would scare everybody by doing taste tests and then stagger around the room pretending to die. I'm too nervous to pick them on my own, though."

"My family was seriously into wild mushrooms," Marc said. "It's very European, and in Oregon, with all the wet, it's always mushroom season."

Phil built up the fire and they moved their chairs to it. Brian got out his Hemingway and found a story to read, *The Three-Day Blow*. After Marc moved the lantern closer, Phil took the first turn. Then Susan, then Marc, then Brian. Each read three pages or so. The spare prose and the images of friendship and heartbreak had a welcome unifying effect.

"It's a guy-type story," Susan said, "but I've always liked it. And knowing we're camped probably five miles from where Hem shot himself makes things pretty heavy."

"Sure does," Brian reflected. "Not to mention coyotes howling in the distance and more stars than any two of us have seen before."

A short time later, the fire died back and they all went to bed. Looking out the side of the tent at the sky beyond the overhanging pines, Phil sensed that Marc, lying next to him, was awake. Obviously, neither of them wanted to talk, or not then, anyway. The Big Wood splashed and gurgled in its meandering channel, an owl hooted, and Phil felt the pull of sleep. But above the night noises, he began to hear from the van muffled voices that were not happy voices. The intensity rose and fell. Brian said the name Vera distinctly at least twice, the second time followed by a semi-audible outburst from Susan. "Forget Vera!" she exclaimed, "...done with that...One more stupid crack about Josette...the next...in the chili pot...your head!...Bad enough...private, but...embarrass me in front of...!"

Finally the voices faded and fell silent. Good, Phil thought. Something needed to be said, and he was glad he didn't have to say it. Phil heard Marc stir and roll over. "Ughhhh," came an exasperated breath from that direction. "How can Brian be so cool one minute and such an asshole the next?" Though Phil had no answer, it was the right question.

The Josette jokes stopped and Tuesday set an agreeable pattern for the days that followed. The McAlpins seemed to lack their customary ease with each other, but Susan's foraging for wild foods continued while the men fished, took photographs or read. She read, too, along with sunning and resting, having brought Barbara Tuchman's celebrated WWI book, *Guns of August*, which led her into many lively conversations with Marc. As a historian, his specialty was 19th and 20th century Europe, so he was well acquainted with the bizarre details of the Sarajevo assassination and the Zimmermann telegram. Susan also oversaw the demise of her centerpiece, removing the broccoli from the bouquet and stir-frying it with wild radish and fresh sage. And after dinner, around the fire, there was more wine, more singing, more autoharp, more dope and more Hemingway.

On Wednesday, the four of them made a day-trip to upper Trail Creek, beyond

Sun Valley, for a picnic and some excellent fishing. To find fishing of that quality near any paved road in California, everyone agreed, had become impossible. Thursday they went to the headwaters of the Salmon River, above Galena Summit, a high, cold, tundra-like meadow laced with innumerable creeks and rills draining the spectacular, snow-streaked Sawtooth Mountains. Mediocre fishing, but with scenery that Marc claimed was Switzerland all the way. The outing also yielded Susan something exotic for dessert. She filled her pockets with enough wild gooseberries to make a topping for that night's round of baked apples.

Friday presented logistical problems. Realizing at breakfast that it was their last full day in Idaho, Brian wanted to photograph the Sawtooths, while Marc was looking for another chance at Trail Creek, where he'd lost a big trout two days before. Phil knew they would be cooped up in the van for the return trip to California, so he wanted to stay around camp, while Susan wanted to check out the boutiques in Ketchum. With one vehicle to share, everybody's plans except Phil's were subject to compromise. But after an animated private huddle with Susan, Brian apparently decided he could photograph just as well near the Big Wood, and that she should run Marc out to Trail Creek, circle back to Ketchum, and then pick Marc up at the end of the afternoon.

"You sure, man?" Marc asked, doing a poor job of concealing his satisfaction.

"Go for it," Brian insisted. "I'm no photographer if I can't find stuff to work with right here." This seemed sincere, and Phil hoped it was.

They all lingered in camp to do dishes and drink coffee until late morning, enjoying the setting and the companionship. Marc and Susan took off after she left apples, cheese and bread for Phil and Brian's lunch. Those two split the food into separate picnics and parted company shortly before noon. Phil knew exactly where he would go. Upstream, where he'd gone the first afternoon, near the remains of a ruined bridge, was a wider area with potholes among the rocks and gravel bars that looked like good holding water. He'd bypassed it previously, thinking to return, but had not had the chance.

Changing flies several times, Phil fished diligently and without result. Too bright. Noting where the sun would be later, he moved further upstream to see what he could do. There he fished, picked up a few small ones for tomorrow's breakfast, ate lunch, read, took a nap, and fished some more. It was a heavenly day.

A little after 4 P.M., Phil threaded his way through the willows and knee-high grass back to the old bridge. Rounding a corner, he found himself a dozen feet from Brian's flannel-clad back, which was bent forward over a tripod-mounted, 4 x 5 camera. Phil could see that a cluster of unusually beveled rocks against the dark timbers of two surviving pilings was the intended subject.

"Hey, Brian," Phil called, "Don't want to scare you."

"Whoa!" Brian threw his arms in the air and jumped in mock fright.

Phil came closer. "This spot looks great, doesn't it? But I didn't do shit here. Hope you have better luck."

"Think I'll do fine, but the light's not right yet."

"Will it screw you up if I fish?"

"Unfortunately, yes. You'll cause unnatural ripples and you might end up where the camera can see you. I'm stopped way down, so everything's in focus."

"I can wait. Light's not right for me either." Phil examined the camera and the care with which Brian had positioned it. "How do you know what this thing sees?" he asked.

"Experience, basically. But I've just always been able to do it. For me, experience comes more in knowing what I can do in the darkroom."

"Which is?"

"The power to play with reality. That's the real kick."

"What are you going for here?"

"When the light is right, say a half-hour from now, those pilings will be completely in shade except for what is reflected back at them from the water. At the same time, the rocks themselves will be obliquely lit, and every little crack and striation will show up."

"Yeah, I can see it in my mind."

"What I'm not sure about is the exact moment to get the water. That's why I'll have to shoot maybe four or five exposures."

"I don't follow."

"There'll be one instant when the rocks and pilings will behave pretty much like I want, and the water will come up with a pulsing, three-dimensional sheen. With that, I have a negative I can work with. Otherwise, I don't."

"Oh."

"So what we do is relax and wait."

Leaving the camera where it was, Brian and Phil sat against a grassy mound that must have been the approach to the old bridge. Phil put his fly rod aside and took off his vest.

"I've been wanting to talk to you anyway," Brian began.

"Yeah, we haven't had much time together, have we?"

"Look...Whatever he thinks, I don't owe Marc an explanation about Winnemucca, but I owe you one."

"You don't. I'd rather let it go."

"Well, things got out of hand," Brian continued. "I'm still trying to work it through with Susan, and I don't want to drive wedges between us and you. No mystery where it came from. You've seen or heard about our pranks in the past. This was just one more."

"Sure," Phil responded, "before you were married, there was that summer canoe trip through the most crowded stretch of the Russian River wearing gorilla suits...there was having sex in the Sierra Club elevator one night when Susan was working late...and then your whacked-out, costume-party wedding reception in the underground parking garage at S.F. city hall after the judge married you."

"Right," Brian answered with evident pride. "And other stuff like pretending to shop for an engagement ring down at Union Square dressed as a nun and a priest…and the party last Christmas when Susan deliberately served hot mulled vinegar to people, but with such style that some of them asked for the recipe before they left."

"Yeah, I remember, and you also had the fucked-up tree with almost no needles and about two ornaments. I think Karen and I are glad we went to her folks for Hanukkah instead."

"Oh, we'd have let you in on it. We used some of our closest friends as shills to get other folks cranked up. And you were sort of a co-conspirator in Winnemucca."

"Yeah, I guess I was."

"But there's one you don't know about. We call it 'Vera,' and we did it last spring."

"How come you never told me?" Phil didn't let on he recognized the name.

"We were going to do it on you, too. But now, after Winnemucca, we're afraid maybe you couldn't handle it."

"Who was the lucky winner?" Phil asked, trying to hide his dismay.

"We pulled it on Sid. You know him. Met him at our place."

"Sid Hartley? Yeah, I know him. The guy who introduced you to Susan."

"Right. Great photographer. Been a friend for years."

"And who or what is 'Vera'?"

"An imaginary mistress Susan and I dreamed up. No way to say whose idea it was. I have this album of classic Avedon fashion photographs, and one of a model named Vera Moskoya got me joking to Susan about her. Things took off from there.

"Pretty soon after that, Susan was alone with Sid for a while at our place one Saturday when he'd come to pick me up for a shoot at Devil's Slide. I'd been called into the office on some emergency and got home later than planned. Anyway, she proceeds to tell Sid she's almost sure I'm having an affair and she doesn't know what to do about it, and would he talk to me, and so on."

"Oh, shit."

"Oh shit, is right. I mean we'd kicked it around, and kind of zeroed in on Sid, but I had no idea Susan was going to put the ball in play. But she did, and it was my turn. She clued me before Sid and I left, and he acted completely weird the rest of the day. Then, a few weeks later, Sid and I are out somewhere and I tell him I have to leave unexpectedly. Of course, he's suspicious. So I take him into my confidence, and tell him about Vera, and how I want him to meet her sometime and all that. Well, the poor bastard doesn't know what to do, and we just let him dangle."

"You guys were right. Better him than me. And I mean that, by the way."

"Finally, Sid makes a date to talk to me. Lunch somewhere down by the office. It's obvious what it's about, so I have Susan come, too. But she waits in the car. I have to prod Sid to get to the point, but he does. You know, he says do I realize what I'm doing, and think about Susan, and everything a friend would say. I'm contrite and I fumble around and then I work it to go to the restroom. I go out, get Susan and bring her into the restaurant. We tried not to mock him or anything, but we laughed our asses off. At first he was dumbstruck, then he got so pissed he walked out."

"You still friends?"

"He got over it," Brian smiled. "Told Enid, his wife, and they both think it's funny now. But for a while, it put a real strain on things. That's the first one that ever backfired."

"Surely you can see why?"

"Yeah...But I've got to tell you that this shit, these pranks, have been fundamental to Susan's and my whole relationship. It's something we both get off over. Starting with the first one, there was more joy in that canoe the day we wore the gorilla suits than my parents had in thirty-five years of marriage. If I thought I had to copy their style, I'd never get married at all."

"By your logic, that led to Winnemucca."

"Right. I told Susan how you and I were joking about the red light district, and she came up with the basic idea. But it got to be something where I went as far as I did because I had to live up to her expectations, and she thought the same about how far she went. It's like the fucking Vietnam war. An escalation we should have stopped, but didn't."

"OK. Thanks for filling me in. That's all I want to know."

"Well, what you've heard from Susan or me is all you can know. Nobody else except Josette actually knows what happened, and even if you tracked her down and got a different story, how would you know she was telling the truth?"

"Sure," Phil said resignedly. "I've watched *Perry Mason*. But the same applies with Susan. How does she know you're telling the truth?" Phil could see from Brian's expression that this was not a new thought, and he could also see he'd struck a nerve.

"Hey, man, if I was lying to Susan, wouldn't I come up with something more bland than what she told you and Marc in the van last Sunday?"

"What she told us and what you told her may not be the same. That's why I don't want to know more. I'll never be able to believe any of it. From you or her."

"I don't get it!" Brian protested. "Why has this become such a big deal?" He sat forward and looked away for what seemed like a long time. Then he pushed himself abruptly to his feet. "The light!" he said. "Shit, I nearly missed it."

Phil stood, too, but when he put his vest back on and picked up his fly rod, he found he no longer wanted to fish. Brian, meanwhile, was at the river's edge, once again bent over his camera.

"See you in camp," Phil called, heading off through the trees. As far as he could tell, Brian made no reply.

No sooner had Phil arrived at the fire pit, than the van rolled in with a muted toot of the horn to announce Marc and Susan's return. They jumped out and walked toward him, animated and smiling.

"Only five o'clock," he greeted them. "I didn't expect you guys so early."

"Had to get back," Marc responded. "So we can all go out on the town."

"Yeah," Susan followed. "We learned about this cool street fair, barbecue and dance up in Stanley. There were posters all over, and lots of locals from Ketchum are going."

"It's some kind of festival, including the annual rodeo and parade tomorrow," Marc put in. "Won't be able to make that, but tonight is party time."

Whipsawed between their high spirits and feelings left by his conversation with Brian, Phil managed to sound a positive note. "I could probably get up for that."

"You'll have to," Susan stated. "Marc says he's ready to boogie, and the cook's going off duty. Where's Brian, by the way?"

"Working on a photograph this side of the old bridge," Phil answered, wondering how Brian would react to the new turn of events. She nodded and walked toward the side door of the van.

"Get any fish?" Marc asked.

"No great shakes. Three more breakfast-size. How'd you do?"

"Only kept one." Marc extracted another beautiful fifteen-inch rainbow from his bag. "Had a couple of smaller ones, too, but no sign of my lunker. Guess I left him with a sore mouth the other day."

Marc, Susan, and Phil set about getting cleaned up and dressed for the evening. Brian returned to camp at 5:30, and Phil touched him lightly on the shoulder as he passed, getting a strange, raised-eyebrow look in return. Acquiescing quietly to Susan's idea of going out, Brian stowed his camera gear, combed his hair, grabbed his western hat and jeans jacket, and said he was ready. Susan was again in her denim jumper, but added a Mexican shawl for warmth. Marc reverted to his turtleneck, worn under a red-and-black checked Pendleton, while Phil went cowboy, as he had in Winnemucca. At Susan's insistence, he even wore the McAlpins extra hat and jeans jacket. By quarter to 6, with Phil at the wheel, they were on the road. Susan joined him in front, leaving Brian and Marc on the benches behind.

"How far is Stanley?" Phil asked, after he'd turned north and begun to climb Galena Summit.

"People said fifty miles from Ketchum," Susan answered, "so more like forty from our camp."

At the summit they had a heart-stopping view of sunset over the Sawtooths against a row of indigo clouds building to the west. Susan and Marc kept up alternating monologues describing their day's activities, while Brian remained subdued. Gradually, they lost most of the altitude they'd gained and began to run along the banks of the famed Salmon River. A few miles before Stanley, Brian came to life and pointed at an upcoming overlook.

"Let's check out the 'River of No Return' while there's still enough light to see," he urged. Phil eased off the pavement into a fringe of brush.

One step from the van a ten-foot bank sloped to the water, and even here, a few miles below its source, the Salmon made the Big Wood look like a toy. It was a formidable stream, a good thirty feet wide, and deep, with a swift, dark, powerful current.

"Big water, big fish," said Marc. "Wish we'd come here."

"Maybe," Brian conceded. "But how'd you ever wade that baby?"

"Put in one leg at a time," Phil joked. "Bet it's cold as hell, too."

Brian used these few moments in the lee of the van to start a joint around, and they all partook freely. Anticipation of the lights and action in Stanley lent an edge that none of them had felt during their nights camped under the stars.

"It's a long time since I got stoned and went dancing," Marc enthused while Phil found a break in traffic and pulled the van onto the road. "And am I ready. Reminds me of old times in Berkeley."

Phil felt the same, and recalled that it was Marc who kindled Phil's own interest in dancing back in their college days. And Marc did like to smoke a little when he was on the prowl.

"Dope doesn't have that effect on Brian," Susan mused. "Maybe we should've made him take some extra tokes."

"I did," Brian said flatly. "That way my mind can dance while my body hangs out at the bar."

The traffic, the marijuana, and the gathering darkness made the last three miles into town slow going. Finally, they began to pass between columns of parked cars along the sides of the highway and saw the town itself off to their left. Phil turned around and pulled into the first available place on the grassy shoulder. The lights and rinky-tink music of a carnival area defined the edge of a cluster of buildings a hundred yards away. A small Ferris wheel roughly thirty feet high shimmered over everything, emitting waves of children's squeals that seemed to draw walking figures toward it from all directions.

Stanley was a hamlet of a hundred or so structures, some of brick, some of logs, some of clapboard, and all modest. A town that looked exactly like what it was: a jumping-off place for pack trips into the Sawtooths, float trips down the Salmon, and other kinds of outdoor recreation. In addition, it was home to a Grayrock County branch government center, a state highway maintenance yard, and a Forest Service ranger station. There were a couple of food stores, a small hardware, a post office, a laundromat, a gas station, a ramshackle barber shop, two restaurants, and three bars. Tonight, however, the barricaded main streets were free of cars and host to swarms of people.

Western dress predominated, so Phil fit right in, but the other three had enough Ketchum chic to look like no more than visitors from the next town. In it's classic, rural-America way, Stanley's festival was dazzling, even more so if you were stoned.

"What I heard was that they do this after Labor Day and on a Friday night to make sure it's mainly locals," Susan said. They had stopped at a boarded-up building sporting an elaborate poster for the event, and were attempting to get oriented.

"Locals and polite outsiders like you folks," smiled a burly man to their right who had a tow-headed, 5 year-old cowboy perched on his shoulders.

"Let's see," Marc read, " tomorrow's the parade, the presentation of stock and the rodeo. What the he...heck is the presentation of stock?"

The little boy piped up immediately, "That's the cattle drive! Real cowboys bring the horses and cows and everything for the rodeo right down this street!"

"Wow!" Marc responded, lightly pinching the toe of the boy's boot. Then, turning to his companions, "Can you believe it?" he laughed. "The running of the bulls, and we're going to miss out."

"Means we have all our fun tonight," Brian said, materializing with four foaming cups and passing them around.

Along with the Ferris wheel, the midway had a pop-the-balloon dart game, a pair of wise-ass clowns, a BB-gun shooting gallery, and a merry-go-round. Adults and kids wandered about, many carrying bright-pink stuffed animals or almost-as-pink cotton candy. Groups of teenagers lounged wherever there were shadows. And beyond the midway, under a blanketing aroma of roasting meat, the bars, restaurants and other businesses had moved their operations into the street.

As served at the Stanley Lion's Club booth, barbecue was a large paper plate of cole slaw and ranch beans overlaid with corn bread and a stack of dripping back-ribs. Rainier ale was the official beverage, and cups of it stood almost rim-to-rim on every flat surface. The four friends squeezed onto the end of a picnic table in front of the River Rat Saloon, where they began to eat with abandon. Marc, then Phil, then Brian, bought additional rounds of ale from a far-from-sober barmaid, and they all drained their cups between bites.

"Not the equal of Susan's cooking, but still damn good," Phil said, working to keep the sleeve of his borrowed denim jacket clear of barbecue sauce.

"One of the cooks was taking a break," Susan added, "and told me the secret ingredients in the sauce are molasses and coffee. I'm going to try it at home."

"Go back and ask about the beans," said Marc. "I can make pretty mean corn bread, but I've never had beans like this before."

"Bay leaf, cumin and coriander," Susan replied, thinking out loud. "But you're right, there's a bunch more I can't pick up, either."

"Yeah, and see how they make the beer," joked Brian, though he continued in a maudlin tone, "A shame S.F.'s getting so wimpy you can't find Rainier ale anymore."

"Brisbane, down by South City," Marc got out around a mouthful of ribs. "There's a big C&W bar with Rainier on tap and clientele right off the streets of Stanley. I'll take you sometime when we get home."

"Shows what I know," Brian said, apparently to himself.

Their next cycle of cruising brought them down a dark side street past a crude metal tower in front of the volunteer fire department, and then to the Stanley

Free Library, in the garage of what appeared to be a private home. The lights at the end of the block were the community center, where the sound of tuning guitars and random drum beats meant the dance was about to get underway.

They went to the door and looked in. It was a large, high-ceilinged, double-bay, log building with a smooth hardwood floor and drapings of crepe paper. A temporary bar had been installed to the left of the stage in a back corner. On the stage, an all-male, five-piece band in red satin shirts and white Stetsons was finishing its sound check. A pale, fey, peroxide-blonde singer in a blue-dyed cow-skin skirt and matching top stood to the side, untangling and re-looping her mike cord.

At this point, the house lights went down and the four of them became part of the crowd pushing into the hall. The band struck up *I Fall to Pieces*, and the singer proved to have a flair for imitating Patsy Cline. Phil found himself dancing with Susan as the floor filled around them. Over her shoulder, he saw Marc and Brian head toward the left rear, but Marc veered further left and Brian continued to the bar.

"Karen isn't a dancer, is she?" Susan asked quietly.

"No," Phil responded, "Just not her thing."

"Also, as you know, not Brian's."

"But I only miss it when I'm actually dancing," Phil said. "Like now."

"Me, too. And it's no good to harp on that one fault when they both have so much else to offer."

During an almost rock-and-roll version of *Tulsa Time* featuring the lead guitarist's picking and singing, Phil stashed his jacket, hat and Susan's shawl under a chair. They stayed on the floor for a two-step arrangement of *Walkin' After Midnight*, and then danced slowly to *Hello Walls*. Marc slid by in the arms of a plain-looking young woman with brownish-blonde hair in the frizzy, above-the-shoulder style that was just coming into vogue. Brian was at the bar, chatting up a perky cowgirl bartender. He was drinking highballs. A partially filled glass of ice and amber liquid rested beneath his fingers, and the bartender was placing another next to it. This was a Brian that Phil hadn't seen before.

"You smell unbelievably good," Phil said, nuzzling Susan's hair and amazed at his own forwardness.

"Thanks. I crushed a handful of fresh pine needles just before we left camp and rubbed the essence behind my ears and down my neck. I can smell it, too."

"You see Brian?"

"Yes," she answered. "Looks like he's going to get plastered. Once or twice a year he'll do that if something's really bothering him. Then he just sleeps it off."

"Hope I'm not what's bothering him."

"Not likely. Why, did something happen?"

"We had a discussion today."

"Oh."

"About..." Phil hesitated to find a word, "pranksterism."

"That's kind of a loaded subject right now. What did you say?"

"Essentially, that the kind of pranksterism you guys are getting into destroys trust, and trust is a heavy-duty thing to mess with. Brian also told me about 'Vera' and Sid, and how I was going to be next."

"I'm sorry about that. It's good he told you, but I'm sorry." She squeezed Phil's arm and shoulder as they danced.

"And we talked some about Winnemucca, too."

"That's been a watershed. We wanted to shock you and Marc, but we ended up shocking ourselves. It's like Brian and I suddenly weren't on the same team. See, the plan was..."

"Stop. I don't want to hear it. I told Brian the same thing."

"OK, OK...But to him, if we give up that stuff, we might as well have kids and move to the suburbs."

"So it's pranks or kids?"

"No. I don't know. I mean I do want to have kids, and I think Brian does, too, but I don't know if that means moving to the suburbs or not."

The music faded and Phil felt someone tapping his shoulder. "I'm cutting in," came Marc's voice from behind, "but I want to introduce you to somebody."

Phil separated from Susan and turned right into the face of the frizzy-haired girl. Her eyes held his while he registered her plaid western shirt and nicely fitting jeans.

"Phil," Marc smiled mischievously beneath his mustache, "meet Rose. Rose, this is Phil."

"Hi," she said, extending her hand. "Rose Laing."

"Hi," he answered, completing the handshake. "Phil Beaumont." There was a deep chord of humor to the situation, but it would clearly be the wrong time to laugh.

The band switched to *Okie From Muskogee*, and Marc started to dance away with Susan. "No, wait," Phil heard her say. "Brian loves this one. Let's go talk to him a minute." They swung in the direction of the bar.

"You still dancing?" Rose asked.

"Sure," Phil answered, reaching for her.

"Your friend said you wanted to meet me but you're shy."

"He says a lot of things, but this time mostly true."

"I saw you guys in the store last Monday. And I kind of thought you gave me the eye."

Phil had a flash of recognition. He had seen her before. "You work at All Season Sports, right? Or were you a customer?"

"Why...do they make customers stock shelves where you're from?"

"Only when they misbehave," Phil laughed. Beyond her deep suntan, she had a casual vivaciousness that made her seem to float as they danced.

"Your friend's a good dancer," she offered, "and you are, too."

"Thanks. Same goes for you. What else did he say—Marc, that is?"

"You're from Berkeley. I could have guessed, though. We don't see many people here like that other guy with you, the one with the pony tail, who aren't from California someplace."

Phil smiled. Maybe it was the dope, but it was unprecedented for him to feel so comfortable with a woman he'd barely met. "And what about you?" he asked. "Where you from, and what do you do besides work at All Season Sports?"

"I grew up in Twin Falls. I'm working now to save money for grad school. My brother-in-law owns All Season, and I've worked there a lot of summers. Winters I work as a ski instructor at Sun Valley. Free skiing, and I earn a lot more."

Suddenly it was break time for the band, and everyone made a rush for the bar. Phil and Rose hung back, and Phil couldn't see Brian or Susan or Marc through the crowd. He followed Rose to a side-door landing at the top of some narrow stairs where they continued to talk.

"What kind of grad school?"

"I plan to get a teaching credential from U. of Idaho. I graduated there two years ago. Ketchum's been fun, but ultimately I want to do something more serious with my life."

"You'll be a great teacher," Phil said. "I can already see you have the, the... presence to connect with kids in any subject."

"Gee," she smiled. "Thanks. I'm shooting for sixth grade or something like that."

They proceeded to talk and dance into the next set. By then Rose knew Phil's background with Marc and the McAlpins, knew about his job and about his love of fishing and mountaineering. And he knew at least as much about her. As they were dancing slowly to *Make The World Go Away*, Brian approached unsteadily behind Rose and pantomimed to Phil that he was going out to the van to sleep.

"There goes the guy with the pony tail," Rose said as Brian went by. "Sure looks wrecked."

"I'm afraid he is," Phil acknowledged.

"Did you say that woman you were dancing with is married to Marc or the other guy? She's very pretty."

"Susan? She is pretty, and she's married to the guy who just left."

"Well, from what I'm seeing," Rose joked, "I thought you were going to say she was married to them both. I mean you are from Berkeley and all."

He gave a grudging smile. "We're weird, but not that weird."

"Well, what about you? Do you have a girlfriend there in Berkeley?"

"Yes," Phil heard himself say, "but no one serious." It was a lie, of course, though just then it didn't feel like a lie. In the background, he saw Marc and Susan dancing together about halfway across the floor.

The band cut to a Texas country blues number, and Phil swung apart from Rose to dance fast. Why was it, when he used to go out to bars and clubs in the Bay Area, that he never, never met anyone like Rose Laing? A sprightly, waltz-time version of *Jambalaya* was next, and he thought about disengaging from her to follow the majority of dancers leaving the floor. Instead Phil asked if she could waltz.

"Yes," she answered, flashing her eyes. "And I bet I'm the only one my age within two hundred miles of here that can."

"Good," he said, and they began to glide together, enjoying the newly-available space around them. Marc and Susan were waltzing, too, along with a smattering of older couples.

"How did you learn?" Phil asked her.

"My father. He taught my sister and me, and had us teach our brother. Said he didn't want any of us to be embarrassed at our weddings because we couldn't waltz."

"A practical and far-seeing man."

"True. How did you learn?"

Phil now had goosebumps. "From my mother," he answered. "My dad traveled a lot, and she was lonely. So for fun, she danced me around the living room until I was in high school."

"What a sweet story. Where is she now?"

"Still with my dad, in the suburbs of Columbus, Ohio."

"Let's see if we can get the band to play another waltz," Rose suggested.

"OK. But how? I haven't heard them taking requests."

"Easy. The bass player is my roommate's boyfriend. And Debbie, my room-mate, is the cowgirl bartender over there."

Rose steered them toward the stage and motioned the bass player toward her. And when *Jambalaya* ended, the guitar-playing male singer kept the mike rather than returning it to his female partner.

"Well, folks," he announced, "I see we've got some waltz fans here tonight. So stay on the floor, we'll do another one before we take our break." He waved an arm, and the familiar strains of *The Tennessee Waltz* began, nice and slow.

"Oooh," Rose sighed. "He knows it's my favorite." This was somehow so in-evitable that Phil shouldn't have been surprised, but he hesitated momentarily before gathering her to dance.

"What was that about?" Rose asked.

"Just that this song has gotten to be my favorite, too."

"Maybe what you need is an Idaho girlfriend," she teased.

Phil's sense of inevitability grew as he and Rose exchanged more whispered conversation and danced out the rest of the song. Then the band did break, and Phil went to hunt up Marc and Susan while Rose talked to Debbie at the bar. Phil could still feel the warm imprint of Rose's lithe body and firm breasts against him as he walked. He found his two friends sitting in adjoining chairs along the edge of the floor playfully arguing some facet of WWI.

"My, my," Susan greeted him. "What's this thing you have for women named Rose? You should see the two of you!"

Phil thought he heard a tinge of jealousy in this remark, though she was more likely expressing disapproval on Karen's behalf. But watching Susan dance with Marc all night hadn't inclined Phil toward concern for her feelings. He deflected all these issues by saying, "Brian went out to the van to crash. Did you see him?"

"Oh yeah, he told us," Marc replied.

"He's going to be one sick puppy tomorrow," Susan added.

"You guys OK to drive by now?" Phil asked.

"I can if I need to," Susan answered. "Why? You still stoned?"

Here it came. "No, I'm going home with Rose. She'll drop me at camp early tomorrow on her way to work."

Marc's face simultaneously signaled approval, disapproval and amazement, and he undoubtedly felt all three. Susan looked down at her lap. "OK," she said. "We'll see you then." Phil handed her the van keys, retrieved his hat and jacket, and headed to the bar.

Walking out of the dance with Rose and through town to her car was completely surreal for Phil. His every pore picked up night smells, cricket sounds, glints of moonlight and her faint perfume. Rose drove an old but serviceable VW bug, and she was so familiar with the highway south to Ketchum that she barely had to pay attention.

"Debbie thought I was nuts when I told her what I was doing," Rose confided once they were underway. "But she agreed you didn't look like an ax murderer."

"Comforting to all concerned," Phil laughed, and she chimed in.

"Anyway," Rose went on, "Debbie won't be home for a while, but she'll be bringing Rich with her after the dance."

The Sawtooths by moonlight, framed against fingers of clouds, were the best piece of Idaho scenery Phil had seen yet, and he was thankful to have the chance, especially under these circumstances.

"Spectacular, aren't they?" Rose said. "I never get tired of them. That's a big part of why I don't think I'll ever want to live anywhere else."

"Makes sense," said Phil.

"But you've got beautiful country in California, too. Yosemite and Big Sur and all. I've been there with my parents."

"Yeah, beautiful country, but getting to be twenty million people to go with it." The downhill run from the summit was so easy the car seemed to drive itself. Phil relaxed and let everything flow by.

"That's the turnoff to our camp," he pointed as they zoomed past.

"Oh, you're at Peebles Meadow, just below the old bridge. I only live about three miles from there."

"We didn't know the name, but that's the place, all right."

Rose and Debbie had a small, nicely-finished, bat-and-board cabin off the highway to the right overlooking the Big Wood valley. They had to share the one bedroom during cold weather, but in summer, Rose converted the firewood storage porch at the back into a private room for herself. She had a large mattress on the floor looking up into the trees through a double window with criss-cross molding. Two small skylights let the stars shine in through the sloped roof. Between the surrounding forest and the lingering scent of firewood, it was as much like being outside as being inside could be.

"Nice place," Phil said to fill the silence.

"Thanks. But, you know, actually having you here is odder than I expected. I mean, the idea is to run a scam on your friends because they think you're a wimp?"

"Could be it's me who thinks I'm a wimp. They're always into crazy pranks and mind games. If I told you, you wouldn't believe half of it. I'm usually on the sidelines, but not tonight."

"I guess I'll need to understand that mind game stuff when I finish grad school. Kids try to run them on teachers all the time. But for now, you're going to sleep in my room and I'll be in Debbie's till she gets home, then I'll move to the couch."

"Why not let me have the couch so you don't have to move?"

"Because I have more control this way, and you promised you'd do exactly what I said if I let you stay."

"Right. That's the deal."

"How about you use the potty while I get a few things out of my room? After that, it's all yours."

Later, when Phil was curled in her bed, hints of Rose's perfume and her own lightly musky smell exuded from her pillow and mixed with the pine-scented air. This had turned out to be a mighty horny fishing trip, and he couldn't help wishing Rose was in bed with him. He knew she was interested, but he also knew she wasn't going to do a one-night stand with some guy who was just passing through. And overall, it was hard to see how things could have worked out better. What Phil hoped now was that Karen would be as horny as he was by the time he got home.

The next thing Phil knew, it was light and the birds were awake and the sound of running water told him someone was taking a shower. He felt great, and was already looking forward to rolling into camp and getting everybody's reaction. Reaching from inside the bed, he located his clothes and put them on. When he was dressed, he got out and started loosening the laces of his shoes so he could push his feet into them. A minute or so later, the water went off and Phil heard Rose's voice accompanied by loud knocking on his door.

"Wake up time!"

"I'm awake," he answered. "Come on in."

Rose, looking smaller and prettier than he remembered her, was in a paisley print robe and flip-flops, and had her hair wrapped in a towel.

"Hi," she said. "Sleep OK?"

"Absolutely," he assured her. "This is a wonderful room. How 'bout you?"

"Just fine, but we need to be out the door as soon as I'm dressed so I can run you up to Peebles Meadow and still get to work on time."

Clouds had filled the Big Wood valley overnight and a weather change was clearly at hand. But the mood in Rose's car was one of intimacy, more so by far than the night before, and more so, Phil thought, than would have resulted from a typical one-night stand. Not that he had any experience along those lines, but it seemed easy enough to project.

"Looks like I'll be driving out of Idaho in the rain," Phil said.

"No surprise. It's time to clear my bed out of that porch and move the firewood in. Fall comes overnight in this country, and you could see it in the clouds behind the Sawtooths on our way back from Stanley."

"You could, you mean. Not me."

"That's right, you're not from around here. Think you'd recognize this valley with eight feet of snow on the ground? That's what we have most winters."

"Wow. Hard to picture. But hey, thanks again for going along with this. There's no way to explain why it's so important, but it is."

"What kind of hot stories will you tell your friends about me?" she teased.

"None. And they won't ask. But it'll mess with their minds. Hope we didn't do your reputation any damage. You're not leaving town today like I am."

"Actually, it might help my reputation," she joked.

"When did Debbie get in last night, anyway? I didn't hear a thing."

"She didn't come home, and I didn't figure she would. I just wanted you to think I had a bodyguard." They arrived at the Peebles Meadow turnoff, and Rose pulled onto the wide shoulder beyond it.

"Another thing," Rose continued, "now that I know I can trust you, you wouldn't be sleeping in my bed alone if you ever came back here. You're a very sweet guy." She leaned, put her hand behind his neck and gave him a lingering kiss.

He returned her kiss and drank in her smell. "Thanks for everything, Rose. When it comes to sweet, I'm not in your league."

"You OK to walk from here? I don't want to feel like I'm on display."

"Sure," he said, getting out. "I'd rather walk." She gunned the VW's metallically chugging engine, gave him a last look, swung a U-turn in the carpet of pine needles and roared off toward Ketchum.

Phil watched her go with a genuine sense of loss. End of Rose, end of vacation, end of summer. But as he walked down the dirt access road under the dark trees and gray sky, he alternated between smiling and whistling snatches of *The Tennessee Waltz*. He was going to have a lot of fun with this situation, and he might even stoop to describing his nighttime activities with the pun, bed of Rose's. They'd all get a groan out of that.

Susan was up and puttering at the fire pit when Phil came into view. Adapting to the weather, she had on a purple watch cap and a heavy woolen overshirt. A narrow plume of smoke lifted from a small fire she had built. The coffee pot was on the lighted Coleman stove, but no coffee smell was yet in the air.

"Hi," he called. Susan looked up, gave a strange smile and started toward him. He could see immediately that things hadn't gone well on this end.

"Hi," she said. "I'm really glad you're back."

"What happened?" he asked.

"I know I have to tell you, but I don't want to."

If Phil's mood the moment before had been that of the cat who swallowed the canary, he suddenly felt like the canary. Brian was so drunk, anything could have happened, and Susan looked as though it had. He followed her to the fire pit and sank into one of the chairs.

"Where's Brian," Phil asked nervously.

"Still asleep. I unzipped his down bag into a comforter and wrapped it around him when we got back, and he's hardly moved since. He's still breathing is all I can say, but I'm sure he'll wake up soon."

"And Marc?" Phil went on, daring to relax a little.

"He's gone," she said. "Took his pack and sleeping bag and must have caught a ride up on the highway." Phil looked over to see that Marc's half of their open-sided tent had been cleared out except for a deflated and folded air mattress.

"What the hell?" Phil felt a surge of adrenaline.

"Marc came on to me last night," Susan explained in a barely audible voice. "He built up the fire when we got here, and I joined him after I was sure Brian was settled. Marc put his arm around me, and that was OK, but then he started kissing me. I tried to put him off, but he wouldn't stop holding my arm and stroking my hair."

"Oh, shit."

"We were both probably a little stoned. He kept talking about Winnemucca, like I would want to ball him to get back at Brian. Maybe not right then, but after we got home."

"Of course," Phil said, feeling stupid for not expecting this outcome. "That's exactly what Marc would think. He said he did some major revenge-fucking in Denver last year when his wife got into her sneaky-Pete affair with this professor she's marrying next."

"Oh, god, what a mess."

"So he eventually got the idea and backed off?"

"No. I ended it by walking away and closing myself in the van. He followed me a few steps, and was pulling at my shoulder."

"How do you know he's gone?"

"I heard some banging around while it was still dark, and he left this on the table."

She handed Phil a folded-over page that Marc had torn from his journal. The name Susan was scrawled on the outside. Unfolding it, Phil read:

Dear Susan,
   Please forgive my thoughtless actions last night. Your own behavior was without fault, and I should never have put you in that situation.

I'd also rather not face anybody in the aftermath of this just yet. Since riding the rails is something I've meant to try, I decided to hitch to Winnemucca and catch a freight from there. If that doesn't work, I have money for a bus ticket.

I took the gear I could carry, but I'd appreciate your leaving my other stuff with Phil when you guys get home. Thanks.

Marc

"Wow," Phil sighed, mustering a reluctant smile at the thought of Marc, that crazy bastard, hunkered into a westbound boxcar. "Maybe he was a jerk, but he's sure being a stand-up guy."

"He is," Susan agreed, sniffing back a tear. "And it wasn't all his fault."

"Why? Because you danced with him the whole time last night? Were you running some kind of tease?"

"I'd never do that. Not consciously, anyway. And it wasn't just the dancing. I spent most of yesterday with Marc, too." She squeezed her eyes closed and sniffed again. "What makes me feel awful is that I was mad at Brian for getting so drunk, and I've been mad at him about Winnemucca, even though I'm as much to blame for what happened. Marc picked up those vibes. They were real. I used Marc without knowing it."

"Don't be too hard on yourself. He was plenty willing to be used, especially at the time."

Susan wiped her eyes with the cuffs of her shirt. "Marc's a great looking guy, but what's really weird, Mr. Phil Beaumont, is if I were going to get it on with anyone besides Brian—which I'm not, by the way—it would be you."

Jesus! Phil thought. Was it possible to pack more conflicting emotions into a single clock hour? This must be how it would feel to get in one of those big machines at the laundromat in Berkeley and have somebody turn it on. No matter how you went in, you'd come out limp. "Sorry," he finally managed, avoiding her eyes. "I don't know what to say to that."

"Don't say anything. Just don't think I'm leading you on." She then continued in a different tone, "What about you? Did Idaho Rose turn out better than Winnemucca Rose?" Susan dropped Marc's note into the fire.

"Yes," Phil said, brightening. "Way, way better. A real sweetheart."

The pot had been perking for several minutes while they talked, and a strong smell of coffee swirled around them. "Seems like it's ready," Susan said, getting up. She turned off the stove and poured out two cups. "Careful, very hot." She handed Phil his and sat back down.

"You understand that Karen isn't going to know about Rose or any of this when we get home," Phil said to her.

"Not from me, she isn't," Susan replied forthrightly. "How's that for women sticking together? Oh...and Brian doesn't need to know about that note, either."

"Fine."

The coffee was strong and good. They drank a few swallows and listened to the rushing sounds of the river. Phil got up to feed the fire, and Susan went to the food chest, placed her cup on the nearby table, and started to rattle around some breakfast things.

Without bitterness, Phil realized his own little prank had been upstaged. By Marc and by reality, apparently, though it could be Susan had merely set him up for Brian and Marc to emerge laughing from the van at any moment. But no. Marc was gone and none of this was aimed at Phil. Susan had deliberately burned the exonerating evidence, and coming next was Brian's turn to wrestle with awkward sexual possibilities.

Somehow these developments heightened the atmosphere rather than poisoning it. Phil felt keen and aware and alive. He raised his head and saw Susan looking at him over her shoulder.

"I've still got a cup of the blackberries I picked the other day," she said. "Thought I'd try a batch of blackberry pancakes. Tell me you want some."

"Yes, definitely," Phil answered, walking toward her. "I want some."

MARRIED SEX

AFTER SWIRLING HER GLASS AND BREATHING THE WINE'S AROMA, CARRIE HELD A SIP in her mouth and swallowed slowly. "You're right," she said, turning her golden brown eyes on Steve. "It's a really, really good one. Not like the jug reds we drink at home."

"I thought you'd like it," he responded. "Let's buy a bottle to have with dinner. You can't get it anywhere else."

Steve drank the rest of his and Carrie sipped again. "The color's so deep it's almost black in this light," she said.

They were at the bar in the wood-paneled basement tasting room of the Balducci Winery, and they were alone except for the attendant, an awkward, college-age boy whom Steve guessed was a Balducci family member. It was a mid-April Friday afternoon in 1980, and things were slow. The winery, small and off the beaten track in southern Mendocino County, was set into a redwood-laced hillside about thirty miles from the coast, with open vineyards rolling away to the east and south. Steve and Carrie had sampled the two other wines on offer, a nice riesling and a too-brawny barbera, before reaching the 1975 reserve zin. This one was worth rinsing your glass for and cleansing your palate with a bite of soda cracker.

Catching their favorable comment, the young attendant poured them each another ounce before walking away to transfer some dirty glasses, towels and crockware into a separate service kitchen. This was the first time since Carrie came in that the boy had taken his eyes off her. Though she always dressed to conceal it, like today in scuffed hiking boots, baggy jeans, an ill-fitting rugby shirt and no make-up, she was a looker. Her athletic body, her tawny shoulder-length blonde hair, her glowing year-round tan and her exotic Ingrid Bergman face resisted all disguises. Steve should know, he'd seen most of the disguises and he couldn't stop looking at her either.

The moment the attendant departed Carrie stretched across the bar, grabbed the zinfandel from the sinktop, eased out the cork, poured herself a generous half-glass and returned the bottle, cork in place, to precisely its former location. Then she turned her back to the bar, ensuring that she would screen the attendant's view, and mugged innocently at Steve while pouring a share of the take from her glass into his. He exhaled a quiet laugh of amazement.

"Ever had a zinfandel kiss?" she asked.

"Can't say as I have." Steve heard the attendant's returning footsteps arrive behind the bar, but he kept his eyes focused on Carrie.

"Well, here's one." She sipped her wine and extended her face upward toward him. Since their bodies barely touched, and they did not hold their lips together long, the kiss must have appeared entirely chaste. But after a second or two she squirted a little jet of warm, blackberry-rich flavor into his mouth including a darting hint of her tongue.

From Carrie's question, Steve had known what was coming, though he was in no way ready for the full sensual charge it produced, heightened by the fact that she abruptly pulled back and went to examine a wildflower poster on the wall near the main door. Refusing to acknowledge the attendant's look of ardent complicity, Steve drank more of his wine and walked toward the cash register.

"I think we'll take a couple of the reserve zin," he said. "It's very good, and we don't get up here that often."

"Sure," the attendant responded. "Where you folks from, anyway." He began to bag the two bottles Steve had asked for.

"Berkeley. We work on campus at IER, the Institute for Economic Research."

"Berzerkley, huh? I'm thinking about transferring to business school down there when I finish JC. Unless I study wine-making at Davis."

Steve and Carrie walked together through the shade of the graveled parking lot. He then laid the wine carefully on the back seat of his beige Volvo sedan, aligned with the depressions in the upholstery that marked where his son's padded car seat was usually installed. Easing behind the wheel, Steve started the engine and they began the long, winding ascent that would take them over damp ridges of Douglas fir and late-blooming dogwood on a backroad route to the sea. They were headed for the Cormorant Inn in Mendocino village for what Steve intended as a romantic getaway.

Steve Parker had a Ph.D. in Economics from the University of Michigan, where he had studied after getting his BA at Princeton. Not bad, he thought, for a scholarship boy from the Minneapolis public schools. Coming to Berkeley had been a chance to work as a post-doc under the celebrated Anton Suslow, IER Director, advisor to Presidents, and probable Nobel laureate. And as luck would have it, Steve caught on there as a full-time researcher when his fellowship ended. The pay wasn't great, and it wasn't tenure-track, but it was still a miracle. Academic jobs of any kind were as tough to get in the Bay Area as finding a pearl by diving off the Berkeley Pier in your street clothes. He was thirty-two, a nice looking man, somewhat athletic, with sandy-reddish hair, married and living comfortably in the Berkeley hills about a mile north of campus. He was not, however, married to Carrie Henson.

In fact, Steve was well aware that he had no legitimate reason for going to Mendocino or anywhere else with her. He also had no intention of leaving his wife to take up with a twenty-four-year-old graduate student. But Steve was insanely attracted to Carrie, thought about her constantly, and couldn't bear the idea of living the rest of his life knowing he'd turned his back on such an attraction. It was carpe diem versus drawing strength from resisting temptation, and carpe diem won out.

Steve was married to Ellen Zemlick, an attractive, dark-haired woman he had met six years ago when she was finishing law school at Boalt Hall. Ellen and their eighteen-month-old son, Matt, were now nearing the end of a ten-day visit with her parents in Chicago and would be back in two days, on Sunday evening. This family trip of hers had been Steve's big chance, and he began pursuing the Mendocino idea with Carrie the moment he learned of Ellen's schedule.

The real question was why Carrie had agreed to come. She'd certainly taken some persuading. First she could but wouldn't, then she would but couldn't, and finally she would and did. The zinfandel kiss was only the third she and Steve had ever exchanged, and was the first to have been truly sexual. But male mammals in full rut rarely stop to consider the motives of their would-be partners.

Though she was single, Carrie lived with her long-time boyfriend, Eddie Boyne, and another couple in a dilapidated, south-Berkeley bungalow near Ashby Avenue. They had all known one another from community college some years before. At this point, Carrie was the only full-time student among the group, and the only graduate student. Her new sixteen-hour a week job at IER, writing Fortran programs and helping set up econometric models, was far preferable to being a math TA, she said. And it had been clear to Steve from day one that she was plenty sharp.

Eddie, a writer, had dropped out of an English major in what would have been his senior year. He'd gotten two stories published and was now working on a novel. Eddie made his living repairing cars and motorcycles in the driveway of their house, and was apparently good at it. He cultivated a biker image, with a woolly beard, tattoos and leather, and got around town on an old Norton. All this Steve knew from conversations with Carrie at lunch and on their one previous date. He had met Eddie briefly on that occasion, too—memorably so.

As the Volvo reached the west face of the last ridge, the country opened up and they plunged toward Highway 1 and the Pacific through nearly vertical green hillsides painted with buttery swaths of California poppies and patches of sky-blue lupine. Steve fought the wheel and the brakes while he and Carrie craned to look. The fog hung a few miles offshore, low on the horizon, with the spring sun angling sharply across the top to highlight the azure tones of the roiling waves.

Steve had been all along the north coast photographing during his Berkeley years. It was his one serious hobby, and he was a regular user of the extensive campus darkroom facility. He worked in black-and-white, and his camera equipment was in the trunk of the car. That was the ostensible reason for this Mendocino outing, and the coastal light reminded Steve that he would have come anyway, even if Carrie had refused. But she had seen mounted prints of his work on his office walls, admired them, and expressed an interest in seeing how they originated. One he had gotten at Point Reyes of an ominous wave poised to shatter the calm of a sunlit tide pool she particularly liked, and he'd made her a custom print. That was two months ago, shortly after she started working at IER.

Carrie said now the same thing she had said then. "Gee, I love the coast. The ocean was so great at Pedro Point when I was growing up." Pedro Point, a suburban enclave of beach and rocky headlands immediately southwest of San Francisco, is convenient to the airport, her airline-pilot father's home base.

"Anywhere on the coast sounds like heaven to a Midwestern boy like me," Steve responded. "No matter how many times I see it, I forget how beautiful it is."

"Gorgeous. And god, today, springtime! I haven't been to Mendocino since my brother was on a commune here when I was in JC. Must be five years ago. Wow."

"Your brother's older, right? Tell me his name again."

"Daniel. The dark one. He's twenty-seven, and he caused my mom and dad a lot of grief. All of us, really."

"Must have if you call him the dark one."

"I didn't mean it that way, exactly. We called him the dark one because, coloring-wise, he got the Indian blood. My sister Fran, who's finishing high school this year, is pure Swede, and I'm the cross-breed."

"What's this about Indian blood? I'd have never guessed."

"My father's mother was a Blackfoot from Montana. My dad's dark, too. But his dad and my mom's folks are Swedes from Spokane. You know, the Olsons and the Hensons. The Northwest is full of them."

"So that winter tan of yours isn't a sun lamp?"

"Come on, Parker," she laughed. "You can't think I'm so vain I'd waste my time under a sun lamp."

"OK...right. But I don't see Blackfoot when I look at you."

"Yes, you do. Think about my hair color and my brown eyes. They're not exactly Swedish. My eyes have an almond shape to them, too, and I have her mouth, or her full lips anyway. Not that I mind. Her name was Clea, and she was very cool. She died in '78. Too bad she always lived so far away."

So there was the explanation for the face that was keeping Steve awake nights. "Yeah, that is too bad," he said sympathetically. "Sounds like someone I'd have liked to meet... liked to photograph, even. What about the faint scar at the side of your eye? Nothing Indian about that."

Carrie paused momentarily before replying. "Surfing accident. Tip of a board caught me when I was fifteen. Looked pretty bad at the time, but nobody much notices anymore. The doctors did a great job."

Steve glanced at her profile against the passing hillside. "I'd photograph you, too," he said. "The face of a girl who was actually surfing while I was in college listening to the Beach Boys."

"Well...maybe. I'm not that comfortable staring at a camera. And don't make too much of the surfing thing. I was into it more as a way to be cool and hang around with my brother and his friends. They weren't heavy-duty surfers, either. Not really. The waves at the Pedro Pier are nothing you'll ever see in a Bruce Brown film. But we sure talked the talk. I was little Ms. Tomboy in those days."

"Little Ms. Tomboy babe, I'll bet." Steve reached over to touch her shoulder and stroke his hand down her arm. He couldn't read her reaction to this, or tell if there was one.

"My sister Fran's the babe," Carrie said finally. "You should see her."

"If I remember right, you said you had a family thing in Pedro Point this weekend?"

"Yeah, Sunday. That's one reason I almost didn't come here with you. My mom's fiftieth birthday is Wednesday, and we're celebrating early 'cause my dad's home. He's always gone a lot flying. But you and I will be back in Berkeley tomorrow, and I can get to Pedro easy enough the next morning."

Steve had heard about these arrangements before, more or less, but he was relieved to have Carrie be consistent. Her endless ambivalence about the Mendocino trip had been hard for him to take. "Sounds like you'll be seeing Daniel, then," Steve went on.

"No way. He won't be around. There was a big blowup with my parents. He's not living in the Bay Area, and I only see him if I make the effort myself. But mostly I don't."

"What sort of shit was Daniel into?" Steve wanted to show he could talk the talk, too.

"Drugs mainly, and theft and in and out of school, and on and off probation. Let's not talk about it. I really loved him and looked up to him when I was younger, but he's poison."

By now the Volvo had reached Highway 1 and they were approaching Mendocino through stands of windblown trees and meadows of billowing oat grass. The sun had dropped behind the fog, turning its upper edge to purple.

"I picked up a Steely Dan greatest hits tape this week," Steve said, seeking to change the mood. "How about I put it on?" He reached to extract a plastic case from a recess in the dash.

"Great," Carrie answered, perking up. "I love those guys. Here...you drive and I'll do the music." She got the tape deck loaded and the bopping, Latin-beat chorus "Go back, Jack, and do it again..." filled the car.

⁂

Though he didn't protest when the desk clerk assigned it to them, Steve was pretty sure he'd recognize the Cormorant Inn's room 9. And after he and Carrie walked across the iris-rimmed, brick courtyard to inspect it before retrieving their luggage, his uneasiness was confirmed. Early in his marriage, Steve had stayed there with Ellen, and more than once. But the bed must be different by this time, he thought. He hoped.

"Now I'm really glad I came," Carrie smiled, adjusting the curtains and eyeing the bed puff, the fireplace and the farmhouse antique furniture. "Places like this aren't in my budget unless I'm traveling with my parents. You must be trying to snow me, Parker." She sat on the bed and bounced a few times.

"I am. I admit it. Stay here and I'll bring our stuff in. Then we can go for a walk. Our dinner reservation's not 'til seven."

Mendocino is the most picturesque town on the California coast. Any number of movies have been shot there, and Steve had photographed its clapboard Victorian houses, its stark churches, its dramatic headlands and the adjacent pocket beaches many times. That was his cover. Ellen knew where he was. She just had no idea he wasn't alone. And in 1980, Mendocino retained enough of its original funkiness to feel like a real place. Not all the locals—loggers, fishermen, and sixties artist-types—had yet been run off by the tourists and the tourist prices. Perierra Bros. Store and Dick's Place, the bar, seemed changelessly authentic.

On their walk, Carrie took everything in and went giddy from the twilight sky and the ocean air. She and Steve were getting along great—joking, laughing and letting loose. This was why older men had affairs with younger women, he realized. It wasn't only their bodies, it was that they're so unencumbered. Of course Steve was a long way from being old. But for the first time in his life, since Matt was born, he'd begun to feel old: career, wife, mortgage, car payments, kid, babysitters—all the impediments of adult life.

"You can't imagine how much I needed a break like this," Carrie said when they got back to their room. "I'm doing ten units this semester, working at IER plus trying to keep up with Eddie and my family. It's too much. But I would never take a Friday off if you hadn't pushed the idea."

"You're wrong...I can imagine," Steve assured her. "I've been there, remember. I worked every semester at Princeton as part of my scholarship, and I had to grind my way through Michigan on TA-ing and summer jobs. I didn't have a life outside school until I got to Cal." Steve stood up and stripped to the waist to change his shirt for dinner.

"You've got a good body on you for an old guy," Carrie joked. "Must be that bicycling to work everyday."

Steve and Ellen were a one-car family. He rode a Bianchi twelve-speed down to campus each morning and back up to the hills at night. Carrie had oohed and aahed over his eco-friendly commuting and how elegant his bike was.

"If that's a compliment, thanks," Steve joked back, buttoning his sleeves and straightening his green cord trousers. "But basketball helps old guys, too."

In addition to biking, Steve played in a three-on-three rec league at Live Oak Park on Sunday mornings, and one weekend Carrie surprised him by showing up to watch. That's when Steve knew things were on. Or at least that they could be on. He'd already been flirting with her at the office, and there was no other reason for Carrie to be in that part of Berkeley so early on a Sunday.

"I forgot about basketball," she said. "How tall are you, six feet?"

"Yeah, maybe a quarter-inch under."

"You were terrific that day. Ran your butt off and hit a bunch of shots. But you're mainly a passer, aren't you?"

"Point guard is what they call it. I didn't know you followed the game." This was more like it, Steve thought. When Ellen came to the park, she brought Matt in a stroller and just wandered out to the azalea garden with him.

"I don't," Carrie said. "I played in phys. ed. at JC, though. And my sister plays high school varsity. She's 5'7", same as me. Sports are really on the ups for girls now. It's great. But I swim at the women's gym on campus to stay in shape. That's one thing I got from surfing. I'm a good swimmer."

"And you are in shape. Or do you hate hearing that?"

"Oh...I don't mind. I just wish Eddie would do something physical. He's not in shape like you."

"Yeah," Steve cracked, "but you wouldn't want me fixing your car." He wondered why he was sticking up for Eddie. That weirdo should be beyond masculine solidarity. But Steve knew what Carrie meant. Ellen hadn't gotten her waistline back after having Matt, and Steve wished she would.

Carrie laughed. "You're right. When Eddie's good, he's good. But listen, Parker, I have a surprise for you, and I need some privacy. So take the zinfandel you bought and head over to the main building. I'll see you in ten minutes. That plaid shirt looks nice on you, by the way."

Steve did as she asked, and waited for her in the lobby with the wine cradled on his lap. He could hear a low buzz of conversation accompanied by food smells and a light clattering of dishes from the dining room to his left. Guests only, and very good. Steve knew that from before, and there was no problem bringing your own wine. As for Carrie, everything was going according to plan. Beyond plan, actually. She was way more than he had bargained for when she and her beautiful ass first walked into IER at the beginning of the semester. What do you suppose this surprise of hers was? And she was certainly open about Eddie. The last thing Steve wanted to think about or talk about was Ellen, but the Cormorant stirred up a lot of memories.

What had happened? Their sex life was in the tank, that's for sure. Ellen had suffered a deep post-partum depression after Matt was born. Their Lamaze instructor had pretty much warned them about that. It was common, she said. Anyway, things had been rough, and Steve was horny and jacking off all the time. But Matt was terrific. You couldn't ask for a better kid.

Then, after the first four or five months, things got better. He and Ellen started having sex again—good sex—and that lasted until she went back to work when Matt was one. They had excellent childcare, the wife of one of Steve's friends from the campus darkroom, but Ellen was so torn. She made herself miserable and somehow it was Steve's fault. If he said she could stay home another year, he was torpedoing her career, and if he said she would get used to working and everything would be OK, he was a heartless shit and an unfit father. Fortunately, Matt seemed fine, and things showed signs of improving. But how was a guy supposed to deal with it in the meantime?

Carrie strode grandly through the lobby door. "OK, Parker, here's your surprise. The fashion-ramp version of Carrie Henson."

He'd never seen her in anything like this outfit. "Wow, a dress!" he said. "And make-up. I didn't know you spoke the language."

"Not my usual language," Carrie laughed. She did a slow pirouette, primping the hair at the base of her neck. She had pulled it into a French braid, and the effect on her face was stunning. Helen of Troy couldn't have had better cheekbones. "Don't take it for granted, but I thought you deserved something special."

"Oh, I do, I do," Steve clowned, standing to offer his arm. She took it, and they went into the dining room. The dress was a one-piece, woven dirndl in a primitive pattern of reds and blues that went perfectly with the Cormorant's hand-thrown ceramic dinner service, artisan candles, oak tables and fresh flowers. Yet there was nothing revealing about it. The only bare skin from her ankles up was her arms. But she looked gorgeous, and Steve clearly wasn't the only one in the room who thought so.

They got settled and the waiter uncorked and poured their wine. "I see you like my dress," Carrie noted. "Eddie gave it to me. He got it at a boutique in San Francisco. Calls it the Gypsy look. It's actually the only dress I have any more. I'll probably wear it for my mom's birthday, too. She loves to see me looking spiffy."

"I do like it. A lot," Steve answered. "But I also like how you usually look. It's the make-up that blows my mind."

"Just mascara, some blush and a little lip gloss. That's a ton for me, though. Kind of against my principles. Anyway, don't confuse the wrapping with what's inside the package."

"They both seem fine to me." Steve raised his glass in a salute. "Here's my chance to repay you for the extra shot of zin you got us at the winery."

This provoked a truly glamorous smile. "That kind of thing makes life fun," she said. "Do you suppose the dorky kid we saw there will transfer to Berzerkley? Didn't seem the type." She took a mouthful of wine and savored it.

"Who knows. Let's check the menu. I'm starved."

"Me too," she echoed. "And I already know what I want from the specials board. Veal stew with sundried tomatoes."

Steve went for the chicken cacciatore with wild Mendocino mushrooms, something he remembered from a previous visit. It would go extremely well with the wine, but so would Carrie's stew. Steve picked up the serrated knife that came with their crusty, whole-grain bread and began to cut thick slices.

"Between your dress and our waiter's peasant shirt," he joked, "the two of you could be in the same opera." Her breath of laughter led Steve to try a more risky subject.

"Cutting this bread reminds me," he continued in a bantering tone, "what was Eddie doing answering the door with a twelve-inch knife in his hand when I picked you up for our dinner date last month? That was really strange."

"Oooh," she said, chagrined. "You didn't say anything, so I hoped you hadn't noticed."

"Hadn't noticed? I'm not blind."

"You're right. I didn't want to make a big deal and spoil our time, but I should have brought it up."

"Well?"

"He didn't pre-plan or anything. We were doing dishes before you got there, and he was drying knives when the doorbell rang. I had told him this married guy at work was asking me out, and he always said I should go. He fools around... you know, goes to bars sometimes and picks up women and tells me horny stories about them. I don't like it, but Eddie and I have a strong bond. We've been together a long time, and we really accept one another. I don't know if you'd understand. It's just that I've never pushed to have the freedom on my side he tells me I have."

"So he whips out a knife?"

"Oh, come on. He didn't threaten you. It's exactly his weird kind of joke. He calls himself a collector of experience. He deliberately sets up edgy situations to get the feelings he uses in his writing. I respect him for it, in a way. But he was having a hard time being Mr. Cool when I was actually going out with someone. He heard the doorbell, and made some mocking remark like, 'Oh, Carrie, your lover is here. What if I meet him at the door like this?' He tossed down the towel and took the knife out with him. I told him he was being an asshole, but he did it anyway. I was afraid you'd hear me through the door."

"I did. But I couldn't get any of the words."

"What's funny is you earned a lot of points with him by not reacting. You walked right by and over to me, remember? And when I got home, he asked me a bunch of times if you'd said anything while we were out."

"Yeah, I remember what I did. I was so surprised not to find you at the door, it never occurred to me to be frightened. I assumed it was your other roommate... you know, Brad...and maybe he was using the knife to fix something. I couldn't imagine Eddie would be letting me in. Anyway, it wasn't until you introduced him that I saw his eyes, and then the knife started to look like a murder weapon."

"I know. I'm sorry. But after that, remember, Eddie just said hello and went out to the kitchen with the knife pointing at the floor. I still should have said something when we got outside."

"Well, I'm glad Eddie wasn't around when I picked you up this morning. Or was he? You were waiting on the porch."

"He was gone. I made sure of it. Besides, he'd already had that experience. He says he doesn't need to have it again."

"Oh...am I going to be in his novel? You are for sure, aren't you?"

"You? Yeah, you could be. And I probably am, but I don't know. He never shows anybody anything while he's working on it."

The waiter had brought their food, and Carrie was eating her stew with obvious pleasure. Steve's cacciatore was all he had expected, too. He ate a forkful, smiled at her to show things were OK and poured them more wine.

"How do you handle all of this?" he asked. "It would be way too much drama for me."

"I told you, Eddie and I have a special bond. I like that he's exciting, but sometimes I do feel overwhelmed. Math is my retreat, the artificial universe. But I wouldn't want my life to be only that. Like you. You're the first man I've met who knows the differential equations behind those regional Leontieff models of Suslow's and isn't a complete nerd."

"That makes me an incomplete nerd, which I could take as a compliment."

"You should. Anyway, if you want to know about Eddie, read *Nightmove*, the story he got published in the *San Francisco Review*. About his motorcycle accident at Point Richmond. I know I mentioned it to you."

"Yeah, you did."

"I'll loan you a copy sometime. It's worth reading. A biker guy picks up a girl at the Baltic and they go back to her place. They get drunk and stoned and she persuades him to let her drive his bike solo up and down the back alley. She stacks it up, and the story ends with him running toward her yelling, 'My bike! My bike! What the hell did you do?'"

"Low-life all the way, huh? But if you say it's good, I'll read it."

"What makes it good is the way Eddie works the characters. You start out thinking she's a stupid bimbo and the guy's a macho intellectual, then things switch around so that she ends up being pretty cool while he's a total jerk. Eddie's novel will be good, too, I bet."

Carrie was mopping her plate with a piece of bread when their salads arrived. At the Cormorant, salad comes last, in the French style. She looked at Steve and held his eyes.

"You know, Parker, when I said you weren't a nerd, I meant I like how broad your interests are. You've got the physical, intellectual, and artistic sides all covered. Maybe because you're older, you listen to me and take me seriously. You're not just standing around with your fly open like most guys."

Steve bowed his head slightly to acknowledge the kind words. If she only knew. Jimmy Carter might be worried about lustful thoughts, but Steve was going for mortal sin itself. And this listening thing must be the cad's secret weapon. Ellen told him he never listened to her.

"I want to be as up front as I can," Steve said, pushing his empty salad plate aside. "I haven't hidden that I'm married, and you know I'm not looking to leave Ellen. Actually, that I'm married might make me safer as far as Eddie's concerned."

"You're right. He's even said that."

"But I can still see how this could be hard for him. I mean his picking up women now and then, whether it's for purposes of his 'art' or not, is pretty anonymous. Not the same as us working together and you going away with me for the weekend."

"Have you and Eddie been rehearsing? He also said that. But I'm not doing payback. I'm doing what I want to do, just like he does what he wants to do. We don't lie to each other, and there's nothing I'm doing behind his back." Carrie looked at Steve as though she expected him to argue with her.

"You and Ellen have a different deal," she went on. "Ellen doesn't want to know what she doesn't have to know, as long as you're discreet, and vice-versa. A lot of couples operate that way, and if it works for them, fine. Eddie and I are taking another route. We don't believe in marriage. We believe in honesty."

"That's a lofty standard," Steve replied. "I hope you can bring it off." What he didn't say was that it could be a cruel standard as well, especially if strictly adhered to. But Carrie's remark gave him a twinge of guilt. Steve and Ellen had no flexible understanding about marital fidelity, never had and never would. He needed Carrie to think they did, but to even begin negotiations with Ellen on that subject was beyond him. It would destroy everything.

The waiter started to pour Carrie more wine, but she waved him off. "Let's cork it up and save it for lunch tomorrow," she said. Steve nodded his assent.

"I'll split a dessert with you," Carrie continued. "How about a piece of the Booneville apple pie? Then we can go back to our room and change for my next surprise. There's a Friday-night fantasy bit I've always wanted to do, and Dick's Place, that bar we saw, should be perfect."

"Oh, yeah? What's this ab—?"

"Did you bring hiking boots and jeans with you?" she interrupted.

"Sure...for tomorrow."

"Well, I want you to put them on along with that blue workshirt you were wearing this afternoon and be the big studdy guy I pick up in a bar. What do you think?"

Steve gave a muffled laugh. "Oh, I could handle that. Just don't get us into any fights."

"Don't worry, if things get ugly, we'll leave. I've got an outdoorsy shirt that'll look right with my good jeans, and I'll go over to Dick's on my own. After about 20 minutes, you come in, make like you're a loner and sit as far away from me as possible."

"Then what?"

"You'll figure it out," Carrie said, "but ignore me until I start something."

When their pie came, she made airplane noises and fed Steve bites, just like he did feeding Matt.

✳ ✳ ✳

Carrie had now been at Dick's Place fifteen minutes, and Steve was killing time by walking along the dark bluffs at the mouth of the Big River, behind the white bell-tower of the Congregational Church. The sea tumbled against rocky cliffs thirty feet below him and the moon made a weak luminescence behind the gathering fog. Hugging his arms to his body for warmth, Steve glanced occasionally at his watch and then at the lights of Main Street around to his right.

This plan of hers was intriguing, no question, but the couch in their room with a fire in the fireplace and the rest of the zinfandel was more how he envisioned the evening would go. The fact was, his balls were aching from thinking about it. He had a joint of pretty good dope in the room, too. Steve didn't know yet how Carrie would feel about smoking with him, but looking at Eddie, he doubted she'd be shocked. She didn't seem like the type for cocaine, but there was a lot of that around Berkeley now. Steve didn't go for it himself, and didn't have any, so he hoped she wasn't expecting their weekend to include a line of Bolivia's best. What guys seducing beautiful college girls did as of 1980 Steve couldn't pretend to know. He'd been out of the market a long time.

Dick's Place was a one-story structure with a two-story false front and an afterthought porch extending over the wooden sidewalk. Several well-used pickup trucks were parked in front, one of which had a bumper sticker reading "Sierra Club Kiss My Ax." Once he reached the porch, Steve got a faint view into the barroom through the open blinds of two oblong, chest-high windows to the right of the door. Beyond a line of huddled male backs in the foreground was a large mirror and a scatter of the usual beer signs. Steve opened the door. Dick's was dark, smoky, and funky, a classic of its kind.

Carrie, her hair released from its braid, sat at the far right of the bar. In front of her were two beer bottles, and she had the sleeves of her blue and white checked shirt rolled up. She was talking to the bartender, a dumpy looking woman in a red 49ers sweatshirt, who was laughing at whatever Carrie just said. There were no other women in the room. Struggling to avoid meeting Carrie's eyes, Steve turned his attention to an NBA game on the TV, which was balanced on a make-shift shelf at the top of the mahogany back bar. The playoffs, right, he'd forgotten. The Lakers were drubbing the Warriors on the way to what looked like a first-round sweep. If he were in Berkeley, Steve would probably be watching this at his friend Seth's house. Seth played center on Steve's rec league team.

Steve took the end seat at the far left and nodded silently to his nearest neighbor, three stools down. None of the booths behind him were occupied, and the five other guys at the bar, all wearing jeans and hats of some kind, seemed bored and subdued. Two were playing a desultory game of liars dice, while the rest half-watched TV. Not what you'd call a happening place, or a happy one, either. But it was early yet, and the low-lying, chrome-and-neon jukebox held the promise of music.

"What ya' drinkin'?" the bartender asked, moving square in front of Steve. She was a school of hard knocks grad, Portuguese probably, with stringy black hair, a serpent tattoo on the back of her hand, and bright, mischievous eyes.

"I'll take one of those," he answered, pointing to the glowing Lucky Lager sign on the wall. "Just the bottle, don't need a glass."

"That's how we serve 'em, and that's the only kind of lucky most guys get in here." She pushed closer and lowered her voice, "But there's a real sweetcakes at the other end of the bar, in case you didn't notice."

"I noticed," Steve said. "I'm just not in the mood."

"Like I believe that?" the bartender laughed. "My name's Meg, by the way. You just passing through?" She maintained this patter while getting his beer, opening it and sliding it to him along the bar top.

"Passing through," he said, "that's the story. Anyway, I'm Steve. How come it's so quiet for a Friday night?"

"Folks've spent their welfare and unemployment checks already. And the respectables are at the crabfeed in Noyo Harbor or home tryin' to do their income taxes. Pentagon needs money to fight the Ayatollah, and maybe the Russkis in Afghanistan. Hate to see another Vietnam, but a lot of 'em over there need their butts kicked."

"What do I owe you, Meg?" Her Vietnam remark reminded Steve of his good fortune, years before, in drawing a high draft number. And now, being over thirty, whatever happened in the Middle East would involve him as an economist, if at all.

"A buck," Meg answered.

He paid and settled in to watch the Warriors rally behind an injured Phil Smith to an eight point deficit and fall back to fourteen. The beer was cold but flavorless. No wonder there were rumors that Lucky's San Francisco brewery was going out of business. How had they managed to stay around a hundred years with a product this bad? He surreptitiously moved an eye to check on Carrie. She was shaking the leather dice cup and talking to the guy on the next stool. From Steve's angle, the guy appeared to be looking down Carrie's front. Not wise to be distracted while playing dice with a math major. Steve stared vacantly at the TV, thinking that time was going as slow now as when he'd been at Michigan waiting for the final meeting of his dissertation committee. He waved and Meg brought him another beer.

Movement at the corner of Steve's eye turned out to be Carrie heading for the jukebox. Was her walk always that sexy? No, she was vamping, and it was even more out of character than the makeup she'd put on earlier. The deep-cover Carrie Henson he knew in Berkeley was not, Steve was learning, the only Carrie there was. Some of the guys at the bar turned to stare at her openly while the others stole periodic looks. Steve turned away and Meg caught him smiling.

"Still sure you're not in the mood?" she asked.

Carrie stayed a long time at the jukebox, studying the selections carefully. She leaned forward at the waist, resting her palms and her weight on the lighted panel and holding one ankle crossed in front of the other. Women's jeans were designed for a performance like this, and Steve was far enough away to see it all in the back-bar mirror. Carrie made her last selection and started to return to her bar stool, veering as if on impulse directly toward his back. He saw her eyes in the mirror and heard her approaching footsteps just as the first song cranked up. All the regulars in Dick's, and a big chunk of everybody in the U.S., would have recognized Hank Williams' *Your Cheatin' Heart* from just the first few notes, and so did Steve.

Carrie stopped twelve inches behind him and said, "Want to dance?"

"Yeah, I guess," Steve deadpanned. He got up, walked with her toward the juke-box, and took her in his arms. After two steps they collided clumsily and he recoiled to a safer distance.

"I asked you," Carrie stated with quiet determination, "so I'm leading." She stepped into him and planted a hand firmly in the middle of his back.

Their next five or six steps were fumbling and awkward, but Steve slowly got the hang of it. God, just like dancing school when he was a kid, learning his first fox-trot with Lester Talbot and Bobby Tibbetts and taking turns being the girl. "Not a song you picked at random, I guess," he whispered in her ear.

"Why Parker, you shrewd boy, and you can even dance." Carrie's enthusiasm was making it difficult for her to stay in character.

Every so often, she turned him so he could see the bar with Meg's missing-tooth smile behind it, along with the faces of the three guys following them indirectly in the mirror and the two who had swiveled to watch them directly. Finally, country-music's most famous warning about the pitfalls of unfaithful love wound to an end.

Carrie stood on her tiptoes to say, "You're going to love the next one, too, and it's your turn to lead." The Eagles came on, another song Steve recognized instantly, *Lyin' Eyes*.

"Jeez! Are cheatin' songs all they have on that thing?"

"No," she said, letting him pull her close and take control. "Discriminating taste was involved."

They danced slowly, moving once every two beats, and Steve felt her warmth against him as if they were naked. He smelled her hair and her skin and wondered how he could stay standing, much less lead. "Just for the record," he said, "I don't see that either of us fits the kind of cheating in this song. I mean we're not in the relationships we're in for bad reasons."

"Like Eddie says when I over-analyze his stories, 'Don't be so literal-minded.'"

Steve moved his hand to the base of Carrie's neck and felt her hair teasing back and forth on his skin. No couch in front of the fireplace could have been better than this, and he abandoned himself to it. Better yet, *Lyin' Eyes* was a nice long cut.

As its last notes died, Carrie eased away a bit and a song started that Steve couldn't identify. She looked at him with a delicious smile. Then the vocal began and he realized her final selection was Toni Tenile's *Muskrat Love*. He laughed loud enough that she cracked up, too.

They tried to keep dancing, but there wasn't a rhythm they could really sustain. Carrie slid into the nearest booth and Steve went from his end of the bar to hers to collect their beers. He found himself running a gauntlet of incredulous stares.

Returning to sit across from her, Steve reached for her hands. "God, Parker," she said. "This is so much fun."

"Yeah, it is. Now what?"

"We sit here a while to draw out the suspense, and then the bartender is going to come over."

"Meg? How do you know that?"

"She's in on it. I told her."

"So that's what she was laughing about when I first came in."

"Sort of...but I told her the basic idea way before. And that was sure a long twenty minutes. I thought you'd never get here." She squeezed Steve's hands.

"Seemed long to me, too. And you took forever at the jukebox."

"I know, but it was part of the plan. And see, no fights. The TT ratio in here is pretty good."

"TT ratio? What the hell is that?"

"A joke I have with Eddie. He's always talking about these down-and-out bars at the Port of Oakland and along San Pablo where everybody has a lot of tattoos and no teeth. I made a ratio out of it. We'd all be born 0/32, right? If the crowd in here averaged 2 tattoos each and had half their teeth knocked out, the ratio for Dick's would be 1/8. The higher the ratio, the more dangerous the place. Dick's is about 1/12 or 1/10 tonight, so not too bad... get it?"

"It's math run amok," Steve laughed, "but I get it." In fact, the more he thought about it, the funnier it was. "Sounds like something Suslow could model," Steve went on. "Maybe we should write a grant proposal."

"You mean I could publish a paper with Steven G. Parker, Ph.D.?"

"Sure, but I don't see it happening. You picked me up in a bar, remember. Won't I be dumped by tomorrow?" Steve drained the last of his beer.

"Oh yeah, I forgot. But I see more now why Eddie likes the hunt. Being in here and knowing that if I was aggressive I could probably pick up any one of these guys is a kick. Not that I want to, of course. But in the traditional mode, what do the girls get out of it? Why do they go for drunken one-night stands? That's the last thing I'd be...you know, some guy's score to brag about later."

"OK, I agree...but there's a saying about men: 'When the balls are full, the mind is empty.' Something like that must apply for women, too."

Carrie laughed. "Sure...sometimes. But I still don't get it." She began to speak more intensely. "Women take most of the risk. It's not just that men don't get pregnant and don't have to choose between kids and abortions. Women get more venereal diseases, and the ones they get are harder to cure."

Unaware of this conversational turn, Meg appeared alongside their table. "OK lovebirds," she boomed. "Can I sell you some champagne?"

"Don't think so," Carrie said, back in character and slightly projecting her voice. "I've got this one talked in to coming home with me, but he's worried about getting dumped in the morning."

Meg loved that remark and laughed heartily. "C'est la vie, buddy boy," she said. "That's how the game is played. But this place needs music. It's deader'n a spawned-out salmon in here." Meg went to the jukebox, pumped in a few coins and started back to the bar with Mick Jagger and a buzzing guitar riff following her: "I...can't get no...satisfaction...I've tried and I've tried and...but, no, no, no....'

"Order up, losers," Meg demanded when she took her place opposite her customers. "Like it or not, you've got fun to have tonight."

"She's something, isn't she?" Steve marveled.

"Yeah," Carrie answered, "but let's hit it. We're going to be less and less convincing the more we hang around."

They got up and walked to the door with Steve's hand on Carrie's shoulder. Guiding her onto the porch, Steve heard Meg's voice taunting the guy who had been shooting dice with Carrie earlier on. "That could have been you, Smitty! That could have been you!"

The fog was down to the rooftops now and it was cold. They twined their arms around each other's backs while Carrie pushed her face against the nearest of Dick's two windows and surveyed the scene inside.

"Looks like we were never there," she said. "But I bet we blew a few minds." Then she started to laugh, happily and unreservedly. Steve dragged her away in the direction of the Cormorant, gasping with laughter himself. The moon and stars were lost in the swirling damp, and Mendocino's deserted streets echoed with sloshing, rushing ocean noise.

Steve was sure he had never been more horny. Walking renewed the ache in his balls, and his cock was threatening to spring a rod any second. He didn't know what to say, so he said nothing, and Carrie was quiet as well.

Back in their room, she headed immediately to the john while Steve lit a lamp in the far corner, away from the bed. "How about I touch a match to the fireplace?" he asked when she emerged.

"Sounds nice. It got cold in here all of a sudden." Carrie sat on the edge of the bed and wrapped herself in a down jacket without putting her arms through the sleeves.

Steve lit the fire and it took hold quickly. Paper, kindling, and split logs had been put in place by whomever made up their room that morning. He found the remainder of the zinfandel and started to pull the cork.

"I don't think I want more wine," Carrie said hesitantly.

"I've got some dope if you'd rather," Steve replied. A rush of anxiety came from nowhere and pushed him down on the couch.

"No, not that either," she said. "Look, I don't know how to tell you this, but have you ever heard of bundling? You know, like with a bundling board?"

Shit, Steve thought, this couldn't be happening. It just couldn't. "Yes, I know bundling. I know what courtly love is, too," he added sarcastically. "But that doesn't mean I want to practice them."

"I knew this would be hard. I should have told you before. I kept hoping we'd avoid a fight somehow." The firelight brought out her almond eyes and golden skin and made her hair shine against the down jacket. "Anyway, Parker, having sex now is something that wouldn't be right. I want to be in bed together watching the fire, and then go to sleep, but without sex. You said there were no preconditions when you asked me up here, remember?"

"Oh, I remember," he said angrily. "And I meant it, at the time. But what about today? And tonight at Dick's? Wasn't it reasonable for me to draw other conclusions?"

"Yes," she acknowledged. "My fault. I was having fun, and I didn't think ahead. I didn't know you'd get into your part at Dick's like that, either. But sex still wouldn't be right."

"You having your period or something?" he challenged. Women, Steve thought. Christ, it was always something.

"Don't be stupid. We could work around that. I'm talking about who I am and who you are. It's too soon, and we have things we need to talk through. There'll be other times."

"Other times! I just bet!" Steve got up and went to the john, almost slamming the door behind him. He could barely calm down enough to piss. After all this... after all of it, she comes to Mendocino and he ends up going back to Berkeley and beating off because he's hornier than he was when he left. They could drive back now as far as he was concerned.

By the time Steve came out of the bathroom, Carrie had turned off the lamp and gotten in on the left side of the bed. The fire was burning brightly, illuminating her clothes draped on the couch where he had been sitting.

"Come on, Parker," she called softly. "Get undressed and get in. It won't be so bad."

When Steve had removed everything but his underwear, he wavered but decided hell with it, he would get naked whether she liked it or not. The sheets were cool on his body, though he could sense warmth from Carrie's direction. He rolled toward her and reached to pull her to him. She was wearing a ribbed tank-top undershirt and his fingers touched the waistband of what must be panties. She resisted, but moved part way.

"You forgot something," Steve said. "No bundling board." He kissed her face, but she kept her mouth from him and finally pulled back.

"Stop, Parker. I thought I could trust you." Carrie sat up with the covers across her chest. He kept his arm around her waist. "I mean it," she went on. "No sex. We can kiss and you can hold me, but no sex. Or else I'll move to the couch, and if you chase me I'll start screaming."

This jolted Steve. She was serious, and he would never risk a scene with her screaming and the desk clerk banging on the door. Nothing in his experience with women had turned out remotely like that, and he was not going to start now. He had to calm down. "I'm sorry, I'm sorry," he told her. "I don't know what I'm doing. I'm crazy for you."

"I'm sorry, too, Parker. Come on, relax and hold me." Steering him onto his back, Carrie slid next to him, shoulder-to-shoulder, and stretched to kiss the side of his face. When she accidentally grazed the corner of his mouth her breath on him was like an injection of Spanish Fly. He groaned. He ran the palm of his hand up from her tummy until he felt the hard nipples of her uptilting breasts through her shirt. Carrie groaned softly, then, too.

"No fair, Parker. It's not easy for me, either." She stopped kissing him and returned his hand to her stomach. He caressed her there and found muscles toned from swimming. His cock was engorged to the point of pain, sticking out like an iron bar and dribbling pre-ejaculate. To make matters worse, he could swear he caught the musky smell of her pussy under the covers.

"This isn't going to work, is it?" she said flatly. "Roll over, Parker. Put your back to me." She pushed on him and he reluctantly complied, but he turned his head to kiss her mouth before she could avoid him.

"Oh, Parker...," she said against his face with some annoyance. She curled into his back, reached her arm over him and put her hand on the base of his cock, causing a supernova of pleasure. Every nerve ending radiated to his hard-on and the rest of his body went numb. She held his balls for an instant, as if she knew how sore they were, and then she stroked her hand up to the head of his cock and down again.

Steve groaned a second time and rolled more toward her as she moistened the palm of her hand with his juices and began a rhythmic up and down stroking. He couldn't hold back, he couldn't think of holding back, he couldn't think of anything. After a dozen or so strokes he started coming—writhing, groaning and shooting sperm wildly. It was on the sheets, it was on his stomach, and it flooded back down over Carrie's hand. She continued until Steve's brain transformed into the brilliant, white mantle of a lit Coleman lantern. Finally, she stopped.

"My god," he said. "My god."

"Shhh," Carrie responded. She moved her hand onto his stomach and then away. "Oh, Parker," she said. "What a mess you made. Wait so I can do some-thing about it."

Steve could feel her sitting up and he heard a rustling of bed linen. Carrie was shaking one of her pillows out of its cover and she then used the cover as a towel. She wiped his stomach and his pubic hair and his cock gently and absorbed as much of the semen as she could from the damp top sheet. His brain began to function. In addition to relief, Steve suddenly felt embarrassed. He had gone from borderline rapist to messy child in less than ten minutes.

"I'm sorry, Carrie. I really am," he said.

"Shhh... Don't be. Go to sleep." She dropped the wadded pillowcase on the floor and curled against him in a warm semi-circle.

Though the fire was largely burned out by now, Steve couldn't imagine he would sleep. He no longer knew what he felt, or how he should feel. At least his balls had stopped hurting. He heard Carrie breathing behind him and started count-ing her breaths. Before his count reached fifteen, he was out as if having been anesthetized.

Waking four hours later, Steve slid quietly from bed and went to use the toilet. Returning, he could just discern Carrie in the darkness, lying as though she had not moved an inch after giving him that glorious hand job. He leaned over and kissed the side of her face, at the eye socket, where her surfing scar was.

* * *

Steve had breakfast alone in the Cormorant's restaurant, browsing an early edi-tion of the *Chronicle* and drinking coffee. The fog had already begun to break up, and the north coast weather forecast was good.

Carrie was still asleep when he left the room. On his way out, Steve picked up the pillow case she had wiped him with the night before, now dried stiff and smelling of his polleny seed, and deposited it in the bathroom wastebasket. Her hand on him had felt so loving in the dark, but by this morning it was hard to see anything beyond self-preservation on her part. She didn't want to have sex with him, he'd been out of control, and she had defused things by the most direct pos-sible route.

After an hour, Steve took some coffee, fruit, and a basket of pastries back for her and heard that she was in the shower. He knocked, opened the bathroom door a crack and called her name loud enough to register over the drumming spray.

"Carrie, hi...you OK?" he asked.

"Hi...yes, fine. Did you eat?"

"Yes. I brought you some."

"Great. Thanks. I'll be out in a minute."

"I'm going to walk down to the store to get some lunch stuff. See you when I get back."

"OK, good."

Simple as that, Steve thought. He wasn't angry at Carrie, exactly, and she didn t seem angry at him, but his married man's quest for a roll in the hay had turned to farce. He felt not just rejected, but diminished. What was left but to make the best of their planned hiking and photography excursion today, and try to forget it when he got home? Ellen and Matt would be back tomorrow. He'd seen this thing with Carrie as probably being over by then anyway. He did notice, however, that she'd fished the soiled pillow case out of the wastebasket, rinsed it and hung it over one of the towel racks. How oddly domestic that was.

Steve bought cheese, apples, hard rolls and some dry salami, which he brought back and put in his day pack along with the wine they had saved from dinner. Carrie sat in a terrycloth robe letting her hair dry while she had breakfast. Steve bustled around, packing his bag and checking his camera. Carrie was distant, but things seemed fine on the surface. She'd chosen denial, too, Steve figured. Anything to avoid strife was OK with him.

A little after 10, they departed the Cormorant and drove south a few miles across the Big River and out to the grassy headlands where a network of dirt roads led to pocket beaches tucked among the cliffs. They parked, and Steve took Carrie down a brushy trail to a small beach that he knew had monoliths of eroded rock and good orientation to the light at this time of day. His tripod and other camera gear were slung over his shoulders, and she clambered along behind. They were both in jeans, boots and bulky sweaters.

Carrie watched while Steve framed shots of rocks and glistening sand at the water's edge. The tide was ebbing, and the waves were choppy and weak. He made a few exposures, but nothing really captured him. Something to work with in the darkroom, that was all. He might actually be more into it if he were alone. Behind him, Carrie had braced herself against a sunny outcrop near a seep-spring and a blooming profusion of wild nasturtiums.

"Warm enough, but not what you'd call surfing weather," Steve called, walking in her direction.

"You'd have to have a death wish to surf here in any weather," she answered. "There's a wicked rip, and look at those rocks."

"Yeah, you're right."

"Anyway, Parker," Carrie announced, "I've decided I'll pose for you. If you still want me to, that is."

"Sure," Steve said, though he felt indifferent. "I could get a few right here. Even in black-and-white these flowers would add interest."

"That's not what I meant, exactly." She stood with a few strands of her hair blowing crosswise in the light breeze. "I'd like to try some of those abstract nudes with rock formations like that guy Edward Weston used to do. You know, the ones at the Oakland Museum. Eddie and I went to see the California photography show you recommended, and we both really liked it. I forgot to tell you. Eddie went crazy for Dorothea Lange, and I kept going back and back to the Westons. That was a great show."

Here was a mind-bending idea. You never knew what Carrie would come up with next. Steve hadn't worked with nude models before, but so what if his intent was salacious? He would at least get to see what he hadn't been permitted to touch. "OK, I'll give it a try," Steve said. "But I'm no Edward Weston. We'll both be learning as we go."

"I understand...that's OK," Carrie said.

"I thought you didn't like looking at the camera," Steve reminded her.

"I don't, but I want to try having the camera look at me. In those Westons, the model is never face-on. It's all torsos and backs and legs. If there's faces at all, they're angled profiles."

She was right, Steve thought. That was the Weston style, along with his erotically charged still lifes of bell peppers, eggplants, and other vegetables.

"One more thing, Parker," Carrie continued. "No beaver shots." She laughed, but he could tell she meant it. And beaver shots were not part of the Weston style anyway.

He laughed in return. Things were loosening up a little between them. "OK, those are the rules. No facial close-ups and no beaver shots. That still leaves plenty of latitude."

Carrie retreated to the mouth of a shallow cave and undressed, piling her clothes to one side of the opening. She draped her sweater across her shoulders to make a shawl and came gracefully toward Steve looking like the north coast update of a Botticelli nymph. Not a Playboy body, the breasts weren't that large and she was more muscular. But any serious photographer, Weston included, would have thought it was better than a Playboy body. And even by Playboy standards, no airbrushing would be required, unless Steve had to take out stray pubic hair later to preserve the sense of modesty Carrie was insisting on. The pubic hair he saw at the moment was a beguiling half-tone darker than her tawny head.

"Stop there," he waved her to her left with his hand. "I want to start you lying on the beach at the edge of the shadow behind you, so you're lit and the background isn't."

"OK, how about this?" Tossing the sweater behind a rock, Carrie settled onto the pebbles just beyond the shade line and stretched on her side with her back to him, her toes pointed and her face hidden in her arms. Her ass was as smooth and curved as a bead of oil, and her golden complexion gave her an almost uniform color, head to toe. Whether he responded as a man or as a photographer, this was an extraordinary female body—an extraordinary human body.

"You look wonderful," Steve said. "Roll your chest a little more parallel to the beach. Good. It lights your hair better and gives a sharper curve down your back. Can you hold that way?" Salacious intent was forgotten. He'd moved wholly into the realm of form and composition.

"I'll try," her muffled voice answered. "But don't take forever."

Over the next hour, while the light was good, Steve burned a lot of film. He took four of her in that first pose, and then she rearranged herself several times at the same spot. The contrast of light and dark there were tough to beat. Later she moved to drape over various rocks and to brave the shimmering, damp sand close to the water. She was cold, she said, but she wanted to do this.

Somehow, in one visit to the Oakland Museum, Carrie had grasped Weston's aesthetic and knew how to position her body to express it. She was also giving Steve his best photography day in quite a long time. But as the sun moved west, he lost the shadows and the changed angle of the light began to flatten everything. They reluctantly agreed it was time to quit.

"God, Carrie, you were fantastic. Thanks...I really mean it." Steve crouched near her, at the mouth of the cave, while she got her clothes back on. He was busily putting away his camera, lenses and other gear at the same time.

"I like to ignore it, but I do know I'm good looking," she said matter-of-factly.

"Good looking? Try beautiful," Steve replied.

"Sorry, I can't deal with beautiful. Good looking is bad enough, along with all the issues it raises. The thing is, today was different. I could get into being good looking and actually let myself enjoy it." Carrie was dressed above the waist, had just donned her panties, and was now pulling her jeans over her feet.

"You enjoyed being good looking at Dick's Place last night. I'm not going to believe you didn't."

"OK, you're right. I mean a woman wouldn't have to be that great to be a hit at Dick's, but I played it up. I almost never do, but once in a while it's fun."

"And it's got to be nice to have the option."

"I suppose. But I never thought about my looks until my brother's high school friends started going ga-ga over me during puberty. And I sure didn't know how to react. You learn, but it's mostly stuff you wish you didn't have to learn."

"As an average looking guy, I've never had that problem," Steve said.

"You're a nice looking guy, Parker, whether you think so or not. But things aren't the same for men. It's a patriarchal society, and men run everything, more or less. But men don't take good looking women seriously, and they project all kinds of weird shit onto us. We're assumed to be dumb, or we're supposed to be their possessions or we're vehicles for their fantasies, or all three. And dealing with women isn't much better. There's constant rivalry, like I'm going to vamp their men or something, and the ugly ducklings want to hang out with you for reflected glory. I just want to do math and be a regular person."

"Even so," Steve replied, "physical beauty gives you a power over other people that most of us don't have. And not only sexual power. I'm talking about something really primal, and I'll bet it translates into the world of mathematics the same as everywhere else."

"The world of mathematicians, you mean. Depressing...but you're probably right. Eddie says to look at it as insurance. Lead a regular life, but know that in times of war or famine, good looking women don't starve."

"Yeah, like *Sophie's Choice.*"

"Eddie's read that book. I haven't. But it's not the same as being a hooker." Carrie was fully dressed now, and starting to tie her boots.

"No, not at all," Steve acknowledged.

"Remember yesterday," Carrie asked, "when I dressed for dinner, I told you not to confuse the wrapping with what's in the package? The wrapping isn't just my clothes, it's my body."

"Yeah...but a photographer is always interested in the wrapping, because that's what the camera sees. Of course, the photographs we call great are the ones where we believe we see the reality inside."

"Reality?" she scoffed. "My legs are what hold me up when I walk. Maybe I shouldn't shave them, but if somebody thinks they look sexy, that's illusion. And my butt that you shot back and forth and sideways...I sit on that, and I take a shit with it every day, too. Function is what's real, not appearance. Think of my mom...turning fifty. Who knows how I'll look then?"

As an artist, albeit a part-time one, Steve was on familiar ground. "It's all reality, Carrie," he replied. "All of it, right down to the subatomic particles. Even illusions are that person's reality. But in total it's way too complex to comprehend. We have to break it up and approximate it through constructs like language and math...and, well, photographs."

"Maybe, but I'll tell you one thing for sure."

"What's that?"

"Thank god I don't have big tits. There's not one problem I have that wouldn't be worse if I had big tits."

Steve tried not to laugh. "You don't want me to take that as a joke, do you?"

"No. What I want is for you to show me proofs of every shot you took today and make me prints of the ones I like. Oh, and I want our lunch out of your pack. I'm super hungry right now."

"OK," Steve answered. "The lunch I know will be good. Let's hope the proofs are, too."

"I really do hope so. Today gives me a new way to relate to my body. I can visualize myself in harmony with the structure of the earth and not as just a sexual signaling device."

They spread their picnic at the base of the nasturtium-covered outcrop and sat passing the wine bottle back and forth until it was empty. There were only about two swallows each, but Steve had water they shared the same way. He never brought glasses or plates when he was out with his camera, and a Swiss army knife was his only utensil. The food was a bite of this and a bite of that, with no main course and no dessert. When they finished, he leaned back on his elbows, and she lay perpendicular to him with her head on his ankles.

Time to keep his guard up, Steve thought. If Carrie wanted to revive the quirky intimacy of yesterday, she must be oblivious to Steve's feelings about last night, or she was the most cynical cock-tease who ever lived. There was no comfort for him either way. She'd been phenomenal as a nude model, but he wasn't going to take on all the grief of having an affair and not get laid. That was basic.

"There's stuff we need to talk about, Parker," Carrie said, looking at the sky.

OK, here it came. Some damn something about what was behind the big sexual freeze. "What's that?" he asked.

"Do you consider yourself a feminist?"

"A what?" He sounded surprised because he was.

"You know what I mean."

"OK, and you want a serious answer?" His mind raced ahead. Christ...she was all over the map. Where was she going with this?

"I think feminism's a serious question," she affirmed.

"Then, yes, I'm a feminist. I completely accept the idea that women should have equal legal and cultural status with men and that nothing should be closed to them. But do I think that men and women are identical beings except for having different plumbing? No. Some of Ellen's friends make that argument...I don't buy it."

"That's pretty much what I think," Carrie said. "But what I was leading up to is, have you ever heard of Catharine MacKinnon?"

"No. Who's she?"

"A law professor at Yale. In 1977 she wrote a paper called *Sexual Harassment of Working Women* which was published as a book last year and has been extremely influential. I thought Ellen might have talked about it."

"Not that I remember. But the two of us have been pretty busy changing diapers since last year."

"It must be cool to have a kid," Carrie said. "I'd like to meet Matt sometime. He looks adorable in that picture in your office."

"What about the MacKinnon book?" Steve didn't like Carrie's implications regarding feminism, and here she was mentioning Ellen and Matt as though they were all friends.

"Well, MacKinnon has a ton of documentation to show that women being hassled sexually at work is a common thing. They get felt up and hit on and exposed to sleazy talk by their male co-workers all the time, and they routinely get extorted for sex by their bosses."

"And you're trying to say that's what I did to you?" Steve's voice took on an edge, and he felt like a grenade had gone off underneath him in the sand someplace.

"In a way, you did, and I thought you should be aware. I mean you weren't crude about it, and I liked you, but it's an iffy situation."

"Why? I'm not your boss."

"Not directly, but you could probably get me fired if you went to Suslow and complained about something. I'm new, and I'm just a graduate assistant. I felt very vulnerable when you first started coming on to me and asking me to lunch."

"Wow! I would never do anything like try to get you fired or retaliate in any way. How could you think that?"

"How could I tell? I didn't know you. And you're the one with what MacKinnon calls 'institutional power.' It means that our status at work is very unequal."

"I can't believe this." Steve was almost yelling. "I've felt the whole time that you had all the power. You could reject me and tell me to leave you alone. You could go to Suslow yourself and complain. You could go to Judith Bowden, the graduate dean. You could even say something to Ellen. I took a huge risk bringing you here."

"I eventually realized that, which is why I decided it was safe to come. You know I like you, and Eddie was promoting the idea for his own reasons."

"And if things didn't go well, you'd fry me for sexual harassment. Jesus!"

"God, Parker, I'm not trying to get you or anything. I just thought we should discuss it before we went further. If you and I are going to have a relationship, we need to be really careful. The University is getting touchy about that kind of thing, and you don't have tenure, right?"

"Right," Steve said bitterly. "And I probably never will. For sure, not at Berkeley. Maybe I seem like a big cheese to you, but I'm only on research staff. The grant funds run out, and I'm gone at the end of the month. Ellen earns more than I do by quite a bit."

"OK, that's my point. I don't want to get hurt, and I don't want to see you hurt, either. But right now you're pissed off." She looked at him and tried to hold his eyes.

"Hell yes I'm pissed! Not only am I a presumed harasser, with no protection because I don't have tenure, but you have a far better shot at tenure someplace in the next few years than I do. You're smart, good looking, and in a field with damn few women."

"I agree," Carrie replied, "but I'm not staying in academia. I'm getting into the computer industry. You should see what's happening around San Jose now. There actually will be a revolution this time, a computer revolution, and I'm going to be a revolutionary. You could do it, too." She tried again to hold his eyes, but he wouldn't let her.

"We should go," Steve said. "It's a long drive, and I don't want you reminding me that I promised to get you back by early evening."

"I'm not in a big panic over it. And there's something else we should discuss... about what happened last night."

"About what didn't happen, you mean."

"OK, about what didn't happen. But lighten up, Parker. That wasn't easy for me, either."

"I don't think I want to hear it," Steve said combatively. "Not now anyway. I've had the signals changed on me enough in the last twenty-four hours."

"Oh, oh," she said, "the male ego. Handle with care."

✳ ✳ ✳

Saturday afternoon along the coast was more beautiful than Friday, and Steve decided to drive as far down as Bodega Bay before cutting inland to catch the Richmond Bridge. The wildflowers were at their peak, and fast-moving cloud shadows mixed with the sun to turn the hills and bluffs into changing palates of spring color. Steve felt better after they'd been on the road a while, but he remained unsettled. The idea that Carrie already understood how much over a barrel she could have him at IER was something he hadn't figured on. Meanwhile, she played Steely Dan straight through and tried to get Steve singing with her to an old Marvin Gaye tape of Ellen's that she found in the glove box. Another day and Ellen would be home.

On the high cliffs approaching Fort Ross, Carrie persuaded him to pull over so they could get out and see. Sheer walls fell away dizzyingly at their feet, and the Pt. Reyes lighthouse made a vertical sliver of white far to the south. The ocean's rocking, cobalt surface was 800 to 1,000 feet down, and any one person or car was as tiny as a fly speck. They stood side-by-side drinking in the view until Carrie turned and kissed him full on the mouth. Steve responded, but still found himself holding back, and her sudden assertiveness heightened his sense of unease.

"I want to tell you I've had a really wonderful time," Carrie said. "It's the best thing I've done in months." She kissed him again. "Say you're not pissed off anymore."

"I don't know if I am or not," Steve answered, holding her loosely at the sides of her shoulders. "But I'm surprised you've been having such a great time. Let's face it, things could have gone more smoothly."

"Things can always be smooth and phony. Besides, you couldn't have thought I was some bimbo who was going to fall all over you."

Steve looked at her, unsure of how to react. She was right. He hadn't really integrated what was beyond her beautiful face and beautiful body. Yet she'd never behaved, at IER or on this trip, as anything other than a complex and intelligent woman with a strong commitment to personal honesty. But that wasn't the league Steve wanted to play in. He wanted someone who looked like Carrie, with Carrie's brains and sense of humor, who acted like a bimbo. He dropped his hands from her shoulders.

"God, Parker," she said in exasperation, "what do I have to do?" Carrie pulled away, walked to the car and got in. He followed, hands in pockets and silent.

Past Fort Ross, the coast highway loses altitude quickly and drops through the weather-beaten town of Jenner before crossing the estuary of the Russian River on an arched, double-span bridge of WPA vintage. Steve drove across at 25 mph to prolong the view, giving Carrie a slow-motion look at a hitchhiking hippie waving his thumb at them a dozen or so yards beyond the second span. As Steve began to accelerate the Volvo back to highway speed, Carrie swung away from him in her seat and pounded on the window.

"It's Mayo!" she shrieked. "Stop! Stop! It's Mayo!"

Steve jammed on the brakes and pulled off to the right. In the mirror he saw the hippie jogging up to the car carrying a rainbow-striped macramé duffel bag. Carrie had already thrown her door open and gotten out to meet him.

"Mayo! This is amazing. What are you doing here?"

"Sis-ter Car-rie," the hippie smiled, enunciating each syllable. He gave her a huge hug.

She let Mayo into the back seat on her side and resumed her place in front. Steve headed south again amid the added smells of lavender oil, damp wool and sweat. Carrie faced backwards in her seat, radiating happiness. Mayo was in his late twenties, slender, had a fuzzy brown beard and wore a Rastafarian knit cap along with jeans and a Peruvian overshirt. A Bob Marley tattoo had to be under there somewhere, but it wasn't visible at the moment.

"Mayo's from our Pedro Point surfer gang," Carrie said. "An old friend of Daniel's. This is Steve Parker, Mayo. Steve and I work together at the University."

"Hey, man," Mayo touched Steve's shoulder and smiled. "Thanks for the lift. Still doing the school thing, huh Carrie? That's good."

"Yeah. Grad school. Guess where Mayo's name comes from, Parker."

"Let's see," Steve answered, "could be a clinic in Minnesota or a county in Ireland. Am I warm?"

"Nowhere close. It's from Richard Brautigan. The final word of *Trout Fishing in America* is mayonnaise."

"Haven't read it," Steve said, "just seen copies around."

"Mayo loved that book so much he started eating mayonnaise sandwiches." Carrie freely interspersed her story with laughter. "You still eat 'em, Mayo?"

"Not much anymore," he answered. "Sometimes, though. We make really good bread on the commune. That's what I do now. I'm a baker."

"You living at the Berry Farm?" Carrie asked.

"Yeah, off and on. I was in New Mexico for a while. But I like the Farm. I'm just hitching down to the city to see my folks a couple days. I walked the four miles out to Highway 1, got a ride all the way to the Russian River, and five minutes later you come along. Cosmic, huh? Meant to be."

"Ever heard of the Berry Farm?" Carrie asked Steve.

"No, but I could probably guess what they grow."

"Wrong again, Parker," Carrie laughed. "No berries when Daniel lived there."

"We grow some berries now," Mayo put in. And a lot of everything else. But the name comes from Wendell Berry. You heard o' him, man?"

"You know, I have," Steve said. "Enough to say he's a whole-earth, agrarian type from back east." He was relieved not to flunk their entire counterculture quiz.

"Right," Mayo confirmed. "That's about what I know. He was up to the Farm once, though, and the dudes that met him say he's extremely cool. Wrote a bunch of books, too."

"Daniel got thrown off the Farm for drugs," Carrie said. "Heroin or speed or something."

"That's years back," Mayo added. "We've always tried to keep the place drug-free. O' course pot's not a drug to us," he laughed, "it's a natural sacrament."

"Seen any of the rest of the Pedro gang?" Carrie asked.

"No, not in a long time. Danny Boy still in the slammer? That's what I heard."

Carrie lightly squeezed Steve's forearm. "Yeah, he could get out next November, maybe. But probably not. He's been pretty messed up. I can't stand to see him anymore."

"That's the shits," Mayo said. "You never met him, huh?" Mayo asked Steve.

"No, that was way before I came in," Steve answered, understanding much more now about Carrie's attitude toward her brother.

"Well, Daniel was one amazing dude when he wanted to be," Mayo continued. "He's smart as hell, and he could get anybody to do anything. No matter how it worked out, you'd still end up liking him, and you'd jump to sign on for more. Fuckin' tragic the way he screwed his life up. Should've been the next JFK, not sitting in some damn jail."

"I'm going to Pedro tomorrow for my mom's birthday," Carrie said. "You can crash with me and Eddie in Berkeley and I'll drop you at your folks' on my way."

"That would be cool, but how about putting me on BART tonight? I told my dad I'd try to be there for Sunday breakfast. He'll meet me at the Daly City station if I call."

"Sure," Steve said. "We go right by the Richmond BART, and you could be in the city before we're in Berkeley." He liked this plan better than Carrie's. Steve wanted to be alone with her at least a few more minutes before their weekend was over.

"You still with Eddie?" Mayo sounded surprised. "I was going to ask about him, but I couldn't remember his name. Besides, I figured Parker here must be your new squeeze."

"No, Eddie and I are tight as ever. But Parker's got the hots for me, and I'm seeing him, too. Eddie knows about it. Sort of his idea, in a way." Her tone caused Steve's circulatory system to send an alert. Where would she go with this?

"Oh," said Mayo, "ve-ry Berkeley."

"Actually, it is," Carrie went on. "Parker's married. He's a professor type. He even has a kid. We've been in Mendocino catting around."

"Good place for it," Mayo responded. "The Cormorant Inn up there buys Berry Farm bread."

"That's where we stayed," Steve put in. "And the bread was great." He had hoped to change the subject, but no luck.

"Mayo," Carrie said, "you've got to hear what we did. You know Dick's Place, that bar?"

"Yeah, I've been in there. Did you meet Meg? She's a kick."

Steve had left Highway 1 at Valley Ford and the Volvo was coursing along the connector route to Petaluma and the 101 freeway at a good clip. Despite his initial trepidation, he listened with amusement as Carrie related in detail their episode at Dick's. It was fun to hear it from her perspective and get a sense of how the situation had developed before he walked in the door. Steve helped her tell the later stages. Mayo laughed and asked frequent questions.

"What a great story," he said when Carrie described looking back in the window after she and Steve had made their exit. "I can just see Meg yelling at those guys. It's exactly what she'd do."

"You know what's really funny?" Carrie continued, capitalizing on the admiring response she was receiving. "After all that, poor old Parker didn't even get laid." An involuntary twitch of Steve's right foot made the Volvo lurch. "I promised Eddie I wasn't going to have sex this weekend, but Parker was so horny after our scene at Dick's I had to give him the hand job of his life just to keep him sane." She broke into peals of laughter.

Mayo, too, thought this was a hilarious twist, and Steve knew he could cancel the outward effect of Carrie's jab by laughing right along. Instead, it took all his self control to keep the car from veering into the ditch and killing the three of them. To feel like a fool is one thing, but to feel so small you can barely see over the wheel is something else.

"Hey," Mayo gasped, "same as under the Pedro pier. Man, those were strange days!"

He and Carrie launched another round of raucous laughter, though she faltered when the full weight of what she was laughing at settled in. Registering little beyond his own hurt, Steve held the wheel tightly and drove on.

Conversation gradually resumed, mostly between Carrie and Mayo, but it was about scenery, weather, traffic, BART schedules and Jolie, Mayo's girl friend in Santa Fe. Steve had thought things were as weird as they were going to get before Mayo appeared. There were obviously no rules. In any case, twilight was on and traffic picked up when they hit Highway 101. The Richmond Bridge had good views of the bay and the city, if you were looking for that kind of thing. And Steve was amazed at how severe the bridge's superstructure was. He'd crossed it dozens of times and never noticed before.

Mayo gave Carrie another big hug when they dropped him off in Richmond, and he taught Steve an intricate, vertical handshake that felt more like a beginning position for arm-wrestling than it did friendship. Mayo either had no clue that he'd helped drop a nuclear bomb on their ride home, or he deserved an academy award for avoidance. And this from Steve, who was rather skilled at avoidance himself. Not so skilled, however, that he could contain his growing outrage another minute.

"How could you tell him that?" Steve yelled. "How the hell could you tell him?"

"Why not?" Carrie challenged. "It was the truth."

"Truth! Try this one! I already felt bad enough about last night, and you had to know telling that story that way would really make me feel like shit."

"I can stay home and have Eddie yell at me," she said. "I don't need you."

"Fine," Steve responded, though he did cut his decibel level. The Volvo was moving through the dark of Cutting Boulevard, heading for Berkeley. "But do you not get it?"

"What's with you? You don't have to be so uptight. I started to tell you about what I promised Eddie, but when I brought it up, you said you didn't want to know."

"I said tell me later, not tell the fucking world first."

"God, Parker, I wouldn't even be here with you, and I wouldn't have done anything about giving you a hand job, if I didn't like you. I've admitted my fantasy bit at Dick's wasn't fair, and I've said I'm sorry. Why isn't that enough?"

"Maybe it would've been if you sat me down and leveled with me one-on-one. But that's not what you did."

"Parker, I was telling a story to be funny. And it is funny. But I also thought you deserved to be zinged for pushing me away twice this afternoon. What I told Mayo isn't the whole story anyway."

"Oh, really? When do I get to hear the rest? Or are you planning to tell Suslow during coffee break on Monday while I stand by smiling?"

"You can sure be a jerk, can't you? I did it for you, damn it! I did it for us. If I hadn't agreed not to have sex with you, Eddie was going to follow us up there on his Norton and hang out in Mendocino himself. He wasn't going to hassle us, but he was going to be around. He has some part of his novel with a stalker in it, and he was going to work on the experience. How would you have liked that?"

"Jesus Christ, Carrie. If you going out with me is OK with Eddie, and if it's partly his idea, why do you have to agree to anything? This is like the kitchen knife. You two make your arrangement, he freaks out, and I pay the price."

"Bullshit! I had already decided not to have sex with you, so I gave up nothing. It was too soon, and there were things we had to talk through. There still are."

"Let's see, we've covered your hang ups about being good looking, we've covered the sexual harassment angle, and we've covered, ad nauseaum, your situation with Eddie."

"OK, but maybe you can see why it was so hard for me to come to Mendocino with you. You've got Ellen, and I don't want to lose Eddie. I'm damn well going to hold him to the sexual freedom shit he talks all the time, so that's not the issue. I can take care of that. But this weekend I gave my word, and I kept it. It was tough on you, and on me, but it was still right."

"If hand jobs aren't sex and pot isn't a drug, you and Mayo can teach ethics at the divinity school."

"Gee, thanks," Carrie shot back. "We'll have you guest lecture on the sanctity of marriage."

The car had somehow found its way to Ashby Avenue and was approaching Fulton. To the right a half-block was where Carrie and Eddie lived. Steve had been stopped cold by her counterattack. He was not in a strong position to go moralistic, and he wondered where that impulse even came from. Carrie sat biting her lip and watching traffic.

"Don't pull up in front, Parker," she said wearily when he made the turn. "Take this spot, so we can talk in case Eddie's home." Steve eased to the curb in a pool of dark thrown by a high privet hedge.

"What's left to talk about?" Steve asked in a voice as weary as hers. "The Pedro pier?"

"If this weekend went OK, I was going to tell you before our next date," Carrie said quietly. "I've come to terms with it, and I've decided any man I have a relationship with is going to know beforehand. If they can't handle it, I'll cut my losses. My parents don't know. Nobody knows in my life now but Eddie. That's one of the things I liked about you, Parker. I thought you were the kind of guy who could handle it." She gave a deep sigh.

"I was really glad to see Mayo today," Carrie went on. "He was always my friend, but I should have expected something like that when I told him our Dick's Place story. I wanted to zing you a little. I didn't mean to hurt you. Anyway, it ended up hurting me more." She paused. "You probably already know, don't you?"

"Something about Daniel and his friends is all I know." Then Steve felt the pieces fall into place. "What did he do, pimp you out for sex when you were a kid?"

"Yes. For nearly two years, until I was fifteen. Not every day or anything, and it was for drugs, not money. I jacked guys off and gave them head under the pier. Some of them wanted to fuck me, but I wouldn't. Mayo was never part of it, either, if that's what you're thinking. He helped me and tried to keep everything cool. And things didn't turn out too bad. I mean I don't hate men, and sex can be really good."

Steve could imagine himself reaching for Carrie and putting his arms around her, but he didn't do it. "What got you out?" was all he could say.

"The drugs were for Daniel to use or sell. He made it seem like we were in the front lines of the revolution. When I finally woke up and realized what I was doing and what the guys were saying behind my back, I quit. Daniel got so mad he threw me down onto a surf board and the tip nearly took out my eye. But I still covered for him. It was totally sick...We lied to my parents and said it happened in the ocean. There was so much blood...My mom never noticed my bathing suit was dry. I had plastic surgery three times to get the scar down to where it is now."

"How long has Eddie known?"

"Oh, a long time. He's always been unbelievable about it...Never used it against me or anything. That's what I mean when I say we have a really strong bond. And that's why I cut him slack when he needs it."

"You say you covered for Daniel back then...and that was sick...but aren't you cutting Eddie too much slack now? How do you know what he did this weekend while you were being so scrupulous about not fucking me?"

"You really don't get it, do you? He didn't promise anything except not to show up in Mendocino while we were there. He's never lied to me that I know of, and I don't think he would. Even so, I did look around for his bike when we went out for our walk and when I was going over to Dick's ahead of you. But I'd have been absolutely shocked if I'd seen it. I'm not sure I kept my promise to him as well as he kept his to me. I had you to worry about, and I did my best. I'll tell him what happened, though."

"I'm having a hard time with this, Carrie. I'm tremendously attracted to you, but I thought we'd get it on this weekend, have some fun, and maybe there'd be other times and maybe there wouldn't. The way it's ended up, I don't know how I feel."

"Sounds like you were just interested in the wrapping, Parker. I was hoping for something more if I had another relationship besides Eddie. But even if being good looking means I attract the wrong kind of attention, it also means you won't be my last shot." Carrie got out of the car, pulled her overnight bag and jacket from the back seat, closed the door with force and walked purposefully down the sidewalk toward her house. After a dozen steps, she suddenly circled left into the street and back around to the window on Steve's side. He rolled it down.

"Find a way to call me tomorrow night," she said. "I'll be back from Pedro by 9. I know Ellen will be home then, so this is a test. If you want things to go anywhere between us, find a way to call me." She walked away without waiting for an answer.

Knotted in conflict, Steve drove across the west edge of campus on Oxford and then up Euclid into the hills. His cock was urgently demanding that he do whatever it took to get into Carrie's pants, no matter that she was strangely unpredictable and had the power to threaten his family and zap his career. If he were a collector of experience, like Eddie, an affair with Carrie would certainly be one, and perhaps he could enjoy it on that basis. But this was what the old blues song meant about thinking with the wrong head. Steve was no Eddie. Steve did microeconomic risk, not personal risk. Moreover, Carrie kept using the word relationship. Steve already had a relationship—he was married. In fact he had two relationships; he was a father as well.

Steve was so distracted he barely recognized his own neighborhood when he got there. In that part of Berkeley detached garages sit at street level with the houses themselves perched at varying distances on the hillsides above. It took him two trips up the curving brick walkway to get his bag, camera equipment and the other bottle of zinfandel onto the porch. Then he came back down to reinstall Matt's car seat. Steve knew he'd be driving to Live Oak Park to play basket-ball in the morning, and he wanted everything to be as normal as possible.

Matt's amazing baby smell exuded from the padded arms and back of the curved plastic seat assembly that Steve had left on his workbench the last two days so he'd look less suburban when he picked Carrie up. Steve could feel his son's presence vividly as he cinched the unit back into place. Tomorrow at this time Matt would be hanging around his neck. Steve also made sure Carrie hadn't left anything in the Volvo that Ellen might notice.

Once inside the house, Steve switched on a single lamp, powered up the fur-nace and decided to put some music on the stereo. The Modern Jazz Quartet was the antidote he needed, and he let their mellow improvisations take over the room. Now he did feel at home, with the lights of Berkeley and the campus twin-kling in the dark through the fringe of trees outside the picture window he and Ellen had prized so highly when they bought this place. The white interior walls, built-in bookcases, hardwood floors and worn Persian rugs reminded him of where he belonged. The Balducci zinfandel would be a nice treat to share with Ellen at dinner some night later this week. He'd leave the bottle on the kitchen table so she'd be sure to see it.

Of course, Steve could call Carrie tomorrow. It wouldn't really commit him to anything, and the logistics were simple enough. There was a pay phone right outside the Shattuck Co-op, Ellen would be too tired to shop after they all got home from the airport, and Matt would undoubtedly need milk and other things. Steve was certain to be going down there Sunday night, especially if he volunteered.

Fortunately, he didn't have to decide now. He could unpack, try to get a good night's sleep and deal with it when the time came. Steve was looking forward to roundball at the park in the morning, working up a good sweat with Seth and Lenny and Roger and Dave. None of them knew anything about where he had been the last few days, so he'd be free to lose himself in racking up assists, set-ting picks and playing D. Maybe his jumper would even be on, like it was the day Carrie came by.

But Steve didn't think he'd be calling Carrie. He was nearly sure he wouldn't. She had been a kid and all, but still, a girl who gives blow jobs under the pier to feed her brother's drug habit was not the kind of person Steve Parker hangs out with. Especially when you thought about Eddie and his leather jacket, his tattoos and his knives. It wasn't until Steve saw something from the University in the accumulation of mail he'd brought in from the box that he realized he would be seeing Carrie at IER on Monday whether he called her or not. And beyond that, Steve had two rolls of film to develop, rolls that were filled with images of her naked body.

FRIENDS LIKE THAT

ROY AND CORA WERE ANGRY. THEY WERE HURT AND THEY WERE ANGRY. NOT WITH one another, or not yet, though there was blame enough to go around. They were angry at Spence. Roy knew he was driving too fast, which always bothered Cora, but so far she was too angry to notice.

They were on Highway 49, winding down through the pines from Nevada City to Auburn. Traffic in their direction was light. Nobody left a party town like Nevada City at eight o'clock on Saturday night. The only benefit now was the last of what had apparently been a beautiful, mid-August sunset. Roy's gray BMW wasn't a high-end model, and was no longer new, but it would still whip right along. The rear seat was piled with unpacked clothes and other vacation stuff that had mostly been stowed in the trunk two weeks ago when he and Cora came up from Sacramento.

For the drive home, they hadn't had a chance to organize anything. This trip was supposed to be tomorrow night, Sunday, when they had expected to be returning from a glorious, low-key summer getaway. They'd been house-sitting for Spence, and what really pissed them off was that he had begged them to do it. Then he'd come home a day early, in an ugly mood like they'd never seen, and destroyed everything. Roy wished they'd gone to Cabo San Lucas the way they'd originally planned. It was 1990, and the California economy was heading into recession, but they were far from broke.

"Who knew he'd be such a prick?" Cora said after several miles of silence. "Buddhas in every room, a rack of New-Age CDs, and he's still a prick."

"Not to mention the books on mysticism and spiritual development," Roy added, accelerating sharply into the ravine at Alta Sierra. Stars were popping out across the sky as darkness enveloped the northern foothills.

"And he explodes because we moved a table from the upstairs hall? What kind of bullshit is that? We were going to put it back."

Cora thought she had summed things up, and Roy could have let her remark stand, but he didn't want secrets between them. "There's a lot more to this than the table," he said. "A lot more."

"Oh? Like what?"

"I wouldn't say a thing if he hadn't flipped out and attacked us. Or if he'd cooled off and asked me not to. Whatever, I'd figure I owed him as a friend."

"Forget that. He's no friend. And don't even think about not telling me. But for god's sake, Roy, slow down! You're doing 75 and there's a narrow bridge coming."

⚹ ⚹ ⚹

About six weeks earlier Jill had called Cora one morning at work to promote the house-sitting idea, and Cora called Roy right away. She wanted to say yes, and he hadn't taken much persuading. He and Cora had probably spent a half-dozen weekends at Spence's in the past year, and each one had been more fun than the last. Roy told Cora to go ahead and have Spence call them at home to arrange the details.

But to Stan Gardner, Roy's lunch companion later that day, house-sitting in Nevada City seemed an uninspiring vacation choice. The two were having deli sandwiches and Snapple on a shaded bench at the 15th Street end of Capital Park, midway between the State Treasurer's Office, where Roy worked, and the *Sacramento Bee*, where Stan was a metro beat reporter. Noontime joggers and walkers streamed by and the columned walls of the copper-domed capitol building shone white through the trees to the west.

"You get promoted to Assistant Deputy Treasurer," Stan badgered, "and start making the big bucks, but you spend your vacation seventy miles from home house-sitting for some guy out in the boonies who doesn't even have a pool?" Stan, a blocky, slightly balding six-footer, was wearing pinkish-framed glasses, khakis, and a blue dress shirt with the neck unbuttoned and his tie loose. The dry heat of these Sacramento summer days was something he and Roy actually enjoyed.

"If you saw the place, you'd understand," Roy answered. "There's terrific hiking and river swimming nearby, but it's right on the edge of town, not out in the boonies." Roy Havens, a Jew on his mother's side and Irish on his father's, was dark and wiry. Disproving the stereotype, however, he was extremely even-tempered. He wore a well-tailored, olive poplin suit and had loosened his own tie after sitting down.

"What do you mean?" Stan said. "The whole town is out in the boonies. If you want to stay close to home, go to Tahoe."

"Tahoe's a different scene. Nevada City's like a college town, but they forgot to have a college. It's got beautiful buildings from the gold mining days and an amazing cultural life for a population of 3,500. Good restaurants, a couple of theater companies, a film series, four or five places with live music on weekends, decent bookstores and a wacky radio station run by volunteers. And they're always closing the streets for bike races and parades. Nice and cool at night, too, from the altitude."

"You know, I do hear people in the newsroom talking it up. Maybe Beth and I should go sometime. We usually hang around here weekends or zip down to the Bay. Anything interesting for the kids?"

"In summer, definitely. Come up next month when Cora and I are there."

"Can't. This family's off to British Columbia for a real vacation."

"Well, go on your own after that. There's fall color in October, and a day-trip's no problem."

"Sure...suppose we could. But who's this guy with the house? I know you've been spending a lot of time there. He's some friend of Cora's, you said?"

"No, not Cora's. Of her friend, Jill's. Of Jill's husband's, actually."

"Jill is the blonde who went to Davis with Cora, right? Intense, but kind of a babe?"

"Right. You met her at our place a couple of times when she first got back to Sacramento after living on the East Coast. She and Cora have always been real tight.

"Anyway," Roy went on, "Jill got involved with this guy Alex Bernardi, who's a lawyer in Grass Valley, not far from Nevada City, and she all of a sudden married him and moved up there. The guy with the house, Spencer Mallow, is a long-time friend of Alex's. Spence got a teaching job in ag econ at Sac State a few years ago and relocated from San Jose. He only has to be on campus three days a week, so he leased this incredible house in Nevada City and commutes down here. Alex was Spence's roommate at the house before he hooked up with Jill. I don't know where Spence gets the money, but the place is huge and he's always throwing lavish parties with overnight guests."

"OK, I get it. *The Big Chill.*"

"Not far wrong. The house looks like the one in the movie, white clapboard with a wrap-around porch, and it has all these odd-shaped rooms, especially upstairs. We've had really good times there. In fact, I've dreamt about the place more than once. It's at the end of a dead-end road, with big grounds behind, no neighbors and lots of trees. You can walk into town in five minutes, but there's so much privacy Cora and I were sun-bathing naked the last time we were up. And Spence makes killer margaritas."

"Aaaah, now I have the picture...maybe you're not so dumb. Let's see how it wears after two weeks."

"Well, Spence won't be around. He's off to some conference on international trade in Puerto Rico. But we'll have Jill and Alex to hang out with, plus the Yuba River, plenty of blackberries to pick and a summer street fair with local musicians, barbecue and the whole bit."

"All right, sounds appealing. But update me on you and Cora. Beth wants to know if she'll ever have a wedding to go to. You guys've been living together... must be close to three years. I'm looking at the big 4-0 in a couple of months and you're not far behind. Cora's maybe thirty-six. What's the holdup? Election-year career anxiety?"

Marriage was a familiar topic of banter between them, but Roy decided to deflect it. "Nope," he answered. "Doesn't matter to me if Feinstein or Wilson wins as Governor, and the Treasurer's race is looking OK. If the Republicans get Hayes a full term, I'm good for sure. He's the one who put through my promotion after Unruh died. I've always been registered Independent, and that wasn't loyal enough in the Unruh days.

"But if Jerry Brown's sister replaces Hayes, I figure I'm still good. I've got an odd-ball specialty in public housing bonds, I'm not senior enough she'd automatically want her own person in my slot, and she'll see me as having nice, safe Unruh connections. Besides, Young and Stoneberg, the LA investment firm I was with before I started at the State, is close to her, and I've got some strings to pull if I have to."

"Whoa, slow down. That's why I like you as a doubles partner. Tennis or politics, you have the angles covered. But we're talking marriage. You know, the 'M' word."

"OK, OK," Roy laughed, "same answer as always. No fear of commitment. Don't see how I could be more committed. And I'm not opposed to marriage, but neither of us has brought it up in a long time."

"Is that good or bad?" A platoon of the park's ever-present gray squirrels had assembled at their feet, and Stan was tossing the last bits of his sandwich to them.

"Good. We're completely comfortable together. How could it be bad?"

"Probably right. Not like that endless off-again, on-again drama you had with Linda back when you and I first met. But if you do get married, you think Cora'd change her name? To my ear, there's nothing wrong with Havens."

"Doubtful. She'd stay Cora Trigg. That's how she's known professionally, and in her kind of fund raising, name recognition really counts. I'd be fine with it either way." Roy launched a piece of crust at a scrawny squirrel on the edge of the group who ran off with it before eating.

Stan hurriedly glanced at his watch. "Oh, oh, I'm covering the Board of Supervisors this afternoon, and I need to stop at the office first."

"I better go, too. I have a ticklish bond deal to close. Got time for tennis at the club next weekend?"

"Good chance. I'll call you tomorrow. But what's this bond deal?"

"Facilities reconstruction from the Loma Prieta earthquake."

"What's ticklish about that?" Stan didn't bother to feign innocence.

"No news leaks here. Try the Treasurer's press office at 445-3994." Roy shot him a smile.

"Oh, well, not my beat anyway." Stan walked off, scattering squirrels around him.

✳ ✳ ✳

Roy usually waited out rush-hour by working until 5:30 or so before driving east on J Street past Sac State to his place at Campus Commons. Technically, that is, it was his place. He'd already bought a two-bedroom condo on the greenbelt and was living there when he met Cora, though she had taken over decorating responsibilities and caring for the patio garden as soon as she moved in. As a result, he'd long since begun to think of it as their place. He knew married couples whose lives and finances were less entwined than his and Cora's.

Her office at KXJR public radio was near the corner of 51st on his regular drive home, and the night of Jill's call Roy noted that Cora's Mazda sport coupe was gone from the parking lot when he went by. That meant she'd be home ahead of him, or it could mean she was out on business. Cora worked hard and had a very unpredictable schedule. He stopped at the Howe Avenue Safeway for the fresh salmon Cora had asked him to pick up during their morning phone conversation. It was a perfect Central Valley summer evening with an early hint of breeze from the Delta.

And Cora was home, already changed into shorts and outside fussing with the gas grill as Roy came into the kitchen from the garage. Like Roy, she was dark and wiry. People said they could pass for brother and sister, though she did not at all resemble Roy's actual sister. Cora's hair was short, and she had a broad, full-lipped mouth, lively hazel eyes and a graceful nose. She was also a good tennis player. They had met playing mixed doubles and were still one of the toughest teams at the club. Roy, from West LA, grew up on the courts. By contrast, Cora was a natural. She'd grown up on a ranch outside Willows and had barely touched a racquet until college PE.

"Hi," she called over her shoulder. "Would you believe we have a long message on the machine from Spence telling us we're saving his life by agreeing to house-sit? He apparently knows we've said yes, but he can't stop selling."

"He's afraid we'll change our minds." Roy put the package of fish on the counter and poured himself a glass of chardonnay from an open bottle in the fridge. "Stan was skeptical today at lunch, but the more I think about it, the more I like it."

"Me, too." Cora came to the sliding screen patio door. "Thanks for remembering the salmon. You know, going to Spence's will be way cheap for a vacation. That means we can save to go someplace deluxe next winter. Sound OK?"

"Sure. But this summer, cheap and low-key seems right. With the damned impasse on the State budget, I could be called back to the office over something no matter where we went. And what a radical idea. A vacation that's truly restful. Let's talk about it more after I get rid of this tie. Then we'll call Spence and confirm in person."

Later, as they were finishing dinner under the lemon tree overhanging their patio, the phone rang. It was Spence again, in a lather to be sure they had the correct dates and that they understood all the things they'd need to do to care for his house. They took turns reassuring him that everything was fine, and they promised to come up on Friday night while he was still home so he could show them the routine before he left next morning. That was critical, Spence claimed. Also, they already knew Amida, Spence's cat, so Spence was comfortable with their taking care of him, too.

"Fussy, fussy," Roy said after hanging up. "If I didn't know he'd been married and had kids, I'd wonder if Spence is gay. We've only seen him with place-holder type dates who are there more for the party. And think about all those pristine Asian antiques and wall-hangings. He sure likes to have the place just so."

"I know what you mean," Cora responded, "not that being married or having kids is any proof. Oscar Wilde was married and had kids. But Spence isn't gay. Trust me on that. And we'll do fine there. Too bad he hasn't seen how we live. We're not what you'd call messy."

"We've invited him to stop by if he's on campus late. It's right across the river, but he never has. Keeps his distance emotionally, too. Maybe by our doing him this favor he'll open up a bit. I like him OK, but I'd like him more if he was looser."

"I like him fine. It's good that he's different. I like that about us, too. We haven't bought the whole program of marriage, kids, church and TV mass culture."

"You're right about Spence," Roy admitted. "He is different. I enjoy the Nevada City theater people and his RAND and Hoover Institute friends that we meet at his parties. But I don't know how different you and I are, really. I'm just glad you like our life. I know I do."

"We're different enough. We live in one of the most political cities in the country, and we're still non-partisan. You've said it yourself. There's no party for life-style liberals who are fiscal conservatives but don't hate government."

"OK, that's something. And I guess Alex and Jill aren't standard suburbanites either. Could be why Spence keeps all of us around."

*⁀ *⁀ *⁀

Roy got off work early the afternoon of Friday, August 3. They had decided to take his car because of its larger trunk, so he was busy packing and loading when Cora got home. Casual clothes, in layers for Nevada City's warm days and cool nights, were all they would need, plus tennis and swimming gear. It amounted to quite a pile, though, for a two-week stay, especially after Cora added pillows, towels and the specialty foods and wines she figured wouldn't be available in small-town stores.

Their plan was to be on Highway 80 by 6:15, trailing the Sacramento rush but ahead of the Bay Area people who would be passing through later on the way to Tahoe. According to Channel 3, the weather for the next five days would be great, but the news out of Kuwait was getting scary. That wacko Saddam Hussein could do anything, Roy realized. A few years back he invaded Iran and got his butt kicked, then yesterday he turns around and invades Kuwait. Everybody seemed to figure he'd pull out after swaggering a while, but who knew? Saudi Arabia and Israel were in the line of fire this time. And on top of that, oil prices could go nuts.

But once he and Cora were underway, with Roy driving as he usually did when they traveled together, Middle East worries faded and they were in high spirits. The overdue state budget had finally been adopted at the end of July, so neither of them had brought a speck of work to intrude on their summer break. At Roseville, traffic thinned and they began to make good time.

"Those places give me a laugh," Roy said, pointing to a line of low warehouse units along the frontage road. "Self-Storage. Like everybody has all these old selves, and that's where they keep them."

"Oooh, weird! A screenplay for Woody Allen."

"Or sci-fi. A mass escape, followed by 'Night of the Living Selves.'"

Cora laughed, then said, "In a way, I bet the furniture and stuff people store there does represent old selves. They want to let those selves go, but can't, so they hide the symbols in anonymous little sheds out by the freeway."

"Yeah, once the attic and closets are full. But what about our old selves? We don't have a storage unit, and there's only a few pieces of junk in the garage rafters."

"I told you we were different."

"Oh, no, there's old selves someplace. I see a pretty straight line from Cora Trigg, English BA, to Cora Trigg, public radio underwriting director. But before that, there was Cora Trigg, Native Daughter of the Golden West and Queen of the Rodeo. The one whose family helped establish the Sacramento Valley Rice Growers Co-op. What happened to her?"

"She grew up and got a taste of city life. That Cora would have settled for just the role Glenn County society wanted her to play. This is the real me, so I let her go. "

"Let her go? Where? What you're saying is you've got an internal storage unit, not an external one."

"Well, so do you, Mr. Smart Pants." Cora punched him on the shoulder. "Who's in yours?"

"Two old selves, at least. The college bohemian from Occidental who hung around the edges of the Stanley Crouch crowd and thought he was cooler than cool. All-night parties and non-stop social criticism. And then the masochist who put up with Linda and her stupid games year after year. I have a hard time relating to either of them as ever having been me."

"You've told me about Linda, probably more than I want to know, but I never imagined you as a college bohemian. Did you march against Vietnam and all that?"

"A couple of times, yeah. With my parents, even."

"Wish I had. Davis was sleepy, but there were still things I could have done. Of course my parents were freaked out enough by what I did do. My dad asked once if I was smoking LSD. Can you believe that?"

"Funny. What were you doing, snorting pot?"

"You know, a crack like that went through my mind when he asked. It was sad, really. He didn't get it at all. Doesn't yet, and my mom's no better. You've seen when we visit. If your parents encouraged you, why'd you let your bohemian self go?"

"It wasn't really me," Roy shrugged. "Maybe I was just being my dad's alter-ego. Anyway, when he died and Nixon was re-elected, I went numb. I didn't want to deal with any of it. I decided to focus on my own life and what I could do on a personal level. That's where I still am."

"Could there be a time we'd let these selves go, too?" Cora asked soberly.

"Change is sort of how life works," Roy acknowledged. "But I feel so grounded now I can't imagine making a big break. If we keep being open with one another, maybe we can grow together instead of apart. That'd be a good way to be different from most couples we know."

"There goes another one of those Jeep Cherokees," Cora said, gesturing to her left. "You see them all over. If we're going to be coming to the foothills this much to see Alex and Jill and Spence, may be we should get one."

"So much for being different."

"I heard what you said. Staying open with one another would be different in a way that matters. With cars, so what? Different's not important. I'd like to have four-wheel drive for skiing, too."

"Yeah, and gas mileage be damned. One of us would have to drive the thing to work."

"We can afford it."

"That's not my point. You're the one who was all jazzed over Earth Day this spring. But let's talk cars another time. There's something I've been wanting to ask. What did you mean when we were planning this trip and you said 'Trust me, Spence isn't gay'?"

"Oh, I think women have a sense for that. And besides, I know some of the background...from Alex."

"Yeah?"

"There were 'other women'...more than one...involved when Spence's marriage broke up. His ex-wife...her name is something like Marad or Narad...was apparently quite a beauty. She's Thai, you know, tall and light-skinned, from an aristocratic family. Spence fooled around on her anyway, and things really blew. The divorce in San Jose was very bitter."

"That part I've heard. She got full custody of the kids, took them to live in Hawaii and threatened to move to Thailand. Spence is still trying to work out visitation rights. She'll only agree to let one come here at a time, and he wants to have more of a family atmosphere. There's a girl and a boy, right?"

"Right. The girl's about 12 and the boy is maybe 9. It's like their mom is trying to always have a hostage. Like Spence would kidnap them if he had both."

"Revenge and hostages. Classic. But Spence must have known he was taking big risks catting around that way."

"Good-looking guys think it's their due."

"Yeah, but Spence isn't that good-looking."

"Roy, come on. He looks like Sean Connery. James Bond was good-looking on an international scale."

"I see it, a little."

"I see it a lot. And he's not gay."

"Well, too bad Spence's Thai marriage didn't work as well as his Thai economic policy."

"What do you mean?"

"Remember, he was over there most of the 70's. There and the Philippines, working on economic development through U.S. AID. We were doing everything we could to bolster both countries and keep them in the Western camp during and after Vietnam. In Thailand, it was a big success. They're booming economically now, and they're exporting rice again for the first time since World War II."

"I've barely heard about it, but I know you really follow that stuff."

"Yeah, I have to for work. And it's fascinating. The Pacific Rim economy is going to be a big deal for California. But I've also learned from talking to Spence and to the think-tank folks at his parties. Not all the conversation is music and art."

"No, not in that crowd. But I try to stay away from politics. I can handle the touchy-feely anarchists among the locals, but some of his Palo Alto and LA friends are way out on the right."

"I've noticed. But, hey, honey, we're off the freeway in another couple of miles. How about we stop for Mexican at Auburn before we head north? I'm hungry, and we already beat the Bay Area traffic."

"Sure, fine. A tostada sounds great. We'll still be in Nevada City early enough to get a brain dump from Spence on what he wants us to do."

≹ ≹ ≹

Inching the BMW up through town on Broad Street when they arrived gave Roy and Cora a view of Nevada City at its Friday night best. The sidewalks along the brightly-colored, false-front commercial buildings overflowed with a mixed crowd of white-hair, white-shoe tourists, locals from the pickup and horse-trailer set, and hippies of various ages in sandals, cutoffs and Guatemalan shirts. Drinking on the street was legal and widely practiced. Clots of cars at every intersection meant parking was not to be had. It was dusk and the pale-blue sky behind the Methodist Church at the top of the hill was backlit by the fading sun. Roy could hear ragtime piano from the door of Celestina's Cafe and the rhythmic thumping of a drum circle from the little park behind him by the hardware store. Cora, like Roy, was smiling and excited.

"This really is going to be fun," she said. "The hell with Saddam Insane. For the next two weeks I'm forgetting the world. How would I look in a Guatemalan shirt?"

"Let's find out. I'll buy you one tomorrow at that Herb Shop place. Funny, we're not even a hundred miles from home but it feels exotic."

"California's wonderful that way. So much contrast."

Turning left past the church and an imposing B&B in a former mine-owner's mansion, Roy drove the few blocks out to Manzanita Hill where Spence lived. The last rutted cul-de-sac looked more like a driveway than a street, but it served one other house before dead-ending at a graveled apron in front of Spence's. A barn-like garage big enough for three cars stood open in front of them with the house up to the right. Spence's own BMW occupied a corner of the apron. Roy crept by and pulled into the center of the garage. He saw lights inside the house, but the gathering darkness made the green exterior trim look black against the house's white walls. Big trees, pines and cedars, arched over the roof from the sides and back, and crickets chirped loudly all around.

"Hi. You made it," Spence's clear baritone called from somewhere. They could hear his footsteps approaching. "Thank you two again for doin' this." Though he was forty-six and had lived most of his life around the Pacific, Spence still spoke with the rounded vowels of his boyhood. He'd grown up near Baltimore and gone to the University of Virginia, if Roy remembered right. When Spence reached the car, he stopped first on Cora's side to shake her hand through the rolled-down window.

"We should be thanking you," she said. "I know we'll have a wonderful time."

Spence came around to Roy, who got out to meet him. You didn't hug Spence, but a vigorous handshake was mandatory. Spence was tall, perhaps 6'2", with full dark hair, graying at the temples and cut just long enough that he couldn't pass for a military officer. OK, Roy thought, Sean Connery. Cora wasn't entirely making it up. Roy felt Spence grip his hand firmly while Spence's other hand squeezed his forearm.

"Good to see you," Roy said. "This is much better than our coming tomorrow and trying to learn the ropes from written instructions."

"Yes, good to see you," Spence replied. "But there's written instructions, too. Plenty of 'em. I'm leaving a three-ring binder in the kitchen. This is better, though. Can I help you carry anything?"

"Yeah, thanks. From the trunk. Cora can get the back seat on her own." A breeze was drifting down the Deer Creek canyon through town, and Roy felt a chill. "Honey," he said to Cora, "could you reach my sweatsuit jacket from in there?"

The house was, as usual, immaculate, although Spence claimed it was a mess. He had cleared out a cupboard in the kitchen and gave a running commentary on the wine and food they'd brought as Cora put things away. After making a final trip in from the car, Roy piled the towels and pillows with their suitcases and shoulder bags on the living room floor at the foot of the curved wooden staircase.

"Here, I made margaritas," Spence said, coming up behind Roy and handing him a frosted tumbler. "For old times sake, even if we haven't known one another a full year."

"Thanks. Cheers. It does feel like old times. We've had super weekends here."

"Yes, cheers," Cora added, joining the two men near the stairs. She drank from the tumbler Spence had given her while Roy was outside.

"What are you drinking?" she asked Spence. "That's not a margarita."

"Rum and tonic," he said. "White rum. A warm-up for Puerto Rico. Good, too.

I've never been there before, but I'm looking forward to it. I like the tropics. You know that already."

Each of the four main downstairs rooms had large, cross-hatched casement windows and bare, plank floors with oriental rugs or tatami matting. The smooth plaster walls, painted pale apricot or lime against white trim, carried an assortment of framed silk tapestries, watercolor landscape scrolls and wood-block prints. The furnishings were chests, tables, chairs and sideboards of brass-fitted rosewood or lashed bamboo combined with occasional mahogany pieces. Crudely formed pottery, unglazed or partly glazed, along with statuary, heavy candles and a few indoor plants rounded out the decor.

"There's nothing much you need to know about the living room or dining room while I'm gone," Spence continued. "Check the plants and give them enough water to show in the saucer if the soil feels dry when you stick a finger into it. My office back beyond the dining room I'd like you to treat as private and leave the door closed. Same with my bedroom upstairs. The library we'll need to go over in detail. You'll be spending a lot of time there, probably, because it connects the kitchen to the front and back porches and all the other rooms. The stereo and phone machine are there, too. I hope you remember I don't have TV. You might miss it with what's going on in Kuwait."

"We don't watch much TV," Cora replied. "And we're trying to hide out from war news. If something happens, we'll get what we need on the radio."

"Well," Spence pressed on, "Bush is already talking about sending in the 82nd Airborne to bolster the Saudis. Good move if you ask me. Bush is no pansy. He used to be CIA Director." Spence made eye contact with Roy, then with Cora, purposely gauging their reaction.

There wasn't one. Cora met his eyes and changed the subject. "I've told you before, but this is just a lovely place, Spence. You did a sensational job of decorating."

"Thanks," he said, resuming the role of gracious host. "I guess you'd call it pan-Asian funk. A purist would die in here. I've mixed Japanese mats and mingei-ya pots with Cambodian tapestries, Chinese rugs, Maylay furniture and Thai scrolls. I put in the track lighting myself. But if you look closely, you'll see there's a Buddha image of some kind in every room...a statue, a drawing, something."

"I know you're interested in Buddhism," Roy put in. "I'm hoping to browse through your books while I'm here."

"Help yourself. *Zen Mind, Beginner's Mind* by Suzuki is a good place to start. Look for Robert Aitkin, too. You can borrow anything you want, as long as you leave a note showing the titles. There's a whole shelf of East/West metaphysics and philosophy."

"That'd be terrific. Thanks."

"Where did you get all of this?" Cora said. "I've always wanted to ask."

"Mainly stuff I had from my family or that Naret and I collected overseas. But it does look good in here, which you wouldn't expect in a Victorian farmhouse.

Better than it did in San Jose, actually. When Naret took the kids, she left everything else. The things were there, but the people were gone. I think she realized it would make our old place seem more empty. That's why I chose a completely new atmosphere when I moved." Spence's voice betrayed no self-pity, no emotion whatever, in relating this.

"Must have been rough," Roy said, feeling he should. Cora nodded her agreement.

"As for the kitchen and downstairs bath," Spence went on, "use 'em whenever you need to. Just clean up and leave things the way they were. You've been here before, so you know the plumbing's pretty primitive. There's no dishwasher or garbage disposal. If I owned this place, I'd update the plumbing and wiring first thing. And I've got to show you the utility room, off the kitchen. The water heater's cranky, you might need to relight the pilot, but there's a washing machine and dryer you can use. You just can't run them both at the same time or you'll blow a fuse. If one does blow, the fuse box and a bunch of extras are by the water heater. The instructions for everything are in the binder."

"Warts and all, this place still gives me real estate lust," Roy said. "Just fantasy, of course. We couldn't deal with the commute. But I'm surprised you haven't bought it by now."

"Oh, I've tried," Spence responded. "Many times. I'm afraid it's hopeless."

"That's odd," said Cora. "Is the owner planning to come back or something?"

"Maybe they want to subdivide and sell off the land," Roy ventured.

"Nothing that rational. I assumed you knew. It comes up a lot at parties. An elderly man in Carmel is the owner. He's senile, but in a paranoid way. This was his mother's family's house. She inherited it and lived here alone for years after she was widowed, and she died here. Apparently she wasn't found for over a week. He arranged the funeral from down there and now refuses to either set foot in the place or sell it. I pay rent to a lawyer in Monterey who's his conservator." Spence rolled his eyes exaggeratedly.

"Is there a ghost," Cora laughed.

"You'd think, wouldn't you? I've met previous tenants who say yes, but I've never seen a sign. I did get goose bumps once when I was first clearing out the attic. Anyway, no special instructions for taking care of the ghost."

"Glad to hear it," Roy said in a joking tone.

"The cat is a different story. He's in my office. Let's say hello." Spence walked into the dining room and through a door to his left. "Wake up Amida," he called softly. "You have company." Cora and Roy followed, sipping their drinks.

Amida was a neutered male Siamese with unusual amber-gold eyes and an alert, talkative manner. Cora's old brindle, Fred, had died, and both she and Roy had really taken to Amida on past visits. He seemed to like them, too, and purred loudly when Cora crouched next to the desk chair where Amida had been curled in sleep. She began to pet him after letting him smell her hand.

"What a sweet boy," she murmured. Looking up at Roy and Spence she said,

"I'm ready to get another cat now that Fred's been gone a year. And Amida has convinced me a Siamese is what I want."

"That would be cool," Roy agreed.

"They're absolutely the best as far as I'm concerned," Spence stated. "So responsive, but you have to give them lots of attention." He reached down and lifted Amida against his chest, saying with obvious irony, "Come, oh source of wisdom, I'm taking you to the couch." Spence moved away into the dining room and toward the library. "Roy," he called back, "would you please get the light and close the door behind you. There's nothing in there that's your concern, and I want to keep Amida out."

Reaching for the switch, Roy saw that Spence's office, beyond its Asian flair and characteristic neatness, had the usual framed diplomas and professional awards plus a phone, a fax machine, a locked file cabinet, a good-sized computer and a wall of books on geography and economics. Roy might like to browse in here, too, but that would have to wait till Spence was home. He also saw on the desk photos of what must be Spence's kids—separate shots of smiling, coal-haired Eurasian cherubs, a boy and a girl, with delicate, well-formed features. A third photo, more current, showed the two children flanking their mother in a tropical garden. Naret's yard in Hawaii, no doubt. In any case, though she was built like a model and beautiful enough to be one, Naret's posture conveyed a regal assurance that the children, like trophies, were precisely where they belonged. No affection for Spence had been intended by her sending this to him.

When Roy caught up with Spence and Cora in the library, she was receiving a run-through on how the stereo worked while the cat watched from a folded afghan at one end of a small leather couch near the fireplace. A pair of overstuffed chairs were backed against the two front windows, between which was a rosewood platform table holding a vase of fresh flowers, a handsome brass lamp, copies of The Economist and Foreign Affairs, a cordless telephone, and the answering machine.

"That covers the stereo," Spence concluded, "and the CDs are over there. All pretty straightforward. But now that Roy's here, I want to cover the two most important things. One is don't let Amida out at night. The raccoons could tear him to pieces. He doesn't usually want to go, but be careful. He's fine outside by day, and he'll come in for dinner and hunker down after that. He gets wet food then and kibble the rest of the time. The cupboard next to where I had you put your things is all stocked with what he eats. Also be sure he has plenty of water. I don't like him drinking out of the toilet, but that's what he'll do if you don't keep his bowl topped up.

"The second thing—really important—is the phone machine. My old one broke and this one has a lot of features I don't understand. Maybe it's me or maybe the thing is defective, but it erases messages when the tape gets full or if you turn it off. I'm expecting calls while I'm away that I really need to get. If I miss them, I'll be in a big hurt. What I'm going to do is phone in every day or so and use the remote to pick up messages. But that means you can't get calls here that will fill up the tape or where you could lose mine by trying to play your own. Call out all you want, but don't answer any. Seriously. And don't touch the machine. I set it to respond on the first ring so incoming calls won't drive you nuts. Tell your friends or whoever that you don't have a phone here. They can't call you, you'll have to call them. I know it's a hassle, and I should have warned you in advance, but..."

"Spence, it's fine, it's fine. Don't worry." Cora's eyes were twinkling with amusement. "We'll love a vacation from the phone and from TV. It'll be like backpacking or river rafting, but we'll have your fabulous house as a base camp." Roy smiled back at her. Nothing, he realized, was so quirky it should surprise them coming from Spence.

"Oh, good. I'm relieved," Spence said. "Thanks for understanding." He smiled now, too. "Wait a minute." Spence ducked into the kitchen and returned holding in his left hand a two-inch-thick vinyl binder with the spine at about the level of his ears. "This will be on the kitchen counter. I know I've given you a lot to absorb, but except for the phone machine, everything's written down. There's a tabbed section for each room and one for the yard. Oh, I didn't tell you about the yard. It can be a lot of work." Spence lowered the binder to his waist.

"Relax, Spence," Roy assured him. "Let me read about it and follow instructions. Look, we love cats, and we've been missing ours that died, so Amida's no problem. And we live in a condo. I never do yard work. I won't mind a bit. You'll be home before the novelty wears off. Didn't I see a ride-around mower in the garage? What a kick."

"Right, you did. It's no Indy 500, but it runs. And the weed-whacking's not too bad. Dragging the hoses to water different parts of the yard everyday is what gets old."

"Don't be macho about this, Roy," Cora interjected. "I'll be driving that mower, too."

"OK, farm girl, you've got the tractor experience. But anyway, Spence, you must have a lot on your mind with an all-day flight coming up. We'll handle things here. Enjoy your conference. It's only two weeks."

"True. Complicated, but not that long a time. I'm visiting family on my way down and back, so I've booked myself to Puerto Rico via DC. I fly out of Reno at eight A.M. tomorrow and return that last Sunday afternoon. Best connection I could get."

"Reminds me," Cora said. "How do we reach you if we need to?"

"You really can't. I don't know where I'll be on any given day. If it's urgent, call my home number from another phone and leave a message that I can pick up off the machine. I'll find a way to get back to you through Alex to give you the phone for where I am at the time."

"Or call us at our home number in Sacramento," Roy explained. "We'll be picking up messages from there with our remote."

"Yes. Either would work. But if it's some minor repair on the house, I don't need to know. The owner has a fix-it guy in town here, Bill Small. His number's right in the front of the binder. See?" Spence raised the binder in front of him again and held the cover open.

"Let's get us settled so we can all go to bed," Cora told him. "I'm tired, and you'll have to be out of here mighty early to get to Reno."

"Good idea. I've been wired today with all the getting ready, but I do need to sleep if I can. And I'll be gone long before you two are up. Let me help with your bags. I'm putting you in Cirene's room. It's bigger than where I've put you on party weekends, and has nice windows."

"The Serene Room?" Roy was perplexed. "I'm not with you."

"No," Spence replied. "Cirene, C-I-R-E-N-E...my daughter's name. I fixed up a room for her. The best room. There's a special room for Lin, too. L-I-N, my son. It's an affirmation that they're coming. I'd been counting on this summer, but something else will work out."

"We really hope so, Spence," Cora said, and Roy could tell she was touched.

Not long later, Cora and Roy were snuggled together with the lights out in a room that very much lived up to Spence's billing. From where he slept opposite the upstairs bath, it was at the far end of the long central hall and extended the full width of the house. A set of twin dormer windows faced the front yard and another set faced the back. Roy had opened those to let in the moon and the night air along with an eager chorus of cricket sounds. Throughout the upstairs the floors were carpeted and the walls were of white-painted wooden boards. Preparations for Cirene's visit included a Hollywood-style double bed, white wicker furniture with floral cushions, a full-length mirror, pink fru-fru curtains and scattered bouquets of dried herbs. Unusual prints that Spence said were rubbings from intaglio at Angkor Wat hung tastefully about.

"Our king bed is going to seem like a football field when we get home," Cora whispered.

"It's a good thing we like snuggling."

"At least we're here, and everything's going great. Can you believe that ridiculous binder? I was afraid I'd crack up when he started waving it around."

"God, yes," Cora said. "And the answering machine. Could anything be more convoluted? But Spence does seem to prove you can be anal without being an asshole. It's heartbreaking to think of him fixing up these rooms and then the kids not coming."

Roy moved his hand from Cora's hip and slid it to her tummy. "Put me in a small bed on a summer night and I can't avoid the fact that I have the hots for my woman." He began kissing her ear and neck.

"And she has the hots for you, but she's not going to act on it until tomorrow morning when we have the place to ourselves. You bring me a cup of our good Java City French roast about 8:30 or so and who knows what might happen."

"OK, if the ghost doesn't do us in while we're asleep, you're on."

❦ ❦ ❦

Chattering mind. That's what Spence's meditation book called it, and Roy could see why. You choose a peaceful place, assume the appropriate seated posture, breathe deeply and count your breaths. But instead of clearing, your mind dashes every which way.

In Roy's case this meant flashbacks of conversations overheard at last night's street fair, apprehension about what his in-basket would look like when he returned to work, wondering whether he needed a haircut, worrying they didn't have enough wine for their upcoming dinner party, trying to guess the temperature of the South Yuba at Edwards Crossing, and relief that nothing had happened between Amida and the raccoons a few evenings before. By the time one distraction passed the next was introducing itself. His fifth meditation session beneath the Tibetan mandala on Spence's enclosed back porch, and the fifth of his life, was, frustratingly, the worst yet. In the overall picture, though, a small thing.

It was Saturday morning, Spence had been gone a week, and they were having a magical time. Taking his cue from Cora, Roy had simply forgotten the world beyond Nevada City. Neither had looked at a newspaper since the first day, when they'd walked to town to get Cora her Guatemalan shirt, and they hadn't bothered with radio news since Tuesday or Wednesday. He'd finished the Suzuki text for beginners and was now into Robert Aitkin's *Mind of Clover*. Cora had found Maugham's *The Razor's Edge*, and was reading that. They were also working their way through Spence's CD collection, with Andreas Vollenweider, Ottmar Liebert and George Winston being daily favorites. Roy's pattern was to get up early, run the trails in the old hydraulic diggings behind the house, shower, then meditate for twenty minutes before breakfast. Maybe next week they'd get out their tennis rackets and hit some balls down at Pioneer Park, but so far they were too busy with other activities.

Right now Roy had a CD of Tibetan bells playing softly on the auxiliary speakers mounted in the upper corners of the porch wall behind Spence's Nordic Track machine. Spence had a zazen cushion at one end of the narrow floor from which you could face either the wall and the mandala or look up and out a bank of chest-high windows into the tree-tops. Cora was in the yard picking apples. There was a Gravenstein that was already producing, and he could hear her moving among its branches. Since it was her turn to do breakfast, she said she'd make fresh applesauce. Just then the smell of coffee found its way under the porch door and put an end to Roy's session. He stood and saw Cora stride by carrying an armful of rosy, yellow fruit. She looked wonderful, brown as an acorn in her Tevas, hiking shorts and T-shirt with her black hair still shiny-wet from the shower.

Checking his forearm, Roy could tell he was getting darker himself, sunscreen notwithstanding. All over, too, because he and Cora were using the nude beaches upstream from the Edwards bridge rather than the beaches downstream where swim suits were expected. This was an established Nevada City custom that the Sheriff was willing to accept even though public nudity was illegal under county ordinance. Roy and Cora had been swimming nearly every day and were going again this afternoon with Alex and Jill, who would be staying for dinner afterward. Alex had been so consumed in preparing an upcoming court case it was the first chance for the four of them to get together since Roy and Cora's housesitting duties began.

At Roy's encouragement, he and Cora had been out a couple of times to Country Rose and Broad Street Bistro during the week, but tonight they were cooking in. Actually Alex, who was a terrific cook, was bringing chicken, and Cora was taking care of everything else. And the house looked good. So far Spence's binder had been needed only once, to acquaint them with the ride-around mower. Roy couldn't wait to develop the snaps he'd gotten yesterday of Cora wheeling the thing across the yard wearing a work shirt and an old straw hat from Spence's closet. Moving the hoses was a pain, as Spence had warned, but they incorporated it into their routine.

Roy went in from the back porch and turned off the stereo. The phone rang once followed by a click and a prolonged whirring from the answering machine. Spence must be picking up his messages, not that Roy was aware of any messages to be picked up. Of course he and Cora had been out a lot. Roy had heard the same noises from the machine a few days ago, and wondered what time it would be in Puerto Rico. An hour later than New York he guessed, so that meant four hours later than California. On this occasion an even louder whirring from the food processor drowned out the message machine. Fresh applesauce would be a treat with coffee and bagels on the front porch in the morning sun. With a mewing cat suddenly wrapped around his ankles, Roy headed for the kitchen to help Cora set up trays.

"Hi." He kissed the back of her neck and, when she turned around, her mouth. "Amida wants applesauce, too," he said.

"Good morning, seeker of eternal truth," she teased. "And good morning, Amida." She bent to pet him. "You have kibble and water, but maybe Roy will spoil you with a little wet food like he did on Thursday."

"Roy will...as soon as Roy has some coffee." His mug was on the counter near the coffee maker and he poured himself four or five steaming ounces. While it cooled, Roy gave Amida a spoonful of ground up something or other from an open can in the fridge.

"Look at him," Cora said. "you're a hit. His tail's sticking straight up."

"Good. Meditation didn't go well, so I'll earn karma points this way. Ooh, great coffee."

"Thanks. Could you put the bagels in and watch them? I just turned on the oven." Cora shook applesauce out of the food processor into a pottery bowl. "Today should be fun, don't you think?"

"Yes, definitely. It'll seem odd to have Jill and Alex here with Spence not around, but we owe the hospitality, and this way they don't have to drive all the way to Sac." Roy sliced three bagels and lined them up under the broiler.

"Entertaining those two at our place is complicated," Cora agreed. "We can never figure out when Alex has the kids. It's supposed to be every other weekend, but Jill complains it constantly shifts. She thinks Alex lets his ex push him around."

"I admire him for being a responsible father, though."

"Me too, actually. Jill should have known what she was getting into."

"You'd think." Roy smiled. "You know, we've never been to the river with them, even though Alex is the one who turned us on to it. Are we going upstream or down?"

Cora smiled with him. "Silly question. Alex would go either way, I suppose, but Jill won't be swimming at any nude beach. Not her style."

"Darn!"

"So you've been lusting to see my girlfriend naked. Should I be jealous?"

"No, and not lusting, but I wouldn't cover my eyes. Even with the glasses and the corny page-boy hair, she's a woman men notice. That can't be news to you."

"Of course not. But it also can't be news I don't want my man looking up her skirt. Just to remove the suspense, I'll tell you she's a real blonde." Cora tried to look stern but her eyes gave her away.

"Good, that solves that," Roy laughed. "But as adventurous a person as Jill is, her physical reserve seems strange. Doesn't fit with the rest of her."

"I've known her a long time and it's just how she is. But that's part of her appeal to men. They all think they'll be the one to break through and reach the primal woman."

"Maybe Alex finally has. She sure didn't hesitate when he started talking marriage, and I've noticed a little less edge to her lately."

"When Jill came back from Philadelphia I told you she was getting over a train wreck in the relationship department. You didn't know her before, so you weren't aware how much effect it had. Anyway, Alex made her feel safe."

"Safe?"

"Sure, with all his manly bluster. Don't you see? Also, Jill doesn't want kids, and he went right out and got a vasectomy."

"No kidding?" This was news to Roy. "How can guys—Alex, for example—be so un-mysterious to you? Every man I know feels he can never figure women out."

"Because men spend too much time projecting and not enough time observing," Cora answered. She twitched the side of her mouth and added, "I don't think women are mysterious, either."

"Hey, I'm at least halfway observant," Roy protested, "but everybody's mysterious to me...filled with contradictions." He snapped his head around and lunged for the oven. "Aaaak! I almost burned the bagels."

❦ ❦ ❦

Alex, Jill, Roy and Cora were single-file on a twisting, narrow trail above the South Yuba heading back upstream toward their car through broken stands of live oak and pungent bay laurel. The swimming had been good, though the river was crowded by the mid-week standards Roy and Cora were used to. The nude beaches would have been less crowded, but Roy knew there was no sense in putting Jill through the embarrassment of vetoing the idea or in allowing it to provoke discord between her and Alex. He would inevitably make a show of not being shy, along with repartee about seeing Cora naked.

In any case, she and Jill had certainly looked fine in their bathing suits. Jill's shorts now showed the damp outline of her suit underneath, and Roy couldn't help eyeing her tight buns as she walked in front of him. Alex was somewhere ahead of Jill around the next bend and Cora was several yards behind Roy.

His watch said almost 4:30, but they were all wearing hats of some kind to ward off the still-intense August sun. A sauna of solar energy absorbed earlier in the day radiated at them from the rock outcroppings and reddish earth beneath their feet. It felt good after a swim, but you needed sturdy shoes to negotiate the trail and the steep side spurs that gave access to the beaches, and a day-pack for your gear so your hands would be free. The river water, clear with the barest of green highlights when you were paddling around in it, was almost turquoise from up here in simultaneous reflection of the sky, the granite stream bed and the surrounding forest. A number of people were getting their last swim of the afternoon, and Roy could hear the laughter and splashing of frolicking children and the deeper voices of adults and teenagers echoing faintly up the canyon.

"I'm watching your ass move," Cora called in a stage whisper when he slowed so she could catch up. "Not bad in those trunks."

"Thank you, thank you," Roy joked, "I've been watching Jill's."

"Yes, I know. But poor baby, no nudity."

Roy shifted his day-pack to make it more comfortable. "I'll survive somehow. Besides, we have another whole week to go upstream where I can get naked with you."

"I'm for that." They started walking again, Roy still in the lead and Cora carrying a plastic bag bulging with the miscellaneous trash she always scrounged along the way.

In addition to her personal crusade against litter, Cora was a good swimmer and she was as unself-conscious a person as Roy had ever known in terms of baring her body to nature. She sunned and dove by the hour on the low rock palisades upstream near their favorite beach, just like the Indians who had used these Sierra canyons as summer retreats over the centuries. Cora had gotten so dark this past week she could pass for a member of Ishi's band. In his mind Roy could see her spearing pike in one of the Yuba's deep pools or weaving willow baskets near a smoky beach fire. The obsidian ankle bracelet she had been wearing would fit the scene perfectly, and these images filled him with intense feelings of love—for her and for this place.

At the last spot of shade before the trailhead Jill and Alex were waiting under a sun-blasted buckeye tree whose leaves had already dried and begun to fall. The first to leaf and bloom in the spring, pushing their elongated, sweet-smelling, white flowers up and down the canyon as early as April, the buckeye was also the first to declare that summer would not be endless.

"Great idea, you guys," Alex said. "And thanks for driving. Your car's just right for that hairy-ass road getting in here. Jill's Honda isn't big enough to handle the four of us and my king-cab pickup would be off the pavement on both sides." Alex spoke in an engaging, fast-paced vernacular that undoubtedly gained him points in front of a jury. His face was a handsome combination of his Italian father's features and his Cornish mother's complexion, topped with wavy, chestnut hair.

"The water couldn't have been better," Jill added. "I was up at Tahoe last weekend, and swimming there is way too cold for this girl." Jill was flushed from the hike, but seemed relaxed and happy.

"I thought you had the kids last weekend," Cora said.

"Alex did. I took off to get some head space. He was very sweet about it. I've been so busy at work lately and trying to get sets done for the Chekhov we open in September."

"They're not your kids," Alex said matter-of-factly. "And I had a good time with them. You know, I've swum down here since I was a kid myself, but I hardly come any more. It seems like I'm always too busy, and Trudy forbids bringing Paul or Lisa. She thinks it's too dangerous. Can you believe that?"

"Well, I suppose it is a little dangerous," Roy put in, "but there's lots of kids. If they stay in the quiet water near their families, I don't see much risk. Of course, if Trudy requires a lifeguard on duty, that's a standard you can't meet."

"One of many, the bitch," Alex said emphatically. "But don't get me started." He led the last few yards toward the Edwards Crossing bridge where Roy's BMW was parked.

Alex had grown up and been a high school football star in Grass Valley, a neighboring town five miles south of Nevada City. After serving in the Air Force and finishing law school, he returned and began his practice in a well-established local firm where he was now partner. Trudy had been his college sweetheart. He was in his early forties, divorced from her about four years. His two children, Paul, eight, and Lisa, six, lived with their mom in a large house Alex and Trudy had built in a rural area outside town.

Alex and Jill had been together nearly two years and lived in Grass Valley, in a much smaller place, from which Alex could walk to work. Gregarious and personable, he was well-known locally and harbored political ambitions, ideally starting with a city council seat and working upward. Alex was a dutiful father, but he had real enmity toward Trudy, the source of which he didn't share, except perhaps with Jill. Alex and Jill seemed to Roy an unlikely pair, but many couples struck him that way.

Never previously married, Jill had worked in advertising in Sacramento, then Boston, then Philadelphia, then Sacramento again before meeting Alex at a party. She had wanted to change her life at that point, and he had provided an appealing means to do so. In quick succession she went off with Alex for a Reno wedding, moved to Grass Valley, got a part time job in marketing with a nearby high-tech firm, and began to do set design for the Foothill Players, Nevada City's top theater group. She had always been artistic, and was delighted to find a satisfying outlet for her talents.

Jill was not one for happy endings, though, so all this was accompanied by angst and doubts that, by long habit, she expressed to Cora. Serving as Jill's confessor was a key element of their friendship as far as Cora was concerned, and Roy always showed a sympathetic interest when Cora related things to him second-hand.

"I'll light the coals as soon as we get to Spence's," Alex said from the rear seat as the BMW began its winding ascent from the river. "By the time Jill and I shower, they'll be ready for the chicken."

"I'd have been glad to do the whole meal," Cora said. "But you've been so keen on bringing this chicken it must be something special."

"It is," Jill put in. "Armenian. He learned it in Fresno."

"I worked in an Armenian restaurant for a while when I went to Fresno State," Alex explained. "The trick is to marinate your meat twenty-four hours in oil, red wine vinegar, garlic, onion, rosemary, bay, salt and pepper. Works with chicken or lamb. Spence loves it. I cooked Armenian for him a bunch of times when I lived at the house after Trudy and I split."

"Did you do all the cooking?" Cora asked.

"A lot, not all. Spence has his parties catered, but he makes these great spicy Asian soups with coconut milk and lime."

"Yeah, very good," Jill said. "I remember."

Roy slowed to wheel the car around a blind hairpin turn at the base of a huge madrone tree. "Wow," he said, "that's some corner. But fill me in, Alex. How is it you know Spence again?"

"Met him at Cal when I was going to law school after the Air Force. Trudy and I were married and he was still with Naret. They lived in the apartment across the hall."

"What was he doing there?" Cora asked.

"Getting his doctorate," Jill answered.

"Were you in Asia before that, too?" Roy glanced over his shoulder at Alex.

"No. And mighty glad. That was Vietnam back then. Even if we end up with troops in Kuwait, I doubt they'll have it that bad. I was in ROTC and got posted in the States in logistics. I went to Texas and a couple of places in California."

"One of them was Castle," Jill said. "Just think, we could have met ten years sooner. Not that I ever gave fly-boys the time of day."

Roy clicked on the fact that Jill was from Merced and her father had been stationed at Castle Air Force Base near there. Roy himself had sweat out the war with a vulnerable lottery number expecting a draft call that never came. He'd made vague plans to head for Canada rather than serve, but he couldn't say whether he'd have dared to follow through on those plans.

"I was married, anyway," Alex replied, "and married lieutenants don't date the colonel's daughter." He laughed.

"Jill's dad is pretty liberal for a military man," Cora agreed, "but not that liberal."

"How long did you live with Spence?" Roy asked.

"Two years, a little over. God, we had a ball. I was glad as hell to see him. I'd been living in the garage at Trudy's going through all kinds of bullshit around the divorce. Spence shows up, snags that great house and starts fixing it up. I lived downstairs where his office is now. Two divorced guys, lots of booze and lots of parties. Totally therapeutic."

"He seems awfully fussy," Roy responded, thinking of the binder. "You must have really been *The Odd Couple*." He shifted out of low gear, finally, as they left the canyon behind.

"Oh, we worked it out. I mean our styles are different, and we got into it now and again, but basically we trust each other."

"Did you hear about the phone?" Roy continued. "How Cora and I can't answer it, ever, so Spence can get all his messages by remote?"

"Cora was telling us," Alex laughed. "That's Spence to a T. Does make one less thing for you guys to worry about."

"I'm kind of surprised you and Jill didn't house-sit for him," Cora said.

"We might have if you couldn't," Alex answered, "but Jill didn't want to. She likes her own nest. It'll be fun being there tonight, though, don't you think, hon?"

"This is a beautiful drive up on the ridge," Jill said. "You can see way out to the Sierra crest, and those white board fences along the road remind me of back east."

✸ ✸ ✸

Spence's house was dark except for a dozen candles on the dining table and sideboards. Vollenweider's sweet electric harp came from the stereo, they were well into the second bottle of merlot, and Cora had just served Alex more of her hand-picked, home-made blackberry pie. The men had changed to Dockers and long-sleeved T's, Cora was wearing her Guatemalan shirt, and Jill was in a lavender turtleneck that, with her glasses left in their case, turned her blue eyes violet.

"You wouldn't think merlot goes with blackberry pie, but it does," Jill said. "I'm feeling buzzed in a real nice way."

"Tonight merlot goes with everything," Roy joked. "I'm glad you guys like it. And Alex's chicken is worth walking to Fresno for...if you can't get it in Grass Valley, that is."

"Marinating's really the secret," Cora added. "When I grill chicken it always comes out dry and half the time it's burned."

"But very strange not to have Spence around," Alex said. "In fact I can't believe he's not. How are you guys getting along? Still glad you decided to take this place on?"

"God, yes," Roy responded. "It's going by like a dream. I've even been browsing through Spence's books on Buddhism and am trying meditation. He has a zazen cushion on the back porch."

Alex did a brief drum-roll on the table with his fingers and laughed loudly. "I don't know from zazen, whatever that is, but I know the cushion. If he was meditating and I went to use the Nordic Track it'd really bug him. I didn't do it on purpose, generally, I just wouldn't know he was there. But if I wanted to bug him, that always worked."

"Poor Spence," Jill said.

"Yeah," Cora put in. "But Roy is really going spiritual on me. I'm afraid he'll swear off sex like Ghandi." She made air kisses in Roy's direction.

"Not likely," he assured her. "Hey Alex, did you ever see the ghost when you lived here?"

"Hell, no. What ghost? The old lady who supposedly died upstairs? I don't believe in that shit."

"We haven't seen her, either," Cora said. "But I wish Roy would stop joking about it. Kind of creeps me out. Like he's baiting fate. Don't those books tell you to have respect for spirits?"

"Yes, in a big-picture sort of way," Roy answered. "The reincarnation of souls is an important concept."

"Well, I'm not religious, but I believe in the paranormal," Cora went on.

"New Age crystals and that woo-woo stuff?" Alex mocked.

"No. I just know there's powers we don't understand and probably could never understand."

"Like?" Roy probed.

"Like...," Cora struggled. "Look, I'll tell if you all promise to tell me what my story makes you think of. Honestly. What comes to mind from your own life. Deal?"

"Oooh, spooky stories around the campfire," Jill said. She hesitated. "OK, I'll play. But I go last."

"What the hell," Alex said. "I'll go second. You in, Roy?"

"Could I refuse? And we know I'm going third."

"Wait, wait," Jill jumped up. "Spence has this perfect CD. Have you guys found it? The *Novis Magnificat*. Totally ethereal."

"No, put it on," Cora said. "And pour us all more wine, Roy. I'm into this, but I'm taking a bathroom break first."

Roy poured the last of the merlot and popped a bottle of cabernet that he pirated from Spence's wine rack in the utility room. He'd replace it or tell Spence about it and replace it later. While he was rummaging about, music came on that sounded like a lentimento Mozart had written posthumously for electric piano and synthesizer backed by the full celestial choir, two-hundred voices at least. The hairs on Roy's arms and neck prickled. Jill was adjusting the volume down a bit as Roy carried Spence's wine through the library toward the candle-lit dining room. Cora was back at her place, opposite Alex and ready to begin. Jill sat across from Roy a moment later.

"I'm kind of embarrassed, but this is what happened and how it felt," Cora said. "When I was ten, a spirit saved my life. I mean really saved my life."

"Oh, come on, a sp..." Alex challenged before Cora cut him off.

"No! Part of the deal is we get to tell our stories without wisecracks. I forgot to say that. This music is very cool, by the way.

"So...on my parents' ranch one summer when I was a kid I nearly drowned. My brother had some friends over, but they wouldn't let me play with them. It made me mad. I took our black lab, Mandy, and went out behind the house and way into the fields. I was walking along the irrigation ditch in a place I'd never been. Mandy jumped in the ditch, which she did all the time. But in this place the current was strong and the sides were real steep and she couldn't get out. She started whining and crying and I had to run to keep up with her.

"I found a wide spot where I could get down to the water, and Mandy swam to me. I grabbed her collar and got her out, but my foot slipped and I went in myself. Underwater, and it was cold. When I came up, I was being sucked right into a drain pipe beneath a road. The current was really fast. There was a metal grating over the upper part of the pipe to catch branches and trash. You know, so the pipe wouldn't get clogged. The current smashed me into the grating and I banged my head. Not enough to knock me out, but it hurt.

"The current was pulling my legs under the grating into the pipe. I had to hang on to the bars with all my might. I couldn't move. I could just hang on. I started screaming. I knew no one was around, but I couldn't stop screaming. The water would surge and push me down so it rushed past my ears, like it was alive. Pretty soon I could barely scream. My throat wouldn't make noise, and I knew I was going to die.

"Then a man was there. A dark man with a cowboy hat, a blue shirt and a kerchief. A Mexican, maybe. He just crouched down from the road, grabbed under my shoulder and pulled me out. I mean he saved me from drowning and never even got wet. I was probably in shock. He didn't say anything. Didn't smile.

Nothing. Just looked at me. I finally started talking, telling him how scared I was, and he said 'No se, no se.'

"That's Spanish for 'I don't know,' but I thought he was telling me not to say anything, so I shut up. He looked at me a while longer, and walked away. I never saw him again. I didn't tell my parents or anybody what happened. They had yelled at me a thousand times not to go in the ditches. I was mostly dry by the time I got home. I just said Mandy went in and I had to help her get out. Anyway, who was he? What was he doing there? How could he come along like that, from nowhere, to save my life?

"There were no workers in the fields that day, no Mexicans around anywhere. I made up a reason to ask my dad when the workers would come and he said September. And there were never any during mid-summer in the years afterwards. I always checked. I can't explain it any other way than that he was a spirit. Someone who had died working in those fields who had a little girl in Mexico that he didn't get to see before he died. So he saved me. Maybe because I'm so dark."

"God, Cora, that's some story," Roy said. "You never told me." He reached to encircle her wrist and hold it.

"It is a good one," Jill agreed. "Now I'm getting the creeps."

"Why not a Mexican fugitive?" Alex asked. "Why a spirit? Why not somebody running from the 'Migra'?"

"Why not a spirit, Mr. Attorney-at-Law?" Cora shot back. "There's no evidence either way. A spirit is just as plausible."

"OK, OK," Alex conceded. "Hellofa story. Hell—of—a—story. Well, it's my turn, and here's what I thought of listening to Cora. Wait, somebody give me more wine." He held out his glass and Jill poured cabernet for him.

"Thanks," he continued. "I'm going to tell why I stopped hunting. Did you know I used to hunt? Deer...every fall since I was a kid. Not something you three approve of, I'd guess. But I stopped. You don't know this story, Jill, because I've never told anybody but Spence.

"It was when I was living in the garage at the end of my marriage to Trudy. Within weeks after this happened I moved in here. Anyway, I'd been going with my buddies to the old Chalk Bluff Mine along Lowell Hill Road almost every weekend that season. A couple of them got nice bucks, but I never even got a shot off. It was completely the shits and I was frustrated, big time. Finally, Sunday night the last weekend of deer season I was home in the garage and couldn't sleep. Bright moon out, so I went into the back yard. I mean it's country there. A deck and a few sheds with connecting pathways and the rest low brush.

"What do I see right by the garbage shed but a big buck. Bigger than any my friends had got, with a big rack on him. I couldn't stand it. Somehow he didn't spook. I knew it was crazy to be shooting there, but I floated myself inside, got my rifle, loaded up and came around the garage the other way. He was still there. I shot him. Big loud noise. One shot, clean. Went down like a sack of cement.

"Trudy, of course, is freaked. Lights start coming on in the house, and I see her at the kitchen window. She sees me, too, holding my rifle, and I hear my daughter start to cry. I put down the gun and ran to the deer. He's not moving at all. Stone dead. Unbelievable. He's facing away from me, so I reach out and grab his horns to bring his head around where I could see him. I'm thinking trophy. You know, mounted on the wall. Both horns just come off of him and crumble into fragments in my hands.

"I look at him closer. He's diseased. Old and diseased. Teeth rotting and hide all tattered. A grand patriarch ready to die, rooting for garbage in my yard. He stinks terrible. I'm stunned, I mean stunned, and Trudy starts yelling out the window 'What did you do? You scared us to death, you idiot! What did you do?'"

"Holy shit, Alex!" Jill said. "What did you do? I mean after that."

"What could I do? I told Trudy to shut up, that everything was OK. I'd shot a deer and I'd clean it up. She should keep the kids away. I put a tarp over it and the next day I hired a couple of old coots I know in town to haul it out of there on the QT and bury it. End of story."

"You swore off hunting on the spot?" Cora asked.

"No. But I couldn't get that buck out of my mind. I dreamt about him. Like he was my father's ghost or something. I planned to hunt the next year, but I couldn't pick up my rifle, couldn't even think about loading it. Since then I've made excuses to my buddies about being too busy, about meeting Jill and about being newly married, and they finally stopped asking. I don't hunt anymore, and that's why. Sounds wimpy, but there it is."

"I don't see it as wimpy, Alex," Roy said. "More like message sent and message received."

"Exactly," Cora nodded. "Exactly."

"If anything's wimpy," Jill added, "it's that you can't tell people the reason you don't hunt is because hunting's too gross. Don't be using me as an excuse, like the poor, henpecked husband can't go out with the boys anymore." Her tone was fairly light, but it was pointed criticism and it stung.

"Look, babes," Alex defended. "Cora said be honest. At this table, I was honest."

Roy couldn't help wondering if Alex's hunting buddies knew about his vasectomy. Likely not, and Roy wasn't supposed to know either. When Roy had asked if Alex wanted more kids, Alex had said something like, "Don't know, but the old engine still works pretty good." Alex might have told Spence; they seemed to have that kind of friendship.

"OK, I'm off the hook," Alex said. "Let's see where Roy goes with his shot."

Roy had initially been unsure where he would go with his shot, but once he heard Cora and Alex, he knew. And this, on top of the flickering candles and the *Novis Magnificat*'s building finale, made his goose bumps return. He met Cora's eyes. Wine wasn't what he needed for a dry mouth, but he drank some anyway.

"I'm ready," Roy said. "All of you know how I got lost cross-country skiing last winter. The day Cora was with Jill in Grass Valley while my nephew and I went out. Alex was off with his kids to a movie or something."

"I remember," Jill replied.

"This is the story of how I got un-lost."

"You told us," Cora interrupted. "You followed your tracks back."

"That's what I said, but I was actually guided back. I couldn't let myself believe it at the time, so I downplayed the whole thing.

"It was the Saturday between Christmas and New Year's. My nephew, Joel, was up from San Diego. You met him. A nerdy, loner kind of kid who was thirteen. I took him to the Railroad Museum and all that. But he was dying to see the snow, and old Uncle Roy was ready to oblige. So the three of us came up late morning. After lunch, Cora hung around Grass Valley while I rented Joel equipment in Nevada City and got a trail map."

"You went to Alpha-Omega Road, right?" Alex asked.

"Yeah. It looked like a piece of cake on the map. You park on Highway 20 where Alpha-Omega comes in, about 4,500 feet elevation, drop down a ways, head up canyon at the first right turn, loop around to the left till you hit Alpha-Omega again, and back to the car. Four miles, and nothing too steep. A baby run, really, but a big adventure to Joel. He'd barely seen snow before and it's his first time on skis. Of course he falls a lot and he's cold and we don't make steady progress, but he's a good sport. Better than I expected. The snow is five or six feet deep, deeper in the drifts.

"You can tell from the slope and the vegetation where the road is, but there's no trail markers after the first half-mile and only a few skiers have been in there since the last snow. Another problem is, there's a lot more roads than show on the map and the skiers ahead of us turned off on some of them. We're out a couple of miles and I start looping to the left but it turns out to be the wrong road or trail or whatever. By mistake, we get ourselves into a side canyon when I think we're still in the main canyon.

"Suddenly it gets dark and starts snowing. Not even three in the afternoon, but the clouds are down at tree level and you can hardly see. It starts getting colder, too. We make a push, maybe another mile before I realize we're lost. I'm as panicked as I've been in my life, but I've got this thirteen year-old, so I have to stay calm. He's cold and scared and has all his hopes in me. We stopped, ate energy bars, and turned around to retrace our tracks. Longer route, but at least we knew where we were going."

Cora broke in. "This is pretty much what you told us that day, just more detail. You were late and we were almost ready to bring in Search and Rescue. It was nearly six and had been dark for an hour. You called us a bunch of weenies."

"I know. I was defensive about getting lost and I didn't want Joel telling my sister and brother-in-law I almost got him killed. I mean we didn't have food to speak of and no tarp or weather protection. An overnight out there would have been really iffy. Besides, I was weirded out by how it ended.

"See, after half an hour enough snow had fallen and the visibility was so bad it was hard to tell our tracks from the crossing tracks of other skiers. After an hour, it became impossible. I made a wrong turn, but luckily, I caught myself within fifty yards. When we cut back to what I hoped was the main trail is when I first heard the voice."

"What voice?" Alex demanded.

"Let me tell it," Roy protested. "The voice was inside, talking to me, coaching me to follow the right tracks and grunting when I went wrong. The voice alone is not so amazing. Something like that will happen in tennis, say when I'm down Love-40 on my own serve. I hear a voice that tells me to place my serve in a certain spot. If I listen to the voice I can almost always deliver and win the point. This was different. This voice wasn't in English. This voice was in some language I've never heard before and that I don't understand. But I followed it, mainly by avoiding the grunting, which was clearly negative, and we got out. In heavy snow and dark, we got out. When I knew we were on the last little climb up to the car, the voice stopped."

"Shit, that is weird," Alex said.

Cora was now clasping Roy's arm. "It's like Alex's thing with the deer," Roy continued. "I can't stop thinking about it, and that's a big part of why I've been browsing through Spence's library this week."

"I think an Indian spirit saved you," Cora said. "That's why the language was strange. I didn't understand my spirit's language either, but in school, when I began to recognize the sound of Spanish, it was already familiar."

"I don't have any other explanation," Roy concluded. "Time for Jill."

The music by this time had gone silent and a few of the candles had guttered out. Amida was nudging their legs under the table seeking tidbits. Jill looked truly uncomfortable. "Why did you want to go last?" Cora asked her.

"Because I was afraid you'd all have stories like that, and I knew I wouldn't. No spirit has ever talked to me, but I hoped if I heard you guys I might remember something. Here's the only story I can tell.

"When I was in high school in Merced, the summer before my senior year, I had a boyfriend whose family was into fundamentalist-type religion. His name was Chad. I'd had a crush on him for years. Who knows why. I'd always thought Christianity was a crock. But he mocked it, too, and laid it off on his parents. Anyway, I agreed to go with him and a bunch of other kids to a weekend revival camp on a lake up in the mountains. His parents and other members of their church were chaperoning.

"They made it sound like fun, and at first it was. Starting Friday night, we were in girls and boys barracks, a bunch of cots down both sides of a long room and group bathrooms. There was lots of giggling and goosing around. We took turns helping serve meals and cleaning up. I had some girlfriends there, and Chad and I hung out at the lake and sat together in Bible classes. But on Saturday night, it really hit the fan.

"After dinner we went to the assembly hall for a revival meeting. The speaker was a woman in her late thirties. She was Czech or Hungarian, I think, and she had escaped from the Communists with the help of Jesus. She experienced direct spiritual intervention, like Cora and Roy, but hers went on and on because she was on the run for months and had to cross a border somewhere to get free. I mean she was a good speaker, and I still think she was sincere. Her accent made it that much more real.

"When she finished, the preacher of one of the sponsoring churches took the podium and started calling for people who felt the spirit to come up and be blessed. There was a piano player, and she lit into heavy-rocking gospel. A lot of people, kids and adults, went up right away. The preacher made some sign on their heads and yelled out 'born again.' He had the 'legion of the saved,' that's what he called them, stand along the side aisles, and pretty soon ninety percent of the audience was up, even the piano player. Chad and I were the only ones left in our row. Then Chad went, then one-by-one everybody else, and I was alone sitting down.

"The preacher didn't come close to me. I thought he would and I was dreading it. But he focused on me completely, spoke directly to me. And I really, really wanted to feel the spirit. I really did. But I felt nothing. It was just a good performance on their part, and I knew they believed. That was it. I actually thought it would be wrong to go up if I didn't, you know, feel the spirit. Finally he started talking about Satan, like I was possessed or something, but I still didn't budge.

"They gave up on me and dimmed the lights and he started everybody singing a hymn they all knew. They were going to march two-by-two down to the lake and sing more. As they left the hall, each marcher was given a lighted candle. I got up when the church was empty and went out onto the bluff to watch. It was beautiful. They cut a glowing path through the night and the singing made me cry. I watched a long time. When they built a bonfire and started doing marshmallows I went to my barracks and got in bed. I felt awful."

"Jill, Jill, that's the best story of all," Roy said. "I mean it. In my dreams, I don't have that much courage."

"It didn't feel like courage, whatever that is."

"What the hell did you do?" Alex followed.

"You mean after? I pretended to be asleep when the other girls came in. Everybody was pretty subdued. But the next morning, before church service, they were back to giggling and goosing. In the barracks and at breakfast, though, almost no one would speak to me or they just said hello and looked away. Even Chad. I went to the office and made them call my dad to come and pick me up right away. He did, too."

"I'm fascinated by this, Jill," Roy said. "Did you tell your dad? How did he react?"

"Yeah, I told him. He was cool about it. I was nervous he wouldn't be. He and my mom were sort of half-assed Episcopalians. But he said they'd been dubious when I told him where Chad and I wanted to go that weekend. They OK'd it because they thought I should find out for myself. My mom was cool, too. She said what you said...about courage...and that she was proud of me. Anyway, no Jesus in my life yet and no other spirits either. I'm still waiting."

"What happened with the boyfriend?" Roy had to know.

"I assumed he would dump me. In a way, I wanted him to. Instead, he gave me this bullshit that he hadn't really felt the spirit and he only went up to the preacher because his parents were there and what I'd done was right. He said he felt bad about it and so did some of the other kids. He was such a jerk he couldn't understand why that made me furiously pissed. So I got to dump him. Not a shred of remorse on that one."

Alex and Cora had fallen silent, apparently not as taken with Jill's story as Roy was, which surprised him. Amida was in Cora's lap with his head above the table and his citrine eyes batting from one of them to another.

"OK, now it's Amida's turn," Roy joked. "He's a spiritual type all the way. Speak, oh esteemed one." Amida returned Roy's gaze intently.

"Makes me think of Spence," Cora said. "What story would he tell?"

"I know," Jill answered. "The rat mattress. When he thought he saw the ghost upstairs."

"He told us there was no ghost." Cora said.

"He didn't see her. But for a minute, he thought he did. He was cleaning out the attic, at the edges of the upstairs, along the eves, where it's too low to stand. He says there was god-awful junk from years of tenants who had abandoned stuff. He rented a dumpster and got rid of it all to make room for his things and clear out the rats. Before that he used to hear them all the time. And Amida would kill them and drag them around."

"This could be Amida's story, too," Roy added.

"Yuk!" Cora said loudly. "That's worse than ghosts."

"Must have been before I moved in," Alex said. "Never a problem while I was here. I remember Spence saying something about the mess in the attic, but I don't know this story."

"Oh...," Jill said. "Anyway, when Spence was mostly done, he got to a corner, looked around and saw an old woman in a striped dress leaning forward on her knees. Her white hair had fallen over her face and she was whimpering. He said it scared him shitless and then in a flash he saw it was an old mattress, stored rolled up and standing on its side, that had shredded and partly collapsed. The stripes were the cover and the white hair was where the cotton ticking had bulged out the top. When he got closer, the whole thing had been torn up and hollowed out by rats and the whimpering was a brood of rat pups nested in there. He rolled the thing up tight and squished them, tied it with a rope and hauled it to the dumpster."

"Really yuk!" Cora screeched.

Alex was laughing. "Jillie," he said patronizingly, "that might be the story Spence would tell, but if he really took the dare to be honest, he must've seen things ten times that weird in Asia. I mean, he was in the CIA, for Christ sake."

Cora's mouth fell open and she turned away to pet Amida. Sitting upright in his chair, Roy was as much disappointed at his own naiveté as he was shocked. Jill glared at Alex with her lips pressed tight. "What are you bringing that up for?" she said coldly. "I thought you were his friend."

"I am," Alex replied. "A good friend. But Cora and Roy aren't stupid. They have to've guessed already."

Roy wasn't about to correct Alex and tell him they were stupid. "Yeah, it's crossed our minds," he said. "But Spence has been more than decent to us, and he's your friend and Jill's friend. It's all history, anyway." If Cora disagreed, she did nothing to signal it.

"See?" Alex moved his eyes to Jill. "I don't know the details, and I wouldn't pass them on if I did. When I met Spence at Cal, it was pretty clear he had mustered out and was being retrained for civilian life. I wouldn't want to bet Spencer Mallow's his real name. I don't care. I think he's a hellofa guy. But he doesn't live like he does on any professor's salary. He has a little family money, but there's got to be a CIA pension on top of that. He supported himself without working and without student loans his whole way through grad school, and Naret didn't work either."

Jill got up, turned on a lamp and started clearing dishes away. "I'll help with this, Cora. You have a lot of cleanup to do in that small kitchen, and no dishwasher. Somebody put on some jazz or something. Let's change the mood in here."

Roy also came to life. "Cora has a dishwasher," he said. "Me."

Cora joined Roy and Jill's efforts while Alex stayed at the table to finish a glass of cabernet he was pouring himself. They hadn't been playing bridge, and no one was counting, but Alex had saved a trump for last and seemed to be enjoying the effect. It also gave Roy a sense for how Alex must operate in the courtroom. When Alex stood up, he projected his voice so they could hear him in the kitchen. "Hey, I'll do the music."

Roy saw him go into the library and use Spence's filing system to find a CD Alex must have known was there—classic blues from Albert King. Starting with *Born Under a Bad Sign* it was strong stuff straight through. Alex cranked up the volume. Jill had said she wanted a mood change, but Roy doubted this was what she meant. Spiro Gyra would be more her speed. Alex had to know Jill was angry at him for one-upping her rat mattress story with his tantalizing allusions to the CIA. He ignored that, however, and boogied into the kitchen doorway.

"Not enough room in there for me to help," Alex said, "but I'm good for moral support. And how about the sounds? I gave Spence this CD. I loved Albert King in my Air Force days. Spence isn't into it anymore, but he and I used to lay on the floor right in front of those speakers and smoke Thai weed with Albert singing and hitting hot guitar licks. Shit, those were good times."

❦ ❦ ❦

Roy and Cora accompanied their friends out to Spence's driveway under a brilliant, moonless sky and stood arm-in-arm waving as Alex hauled his sleek new pickup around and drove off toward Grass Valley. The last thing Roy saw was the back of Jill's blonde head shining momentarily in the spill of the porch light. On his and Cora's return up the walk they lingered under a towering cedar part way to the house. The stillness and sweetness of the cool air made it seem they were in deep forest.

"That was a really unusual evening," Cora said. "Dinner was a 'ten,' and the conversation went from ten to nearly zero at the end. Jill's story made me sad."

"I think Alex is pretty drunk. I'm worried about him driving."

"Me, too. I guess he'll be OK, but he sure got an attitude, bang, out of nowhere. Like he and Jill were competing."

"Well, she did get on his case about hunting. And what do you think of Sean Connery now?"

Cora gave a rueful laugh. "It's so obvious, I can't believe I was surprised. Besides, they say life imitates art."

"But god, this place suddenly feels like living amid the spoils of empire. How do we know what Spence did over there?"

"I thought you said it was history."

"I did," Roy agreed. "Of course, I was trying to be cool. But it is history. If I had been drafted, and I'd gone, who knows what I'd've done. Maybe he was lucky and can be proud of how it worked out in Thailand without having too much on his conscience."

"Maybe. I hope so. Personally, I'd have a lot harder time if he'd been involved in Guatemala or Chile where the CIA overthrew elected governments. At least in Southeast Asia, it was war. With or without the U.S., a lot of bad shit would have happened. Look at Pol Pot."

"Probably right," Roy said. "But here's a bizarre thought. What if Spence didn't go to Puerto Rico but is off on some kind of mission? Maybe the Middle East? That could be why we can't call him and why he's using his machine as a message drop."

"Get real. You're as drunk as Alex. Spence isn't in the CIA now, we know that. But maybe we can't call him because the relatives he's visiting don't know him by the name Mallow and don't have that name themselves."

"That would explain it. Hey, I love the stars and the crickets but I'm getting cold. Let's go inside." Roy steered Cora toward the porch and through the door into the dimness of the library. He was reaching to switch off the outside light when she pulled him around to face her.

"Before we go to bed, you owe me an explanation," she said.

"What do you mean?"

"What I mean is, why did you wait until tonight to tell me about the voice that brought you and Joel back from your ski trip? Why did you hide it? You're the one who's so big on being open."

"I told you. It weirded me out, and I was embarrassed."

"But you've said you'd tell me anything. That you trust me. I was hurt to have something I'd never heard before come out in front of Jill and Alex."

"I'm sorry for that. It was more an omission than a lie. You never told me about your spirit either."

"Mine was twenty-five years ago. I was a kid. Yours was six months ago and we were together at the time. That's not the same thing."

"You're right. And it was a relief to finally tell it. The setting was perfect. Nobody laughed. Look, Cora, I am sorry. But in the honesty game, somebody has to go first and trust that the other will follow. There's no such thing as simultaneous disclosure. You went first, and I did follow. I wouldn't be embarrassed to tell you anything like that again."

"OK," she said. "Not the best, but OK. And you can make it up to me."

"Oh? How?"

"Starting now, no jokes about ghosts, rats or the CIA."

≱ ≱ ≱

In the succeeding days, neither Saturday night's disturbance between Alex and Jill, news from Kuwait nor anything on Cora and Roy's Sacramento answering machine interfered with their idyll of flawless summer weather and outdoor pleasures. Swimming was a staple, but tennis also got into the picture, and their high level of play drew onlookers from Pioneer Park's adjacent baseball fields and picnic ground. Evenings meant reading at Spence's or sampling the cultural offerings in town. They took in a zany, sub-titled Japanese comedy about a noodle shop at the film series and caught a stellar performance by an eclectic, female-led bluegrass group from Berkeley sponsored by the local radio station. Patio dining at any of several restaurants let them give Spence's kitchen a rest when that suited them. And, aside from the river, it was all within easy walking distance.

Nosing around a used book store on Broad Street one afternoon and visiting the library across from the courthouse gave Roy some insight into how the Nevada City they were enjoying so much had come to be. First, it had been the center of an extremely prosperous gold mining area that flourished for almost a hundred years until the government shut down the mines during World War II. Placer and hydraulic mining had been important early on, but hard rock mining, with miles of shafts and tunnels beneath the surrounding landscape, eventually took over and sustained the economy to such an extent that unemployment was virtually unknown, even during the Great Depression.

A second key point was that Nevada City, unlike the great majority of California's gold towns, had not burned down since the late 1850's, so it retained most of its historic buildings and homes. The buttressed, red-brick Nevada Theater, for instance, where Jill's Foothill Players were housed, had been in use as a performing arts center longer than any other venue in the state.

There was also a long rivalry between Nevada City, the preservationist-oriented county seat, and its more commercially-minded neighbor, Grass Valley. Roy could see a parallel with the better-known rivalry between haughty San Francisco and arriviste Los Angeles, and it struck him as quite funny. What wasn't funny was that Nevada City, after so much time, had come within an ace of burning down just two years ago. A major conflagration known as the 49er Fire had torn through the countryside west of town in September 1988 after having been ignited by someone burning trash. Tens of thousands of acres of brush and woodland were destroyed, and Roy learned that only an unusual, east-to-west wind pattern had kept Nevada City off the casualty list. Roy had seen the fire on the TV news, but he hadn't known Spence then and had only just met Alex, so he hadn't been familiar enough with the area to realize what was at stake.

Thursday of the second week, they got back from the river late and Cora had Roy stop at Bonanza Market so she could do some dinner shopping. The piney mass of Banner Mountain shouldering dreamily over downtown from the east reminded them how little of their time in Nevada City now remained. Cora told Roy to go on to Spence's and feed Amida. She wanted the experience of walking home with the groceries. Expecting nothing out of the ordinary, Roy was surprised to find an official-looking notice wedged in the front door when he arrived. But before he could unfold it, Amida tackled him from behind in anticipation of dinner, and Roy went inside to see what sort of cat food was available. The refrigerator light didn't come on and the house was unfamiliarly quiet.

The notice told him why. It was from PG&E and said they were doing utility pole replacement on Manzanita Hill that day and would have the power off. It went on to apologize for any inconvenience and make assurances that power would be restored as soon as possible, no more than three or four hours. This sounded hopeful, and while Roy stood in the library reading, the refrigerator burped and began to hum, Spence's wall clock started ticking and a whirring came from the phone machine. Good, Roy thought. No harm done. He tossed the notice in the wastebasket and reached to reset the clock. It said 2:35 and his watch said 5:45, so the shutoff had lasted exactly the time PG&E predicted.

But wait! The machine! It had rewound and maybe wiped out Spence's messages, or would start recording over them with the next call. The rewind wouldn't have taken so long if Spence had picked up messages recently. The way Murphy's Law worked, those important calls Spence was waiting for had just been destroyed or were about to be. Roy considered the options and decided he should do something. The machine didn't look so different from their own. He'd probably be able to work it. Nothing in the binder offered guidance, of course, because Spence hadn't wanted them working it. But if he were Spence, under these circumstances, Roy would want his house-sitter to intervene, and the sooner, the better.

Roy got a pad of paper and a pen, sat down near the machine and hit play. It did. The first message was from PG&E, calling Wednesday to warn of Thursday's power outage. Since that was already moot, Roy didn't bother to jot anything down. Next was a call from Sac State about Spence's upcoming teaching schedule. Roy logged the caller's name, question and call-back number. Then came a message that nearly knocked Roy out of his chair. The caller didn't leave a name or number, but he recognized the voice right away. He jotted down the person's name and the message: will call again. His hand was shaking. Another call was from a law office in San Jose, asking Spence to reply regarding some news on his child custody arrangement. Also, Spence's dentist wanted to confirm an appointment for next Monday, August 20.

And finally, there was a call from someone else who didn't leave a name or number, but left a long message. A startling message, actually more startling than the one that had shocked Roy a few minutes before. This caller, he deduced, was Naret. She had a slight accent, but her English was fluent and clearly articulated. And there was no doubt she meant what she said. Roy was too agitated to write it all down, nor did he think he should. He wrote her name and summarized the gist in a few brief phrases. He stopped the tape at the end of Naret's message. Presumably, future calls would append to the ones Roy had already picked up.

Roy dated the piece of paper and wrote the day each message had come in down the left margin. On a second piece of paper he wrote Spence a note explaining what had happened. Then he carried both pages into Spence's office, put them on the seat of the desk chair with the note on top, weighted them with a metal ruler, and carefully reclosed the door on his way out. Roy wrote a note for Cora saying he had decided to take a walk himself, left it in the kitchen, and went into the diggings behind the house where he'd been running in the mornings. He put his head down, walking west, away from town, on every trail through the tangled manzanita that would take him that way.

Unquestionably, Roy had made a terrible mistake. He should never, never have touched that machine. For Spence to lose his messages because PG&E cut the power was a risk Spence had accepted. Besides, all those people would have called back eventually or contacted him in some other way. Spence had concentrated on the greater risk of Cora or Roy's inadvertently receiving his messages, and Roy had thwarted the very steps Spence took to avoid that risk. It didn't matter that Roy deserved at least some credit for good intentions.

But Roy was going to make damn sure none of this got pinned on Cora. He knew she'd have told him not to play those messages. She'd have thought it through more clearly than he did. Cora would be angry that he'd blundered into this mess, and she would be right. She'd also be angry if she found out he hadn't told her about it, but that was the lesser evil compared to getting her involved. He couldn't un-know what he now knew, though he cursed himself for knowing it. He could, however, try like hell to pretend he didn't know. That meant deceiving Cora and deceiving Spence, but so be it.

With luck, Spence would get all his messages off the tape just as though the power hadn't failed. If Spence didn't suspect anything or raise the issue, Roy would destroy the note and the messages he had logged and wash his hands of the whole thing. If Roy ended up having to explain, he would show Spence the note and the messages privately, apologize and swear himself to secrecy. It was the best plan he could come up with at the moment. Maybe tomorrow or Saturday he'd get a better idea.

For some reason the manzanita seemed larger the further Roy went. Down both sides of the trail, an overhanging jungle of dense, multi-trunked stems the color of dried blood branched to support leathery foliage twice the height of his head. Manzanita loved the nutrient-poor tailings and denuded hillsides left when the miners blasted the gold out with giant hydraulic cannons. The hills around Nevada City were dotted with old pits and collapsing cliffs like the ones Roy was exploring, surroundings in which he normally found a strange beauty. But now, thanks to Naret, brutal scenes from long-forgotten TV broadcasts and the movie *Apocalypse Now* flooded his senses. He'd never been in uniform, yet Vietnam had shadowed Roy's life. Veterans and civilians alike, his generation would bear the social, moral and political costs of Vietnam forever.

Scrambling up a slope of crumbled shale at the far end of the diggings, Roy emerged on a west-running ridge with the Deer Creek canyon below to his left and a curve of Highway 49 north to Downieville below on his right. Here smaller manzanita competed with scrub oak, and a hidden blue jay gave out raspy sentinel cries. An abandoned mine portal on the opposite canyon wall made a dark opening that could have led to a warren of underground bunkers. Roy threaded his way along, increasingly wary at being in unknown territory. He would have to face Cora when he got back, and he wanted to be calm and ready. On Sunday he would have to face Spence, too, but he had time to prepare for that.

The staccato tcha-tcha-tcha-tcha of a logging truck riding its jake brake with the day's last inbound load echoed up from the highway like a burst of machine-gun fire. Startled, Roy remembered that rattlesnakes frequent places like this, and he began to watch where he put his feet. Fifty yards further, in sparse and stunted brush, Roy came to the head of a broad, pine-rimmed ravine that was incongruously filled with rusted, wrecked auto bodies, disused industrial equipment and thousands upon thousands of derelict wheels and tires. Through the midst of this wound an unpaved driveway leading to a battered tow truck parked near a barely habitable mobile home. A few clothes hung drying on a line that ran from one corner of the home to a mangled arm of iron protruding from a dismembered bulldozer. Acres of junk, the anti-matter of the modern age, tucked away in the woods under signal flags of laundry.

Framing the ravine, across the hilltops and ridges to the west, the leavings of the 49er Fire showed themselves. Most Sierra wildfires result from lightning strikes, but this one had been manmade. Sticks of blackened trees poked randomly among barren meadows, heat-splintered boulders and the stubs of what used to be brush. He'd last seen this country on TV during the fire with big helicopters swooping over it dropping chemicals. Nevada City had indeed been lucky. Roy wasn't that far from town and manzanita burns explosively. He needed to get back to Cora and use his wits to make a pleasant evening, but the vista had taken him prisoner— in the foreground, a bombed-out motor pool, and beyond it, a landscape fashioned by napalm and agent orange.

☀ ☀ ☀

Despite a great disdain for lying, Roy turned out to be good at it, or good enough, though circumstance also helped. Cora was in the yard picking figs when he returned from his walk, and she playfully pushed one into his mouth as he came up to her. She gave no indication that his recent absence had been unusual or that anything was awry from her end.

"Yum," Roy said, glad for the diversion. "You found a few ripe ones after all."

"Yeah, finally. Next week there'll be lots. We had a fig tree on the ranch when I was a kid. I love them. How was your walk?"

"Neat. I went all the way through the diggings, out the other side and onto a ridge where I could see scars from the big fire two years ago. Really scary. It could have come right through here."

"Wow. Spence's place would have gone up, just like Manderley."

"What's Manderley?"

"The name of a big house. From *Rebecca*, a famous English novel. All this intrigue and foreboding about things from the past, and then the place mysteriously burns to the ground. Spence might have a copy. The author's du Maurier. Look under D."

"In my new spiritual mode," Roy said, attempting irony, "I'll give it a try. A little mystery and intrigue would sure fit with those stories we told last Saturday. How was your walk?"

"Good. I took my time. Glad you weren't worried. I wandered around and came out Spring Street. I guess I'm starting to say good-bye to Nevada City. It's been so wonderful."

"Yeah...Spence will be home three days from right now." Roy kept his voice flat, but he was still getting used to that idea himself.

"I'm kind of bummed 'cause I'm getting my period," Cora said. "Hope I'm not being snippy. I don't want to spoil any of what we have left. Just so you understand. I'll try to roll with it. Let's plan our time to focus on stuff we really like."

"Sure. Such as?" Roy was beginning to feel less tense, and this news about Cora's period might help him explain away any edginess she sensed between them in the days ahead.

"We should do the yard and all the house stuff Sunday," she answered. "That's probably when I'll be feeling worst. As soon as we're done, we can kick back and enjoy the place till Spence gets home. I'd like to swim tomorrow and Saturday, and one morning I want us to try breakfast at Mama Sue's, where I went with Jill for lunch on Tuesday. You'll love it. The owner is queen of the local hippies, and the food is terrific."

"That's what you said. Anyway, good plan on swimming and all the rest. How about going to Cowboy Pizza Saturday night and checking out the reggae dance at Miner's Foundry tomorrow?"

"OK, I'm game. Reggae's always fun. But on Saturday I don't know if I'll want to eat in town or here. It's our last night. Could we decide later and maybe get a pizza to go? The vegetarian Greek pie is a knockout."

"Sounds fine," Roy said. "And speaking of food, it's my turn to cook. What did you find at Bonanza?"

* * *

As Saturday evening approached, Roy and Cora were on their way back from a final excursion to the river, cruising through the woods and meadows of North Bloomfield Road at the outskirts of town. Each curve took them from bright sun to deep shade while silky mountain air streamed through the BMW's open windows.

"That was perfect," Cora said from behind the wheel. "The water was warm enough you could stay in and float, and not many people. Now that I've driven those canyon switchbacks, they seem even more amazing, and you got a chance to catch the scenery."

"Yeah, it was fun being a passenger. Also, after nearly two weeks down there, I didn't get poison oak. It was all along the trails, but somehow I kept clear."

"I saw a lot, too, but I think I'm immune. I mean I've never gotten it. My brother used to every summer on the ranch. Strange he stayed there and I didn't."

"Not really. It would be pretty hard to imagine him in a Guatemalan shirt grooving to a reggae band. Last night was great, wasn't it?"

"Yes. Who was the band, again? They're hot."

"The poster said Strictly Roots. From Chico."

Cora laughed and waved one hand above the steering wheel. "What a riot. When I used to visit Chico in high school, you know, shopping and hanging out, Swiss cheese was exotic. Now they have reggae. What I mainly remember is the fraternity boys looking us up and down and saying S.U.Y.T."

"I don't follow. What's S.U.Y.T.?"

Cora gaped at him with pretended pity. "You really don't know? S.U.Y.T. Show Us Your Tits. They had banners they'd hang out the windows. So stupid. Isn't it cool I'm finally with a guy who doesn't know what that means."

Now Roy laughed. "I'd like to say we were more advanced in Southern California, but the truth is probably just nobody had the idea."

"I meant to compliment you, not Southern California." Cora brushed her fingertips on his cheek, then downshifted to negotiate the turn onto Manzanita Hill. "Well, here we are at Spence's," she said a minute later. "I'm still up for pizza tonight, but I do want take-out. Hey, he's back. What's going on?"

Roy's ribs clutched at his stomach. There, in the middle of the garage, where he and Cora had been parking, sat Spence's car. Cora pulled onto the gravel behind it.

"You go find him," she said. "I'll bring our stuff, but I've got to head straight for the bathroom."

When Roy went in the front door, he heard clomping footsteps from above and started up the stairs. Spence, moving abruptly, looking quite tan in white trousers and a short-sleeve madras shirt, came into view carrying a small teak table Roy had moved out of the hallway to make a nightstand for Cora.

"Spence," Roy called. "Welcome home. We didn't expect you till tomorrow. Cora's still outside." He readied himself for a handshake.

Spence turned. His eyes were wild and his jawline had a tinge of purple. "Who told you to move the goddamned furniture!" he said, almost shouting.

Roy flinched, thinking for a second Spence might swing the table at him, but Spence put it down with a thump. "This place looks like hell!" Spence went on. "The kitchen's a mess and you didn't do the yard!"

"Spence, calm down. We did the yard last week. We planned to do it again tomorrow, along with the other cleanup, so it'd be fresh when you got home. You're early."

"In case you forgot, you snooping little butt, it's my house. Of course that didn't stop you from drinking my wine, listening to my messages or sneaking into my office to read the faxes."

"Christ, Spence, none of that is what you think." Things were already beyond Roy's worst-case scenario, and he was unsure how to react. On their face Spence's accusations were true. In fact, Roy had been in Spence's office twice. Once to drop off the messages; there were no faxes then. The second time was this morning, to reclaim the messages in hope of avoiding a Sunday confrontation if Spence didn't notice anything regarding the phone machine. Today there had been a fax, spewing out on the floor. Roy had seen a letterhead, something like Smythe, Kamakura & Cruz, Attorneys at Law, Honolulu, but he'd read nothing. How could Spence know Roy'd been there? He'd put the metal ruler back exactly where he found it. Or was the desk booby-trapped somehow? Roy heard Cora enter through the library and make her way to the downstairs bath.

"What am I, stupid?" Spence lowered his voice, also aware of Cora's presence. "You tried to cover your tracks, but the machine archived the messages you intercepted. There they were, big as life, when I got home. And Amida was locked in my office. He followed you in and pissed on the carpet after you trapped him when you snuck back out. You ought to be down on your knees cleaning it up."

"Look Spence, I will clean it up. I'll pay to have the rug sent out. I didn't read anything. I went in to find a book. There was a power failure Thursday. That's why your messages got archived."

"Bullshit. I heard the PG&E message. If there'd been a power failure, the messages would have been erased. The only way they get archived is if you listen to them."

Roy was beaten, and he knew it. "OK," he admitted. "I'm sorry. I was alone here when the power came on and I did what I thought was right. I jotted the messages down just in case. They didn't really mean much to me. I'll go get my notes and give them to you right now. Cora doesn't know anything, and I swear I'll keep every bit of it under my hat."

Roy climbed the last two stairs, pushed past Spence and went to Cirene's room. Spence followed right on his heels. Roy saw that Spence had dumped everything from Cora's table onto the floor, her book, her hand cream, her hair brush, her reading glasses, her nail file, her birth control pills. Roy went to his suitcase, unzipped an inner compartment and handed Spence the note and the messages. Spence grabbed them, glaring while he read. Then he crumpled them in his hand.

"Very touching," he said sarcastically. "And you'll carry all of this to the grave. Tell me again why I should trust you."

Roy stood his ground. He was angry now, too. "Because I'm trustworthy. Because you have no choice."

"I don't? Really?"

"Unless you're so far gone you'll have somebody kill me instead."

"You fucking little butt! How dare you!" Spence's voice was filled with venom. "You have no idea what it was like. Not one fucking clue. Draft-dodging pansies aren't worth killing. You don't even have the balls to ask if what Naret said is true."

"I'm not sure I care," Roy said dismissively. "But you don't shy away from covert operations, do you?"

Cora's footsteps came up the stairs and toward them along the hall. "What's going on up here?" she asked. "Hi, Spence," she said brightly. "Nice tan. How was Puerto Rico? You two have sure been stomping around."

Spence clenched his jaw and said nothing. Roy was trembling with rage, but he did everything he could to hide it. In a calm way calculated to irritate Spence as much as possible he said, "Spence objects to our moving the furniture. I had him show me what he meant. Then I asked why he needed to dump all your things on the floor. I'm waiting for an answer."

"Get out of my house!" Spence replied with cold fury. "Both of you. Right away. Tonight. I'll be on the back porch for forty-five minutes. When I come in, I want you gone."

¥ ¥ ¥

Cora was right. The Highway 49 bridge at Wolf Creek was narrow and Roy had been going too fast. He braked lightly as they crossed, using the short uphill after the bridge to slow them further. Having raised the topic, Roy now had to tell Cora what happened with Spence. But where to start?

"Remember Thursday," he said, "when you walked back from the market and I drove home?"

"Yes."

"The power was off when I got there. I fed Amida, and the power suddenly came on."

"Oh, I miss Amida. I miss everything. Spence was such a shit! We didn't get to say good-bye to the house or Amida or Nevada City."

"I know. Anyway, his phone machine went berserko, so I stopped it and played the messages. I wrote them down and thought I'd figured out how to save them on tape."

Cora was stunned. "Are you nuts? He told us never to touch that thing."

"You're right. I knew you'd say that. It's why I didn't tell you. And I was nuts."

"So?"

"Spence had already played the saved messages by the time we got back tonight. He knew what I'd done and what I'd heard before I could tell him."

"So?"

"So, one of the messages was from Jill. They're having an affair."

"I knew that," Cora said.

Roy's stomach, already churning from his scene with Spence, released a surge of hot bile into the back of his throat. He was glad to be driving. It made him focus and gave him something specific to do. "Christ, Cora," he said accusingly, "how could you know and not tell me?"

"You didn't ask. It was...what's the word you used?...an omission."

"I did everything but ask. Remember how you were so sure Spence wasn't gay? And you put us right in the middle of it with this house-sitting. When did you find out?"

"It was girl-talk stuff, between me and Jill. You don't tell girl-talk stuff. But I thought that might be why Spence put his machine off limits. What did her message say?"

It couldn't make Roy feel any more like Cora's puppet to answer, so he did. "That she'd been at the house with us last Saturday, that she missed him terribly, that her 'little problem' had been resolved, that she would call back when he was home, that their weekend at Tahoe had been a treasure. Did you know all that stuff?"

"No, not till she told me at lunch. You know, at Mama Sue's. Her period was late, but it started. That was her little problem."

"Not so little. There's Alex's vasectomy. What does she do, sneak off for an abortion?"

"Not sneak. Vasectomies aren't a hundred percent, Roy. Nothing is."

"Does Alex know? That might explain how he acted last week."

"No. But she's worried he suspects something. Not with Spence, though."

"What could Jill be thinking with this shit? She just got married, and he's her husband's best friend."

"It's been going on since May. Sometimes people don't think. A lot of times."

"And the weekend at Tahoe? We were house-sitting then. Spence said he'd be back east."

"I was shocked, too. That's going too far. I mean, there we were, with Alex and her, the very next weekend, in Spence's house. And I didn't even know."

"You didn't know?" Roy yelled. "I knew nothing. None of it. How do you think that makes me feel?"

"Well, you didn't tell me about the phone machine either. How am I supposed to feel?"

"That's different. I didn't see any obligation to tell you what I should never have known myself."

"I don't see a big difference. You say I put us in the middle by not telling about Jill. But we're under fire because you messed with that machine and tried to cover it up."

"I'm under fire. I protected you."

"Who says I need protecting? What else was on the tape? Anything?" Cora didn't give up easily.

"Spence's dentist," Roy droned. "Sac State and something from PG&E warning about the power outage. That's all, and none of it, including Jill's, any of our business."

Cora had asked a direct question, and for Buddhists, the fourth grave precept is honesty in all things. Roy, however, had deliberately lied. It wasn't a matter of loyalty to Spence. That bridge was burned. But Cora, by her own behavior, had forfeit her right to know. Naret's call would be secret from Cora forever. Roy realized that the relationship he thought they'd had, or could have, was an illusion. Life doesn't permit total honesty, much less reward it. Like unilateral disarmament, it's something life appears to punish.

With strangers or at work, Roy was used to being on guard. Jill, Spence, Cora and Alex weren't strangers, yet they had all lied, to him and to one another, without compunction when it suited their purposes. And Roy had lied to them, too, in the form of telling less than there was to be told about his cross-country ski experience and about the phone machine. But he'd eventually opened up and what had it gotten him? The more closely a person's interests are allied with your own, which can vary from moment to moment, the less likely they are to lie to you. That's the best you can hope for.

"I'm sorry," Cora said after Roy had been quiet for some time. "I want to be honest with you...always. But I don't know how to handle these conflict of obligation situations. Jill and I go way back."

"Who knows," he answered, taking a wounded tone, "maybe someday you can say the same for us." Roy had never wanted to begin thinking tactically with Cora the way he always had to in his relationship with Linda, but he'd gained some leverage from the events of the last hour he wasn't ready to yield.

"The whole thing sucks," Cora admitted. "How do we get back to where we were? I can't just make a joke out of it, show you my tits and everything will be fine."

"No," Roy said quietly.

Cora turned toward him. "OK, then something more serious."

"Oh?" Roy thought he knew what. After all this wreckage, perhaps because of it, she was going to bring up getting married.

"Next week, let's get...a Siamese cat."

"I suppose," Roy said. Was he relieved or disappointed? The problem was, Roy could still hear Naret's Asian-inflected voice in his mind and it drowned out his feelings. Spence had been in Hawaii, not Puerto Rico, something Roy would bet Jill didn't know anymore than Cora. Cirene had seen Spence outside her school one day, talking to Lin, her brother, and had reported that fact to their mother. Naret had kept them both at home the rest of the week and had called the police and her lawyer. Her message concluded with the threat that if Spence ever did anything like that again, she would tell the judge who was deciding his visitation rights Spence's real name, and what he had done with nerve gas to the villagers at Kan Loc, in Laos, in 1974.

With reference to the back cover, independent sources have verified that BILL PIEPER lives in Sacramento and that he is a graduate of both Dartmouth College and the University of Michigan. He has served as an administrator at UC Berkeley, a Deputy Superintendent in the California Department of Education, and as a private consultant. SO TRUST ME is his first published fiction, but he is the author of several technical and non-fiction works as well.

PHOTO BY DAVID DAWSON